THAYNE

SERENITY
HARBOR

HQN™

ISBN-13: 978-0-373-79939-8

Serenity Harbor

Recycling programs
for this product may
not exist in your area.

This edition published by arrangement with Harlequin Books S.A.

For questions and comments about the quality of this book, please contact us at CustomerService@Harlequin.com.

® and TM are trademarks of Harlequin Enterprises Limited or its corporate affiliates. Trademarks indicated with ® are registered in the United States Patent and Trademark Office, the Canadian Intellectual Property Office and in other countries.

www.HQNBooks.com

Printed in U.S.A.

To Donald and Janice Thayne, two of the
best people I've ever had the pleasure to know.
I love and miss you dearly.

CHAPTER ONE

"THAT'S HIM AT your six o'clock, over by the tomatoes. Brown hair, blue eyes, ripped. Don't look. Isn't he *gorgeous*?"

Katrina Bailey barely restrained from rolling her eyes at her best friend. "How am I supposed to know that, if you won't let me even sneak a peek at the man?" she asked Samantha Fremont.

Sam shrugged with another sidelong look in the man's direction. "Okay. You can look. Just make it subtle."

Mere months ago, all vital details about her best friend's latest crush might have been the most fascinating thing the two of them talked about all week. Right now, she found it tough to work up much interest in one more man in a long string of them, especially with everything else she had spinning in her life.

She wanted to ignore Sam's request and continue on with shopping for the things they needed to take to Wynona's shower—but friends didn't blow off their friends' obsessions. She loved Sam and had missed hanging out with her over the last nine months. It made her sad that their interests appeared to have diverged so dramatically, but it wouldn't hurt her to act like she cared about the cute newcomer to Haven Point.

Donning her best ninja spy skills—honed from years of doing this very thing, checking out hot guys without them noticing—she pretended to reach up to grab a can of peas off the shelf. She studied the label intently, all while shifting her gaze toward the other end of the aisle.

About ten feet away, she spotted two men. Considering she knew Darwin Twitchell well—and he was close to eighty years old and cranky as a badger with gout—the other guy had to be Bowie Callahan, the new director of research and development at the Caine Tech facility in town.

Years of habit couldn't be overcome by sheer force of will. That was the only reason her stomach muscles seemed to shiver and her toes curled against the leather of her sandals. Or so she told herself, anyway.

Okay. She got it. Sam was totally right. The man was indeed great-looking: tall, lean, tanned, with sculpted features and brown hair streaked with the sort of blond highlights that didn't come from a salon but from spending time outside.

Under other circumstances, she might have wanted to do more than look. In a different life, perhaps she would have made her way to his end of the aisle, pretended to fumble with an item on the shelf, then dropped it right at his feet so they could "meet" while they both reached to pick it up.

She used to be such an idiot.

The old Katrina might not have been able to look away from such a gorgeous male specimen. But when he aimed a ferocious scowl downward, she shifted her gaze to find him frowning at a boy who looked to be about five or six, trying his best to put a box of sugary cereal into their cart and growing visibly upset when Bowie Callahan kept taking it out and putting it back on the shelf.

Katrina frowned. "You didn't say he had a kid. I thought you had a strict rule. No divorced dads."

"He doesn't have a kid!" Sam exclaimed.

"Then who's the little kid currently winding up for what looks like a world-class tantrum at his feet?"

Ignoring her own stricture about not staring, Sam whirled around. Her eyes widened with confusion. "I have no idea! I heard it straight from Eliza Caine that he's not married and doesn't have a family. He never said anything to me about a kid when I met him at a party at Snow Angel Cove or the other two times I've bumped into him around town this spring. I haven't seen him around for a few weeks. Maybe he has family visiting. Or maybe he's babysitting or something."

That was so patently ridiculous, Katrina had to bite her tongue. Really? Did Sam honestly believe the new director of research and development at

Caine Tech would be offering babysitting services— in the middle of the day and on a Monday, no less?

She sincerely adored Samantha for a million different reasons, but sometimes her friend saw what she wanted to see.

This latest example of how their paths had diverged in recent months made her a little sad. Until a year ago, she and Sam had been—as her mom would say—two peas in the same pod. They shared the same taste in music, movies, clothes. They could spend hours poring over celebrity and fashion magazines, dishing about the latest gossip, shopping for bargains at thrift stores and yard sales.

And men. She didn't even want to think about how many hours of her life she had wasted with Sam, talking about whichever guy they were most interested in that day.

Samantha had been her best friend since they found each other in elementary school in that mysterious way like discovered like.

She still loved her dearly. Sam was kind and generous and funny, but Katrina's own priorities had shifted. After the events of the last year, Katrina was beginning to realize she barely resembled the somewhat shallow, flighty girl she had been before she grabbed her passport and hopped on a plane with Carter Ross.

That was a good thing, she supposed, but she felt a little pang of fear that while on the path to gaining a little maturity, she might end up losing her best friend.

"Babysitting. I suppose it's possible," she said in a noncommittal voice. If so, the guy was really lousy at it. The boy's face had reddened, and tears had started streaming down his features. By all appearances, he was approaching a meltdown, and Bowie Callahan's scowl had shifted to a look of helpless frustration.

"If you want, I can introduce you," Sam said, apparently oblivious to the drama.

Katrina purposely pushed their cart forward, in the opposite direction. "You know, it doesn't look like a good time. I'm sure I'll have a chance to meet him later. I'll be in Haven Point for a month. Between Wyn's wedding and Lake Haven Days, there should be plenty of time to socialize with our newest resident."

"Are you sure?" Sam asked, disappointment clouding her gaze.

"Yeah. Let's just finish shopping so I have time to go home and change before the shower."

Not that her mother's house really felt like home anymore. Yet another radical change in the last nine months.

"I guess you're right," Sam said, after another surreptitious look over Katrina's shoulder. "We waited too long, anyway. Looks like he's moved to another aisle."

They found the items they needed and moved to the next aisle as well but didn't bump into Bowie again. Maybe he had taken the boy, whoever he was, out of the store so he could cope with his meltdown in private.

They were nearly finished shopping when Sam's phone rang with the ominous tone she used to identify her mother.

She pulled the device out of her purse and glared at it. "I wish I dared ignore her, but if I do, I'll hear about it for a week."

That was nothing, she thought. If Katrina ignored *her* mother's calls while she was in town for Wyn's wedding, Charlene would probably mount a search and rescue, which was kind of funny when she thought about it. Charlene hadn't been nearly as smothering when Kat had been living halfway around the world in primitive conditions for the last nine months. But if she dared show up late for dinner, sheer panic ensued.

"I'm at the grocery store with Kat," Samantha said, a crackly layer of irritation in her voice. "I texted you that's where I would be."

Her mother responded something Katrina couldn't hear, which made Sam roll her eyes. To others, Linda Fremont could be demanding and cranky, quick to criticize. Oddly, she had always treated Katrina with tolerance and even a measure of kindness.

"Do you absolutely need it tonight?" Samantha asked, pausing a moment to listen to her mother's answer with obvious impatience written all over her features. "Fine. Yes. I can run over. I only wish you had mentioned this earlier, when I was just hanging around for three hours doing nothing, waiting for someone to show up at the shop. I'll grab it."

She shut off her phone and shoved it back into her little dangly Coach purse that she'd bought for a steal at the Salvation Army in Boise. "I need to stop in next door at the drugstore to pick up one of my mom's prescriptions. Sorry. I know we're in a rush."

"No problem. I'll finish the shopping and check out, then we can meet each other at your car when we're done."

"Hey, I just had a great idea," Sam exclaimed. "After the shower tonight, we should totally head up to Shelter Springs and grab a drink at the Painted Moose!"

Katrina tried not to groan. The last thing she wanted to do amid her lingering jet lag was visit the local bar scene, listening to the same songs, flirting with the same losers, trying to laugh at their same old, tired jokes.

"Let's play it by ear. We might be having so much fun at the shower that we won't want to leave. Plus it's Monday night, and I doubt there will be much going on at the PM."

She didn't have the heart to tell Sam she wasn't the same girl who loved nothing more than dancing with a bunch of half-drunk cowboys—or that she had a feeling she would never be that girl again. Priorities had a way of shifting when a person wasn't looking.

Sam stuck her bottom lip out in an exaggerated

pout. "Don't be such a party pooper! We've only got a month together, and I've missed you *so much*!"

Great. Like she needed more guilt in her life.

"Let's play it by ear. Go grab your mom's prescription, I'll check out and we'll head over to Julia's place. We can figure out our after-party plans, well, after the party."

She could tell by Sam's pout that she would have a hard time escaping a late night with her. Maybe she could talk her into just hanging out by the lakeshore and talking.

"Okay. I guess we'd better hurry if we want to have time to make our salad."

Sam hurried toward the front doors, and Katrina turned back to her list. Only the items from the vegetable aisle, then she would be done. She headed in that direction and spotted a flustered Bowie Callahan trying to keep the boy with him from eating grapes from the display.

"Stop it, Milo. I told you, you can eat as many as you want *after* we buy them."

This only seemed to make the boy more frustrated. She could see by his behavior and his repetitive mannerisms that he quite possibly had some sort of developmental issues. Autism, she would guess at a glance—though that could be a gross generalization, and she was not an expert, anyway.

Whatever the case, Callahan seemed wholly unprepared to deal with it. He hadn't taken the boy out of the store, obviously, to give him a break from the overstimulation. In fact, things seemed to have progressed from bad to worse.

Milo—cute name—reached for another grape despite the warning, and Bowie grabbed his hand and sternly looked down into his face. "I said, stop it. We'll have grapes after we pay for them."

The boy didn't like that. He wrenched his hand away and threw himself to the ground. "No! No! No!" he chanted.

"That's enough," Bowie snapped, loudly enough that other shoppers turned around to stare, which made the man flush.

She could see Milo was gearing up for a nuclear meltdown—and while she reminded herself it was none of her business, she couldn't escape a certain sense of professional obligation to step in.

She wanted to ignore it, to turn into the next aisle, finish her shopping and escape the store as quickly as she could. She could come up with a dozen excuses about why that was the best course of action. Samantha would be waiting for her. She didn't know the man or his frustrated kid. She had plenty of troubles of her own to worry about.

None of that held much weight when compared with the sight of a child who clearly had some special needs in great distress—and an adult who just as clearly didn't know what to do in the situation.

She felt an unexpected pang of sympathy for Bowie Callahan, probably because her mother had told her so many stories about how mortified Charlene had been when Katrina had a seizure in a public place. All the staring, the pointing, the whispers.

The boy continued to chant "no" and began smacking his palm against his forehead in rhythm with each exclamation. A couple of older women she didn't know—tourists, probably—looked askance at the boy, and one muttered something to the other about how some children needed a swat on the behind.

She wanted to tell the old biddies to mind their own business but held her tongue, since she was about to ignore her own advice.

After another minute passed, when Bowie Callahan did nothing but gaze down at the boy with helpless frustration, Katrina knew she had to act. What other choice did she have? She pushed her cart closer. The man briefly met her gaze with a wariness that she chose to ignore. Instead, she plopped onto the ground next to the distressed boy.

In her experience with children of all ages and abilities, they reacted better to someone willing to lower to their level. She wasn't sure if he even noticed she was there, since he didn't stop chanting or smacking his palm against his head.

"Hi there." She spoke in a calm, conversational tone, as if she were chatting with one of her friends at Wynona's shower later in the evening. "What's your name?"

Milo—whose name she knew perfectly well from hearing Bowie use it—barely took a breath. "No! No! No! No!"

"Mine is Katrina," she went on. "Some people call me Kat. You know, kitty-cat. Meow. Meow."

His voice hitched a little, and he lowered his hand but continued chanting, though he didn't sound quite as distressed. "No. No. No."

"Let me guess," she said. "Is your name Batman?"

He frowned. "No. No. No."

"Is it…Anakin Skywalker?"

She picked the name assuming by his Star Wars T-shirt that it would be familiar to him. He shook his head. "No."

"What about Harry Potter?

This time, he looked intrigued at the question or perhaps at her stupidity. He shook his head.

"How about Milo?"

Big blue eyes widened with shock. "No," he said, though his tone gave the word the opposite meaning.

"Milo. Hi there. I like your name. I've never met anybody named Milo. Do you know anybody else named Kat?"

He shook his head.

"Neither do I," she admitted "But I have a cat. Her name is Marshmallow, because she's all white. Do you like marshmallows? The kind you eat, I mean."

He nodded and she smiled. "I do, too. Especially in hot cocoa."

He pantomimed petting a cat and pointed at her.

"You'd like to pet her? She would like that. She lives with my mom now and loves to have anyone pay attention to her. Do you have a cat or a dog, Milo?"

The boy's forehead furrowed, and he shook his head, glaring up at the man beside him, who looked stonily down at both of them.

Apparently that was a touchy subject.

Did the boy talk? She had heard him say only "no" so far. It wasn't uncommon for children on the autism spectrum and with other developmental delays to have much better receptive language skills than expressive skills, and he obviously understood and could get his response across fairly well without words.

"I see lots of delicious things in your cart— including cherries. Those are my favorite. Yum. I must have missed those. Where did you find them?"

He pointed to another area of the produce section, where a gorgeous display of cherries gleamed under the fluorescent lights.

She pretended she didn't see them. Though the boy's tantrum had been averted for now, she didn't think it would hurt anything if she distracted him a little longer. "Do you think you could show me?"

It was a technique she frequently employed with her students who might be struggling, whether that was socially, emotionally or academically. She found that if she enlisted their help—either to assist her or to help out another student—they could often be distracted enough that they forgot whatever had upset them.

Milo craned his neck to look up at Bowie for permission. The man looked down at both of them, a baffled look on his features, but after a moment he shrugged and reached a hand down to help her off the floor.

She didn't need assistance, but it would probably seem rude to ignore him. She placed her hand in his and found it warm and solid and much more calloused than a computer nerd should have. She tried not to pay attention to the little shock of electricity between them or the tug at her nerves.

"Thanks," she mumbled, looking quickly away as she followed the boy, who, she was happy to notice, seemed to have completely forgotten his frustration.

CHAPTER TWO

WHAT WAS GOING on here?

Bowie followed the gorgeous woman with the sleek fall of honey-blond hair, listening to the steady stream of one-sided conversation she seemed to be having with his heretofore nonverbal little brother.

He felt as if he had just slid down a rabbit's hole, into a bizarro world where it wasn't at all out of the ordinary for a woman to take a strange kid under her wing in the grocery store and where a pretty smile could divert an out-of-control boy from a full-blown meltdown.

He didn't know what to think. Who was she? And how had she managed to reach his brother so quickly and so efficiently?

He certainly hadn't been able to pull it off in the three weeks since Milo had been dumped in his lap—the brother he never knew existed, from the mother he hadn't seen or heard from in nearly two decades.

He was no closer to knowing how to avert the frequent meltdowns than he'd been the day he got that phone call from Oregon Social Services and flew immediately to Portland—despite extensive research and training on behavior modification.

Rabbit hole. That accurately described where he'd been the last three weeks, falling down one blind chute after another.

A month ago, he thought he had his world pretty figured out. He had a fantastic job he loved that offered the sort of challenges he craved. Maybe he hadn't been completely thrilled about leaving the excitement and dynamic energy of Silicon Valley at first, but after his first few months in town, Haven Point had been growing on him.

The town was small but charming, with a vast lake and soaring mountains that offered an abundance of recreational opportunities for a guy who loved the outdoors. He had been thrilled to take on the challenge of overseeing all the research and development at the new Caine Tech facility in town.

If he ever stopped to think about it, he couldn't help a spurt of pride at how far he had come, all through his own talent and drive—from a fifteen-year-old homeless kid on the streets of Portland to a major shareholder and the director of R&D at one of the country's most influential and innovative tech companies.

And then had come that phone call less than a month before and the difficult decisions with which he still wrestled.

"Before she died, his mother named you guardian

to your brother," the social worker had said. "It's not legally binding as you had no formal agreement."

"How could we?" he had shot back. "I haven't known where she was for years, and I certainly didn't know she'd had another kid, twenty-five years after she had me."

If he *had* known, he wanted to think he would have tried to rescue Milo, to find some kind of stable situation where his half brother could get the medical and therapeutic treatment he so obviously needed.

"You're under no legal obligation to take custody of Milo," the social worker had gone on as if Bowie hadn't spoken. "If you refuse, he will simply remain in the foster system. You should be aware that he will probably end up institutionalized in a special school, as he's been…difficult."

And just like that, he knew his life was about to change. He couldn't do it. He had spent enough time in and out of foster homes, between Stella's brushes with the law or her frequent court-ordered rehab stints or those times when she simply disappeared for weeks at a time.

How could he inflict the same kind of life on another kid? Somehow warehousing him somewhere—out of sight, out of mind—didn't seem the answer either.

Bowie's skills with a computer had paid off handsomely in shares and patents with Caine Tech, and he had more money than one man could ever spend. Since he had the resources to provide a better life for

Milo, how could he live with himself if he walked away and tried to forget he had a half brother tucked away in an institution somewhere?

He still wanted to think he had made the best decision, going through with the guardianship papers. That didn't necessarily make it an easy one—nor did his almost unlimited resources help him find qualified caregivers who would stick, as the last few days amply demonstrated.

"You think those are better than these? Hmm. You might be right. These are from right here in Idaho." The woman with the dimpled smile held out a clear plastic bag near the cherry display. "I need to fill this bag about halfway. Can you help me do that?"

Milo nodded with an understanding and eagerness that shocked Bowie, who had seen nothing similar in his own interactions with him.

"Thank you, Milo," she said with an approving smile when she apparently judged she had enough cherries. "That's perfect. My friends will really love these. Can you help me find the bananas now? Do you know what a banana is?"

He didn't nod or smile or otherwise give any indication he understood, but he led her directly to the stacks of greenish-yellow bananas.

She followed him there and was reaching for a bunch when a girl with red braids and a couple of missing teeth raced over to them.

"Miss Bailey! Miss Bailey! Hi, Miss Bailey!"

Milo's new friend beamed at the girl, who threw her arms around the woman's waist. "Hannah Lewis," she exclaimed as she hugged her back. "Hello! Look how tall you are! And your hair's gotten long. It's still such a beautiful color. Are you sure we can't trade?"

The girl giggled and tossed her red braids. "I haven't seen you in *forever*! Since last summer, anyway. Are you going to be back teaching this year? I hope so! Mrs. Chatterton, the lady who replaced you, is nice and stuff but not as nice as you. My brother's going into the second grade, and he was so sad that you weren't going to be his teacher. Maybe now you can be!"

For a moment, sadness flickered across the woman's lovely features, but she appeared to make an effort to wipe it away.

"I'm afraid I'm not coming back to Haven Point Elementary right now."

"Why not? Don't you like being a teacher? You're so good at it! I liked having my third-grade teacher last year, Mrs. Morris, and I learned my multiplication tables really good from her, but you're still my favorite."

Miss Bailey—at least he had that much of a name—looked touched. "That's very sweet of you to say, Hannah. Thank you. I'm afraid I'm not back to stay, only for a month, for my sister's wedding. I'll be gone again before school starts up in the fall."

"Oh. That's too bad." Hannah looked as if she wanted to say more, but her mother called her over with a smile and friendly wave at Miss Bailey. "I'd better go. My dad's waiting in the van, and we told him we would only be a second. Bye."

"Good to see you, sweetheart."

She hurried away, and Bowie finally spoke. "You're a teacher. That's why you knew just what to do with Milo."

She looked down at the boy, who was fully concentrating on trying to twist together three ties from the produce bag rack.

"I *was* a teacher. I taught second grade at Haven Point Elementary School for three years. Well, I guess I'm still a teacher. I've spent the last year teaching English in South America. I'm sorry I didn't introduce myself before I took off with Milo to buy cherries. I'm Katrina Bailey."

"Bailey. Any relation to Mike, who runs the auto body shop?"

"That's my uncle—and my stepfather. It's a long story."

He held out a hand. "Bowie Callahan. You've met my brother, Milo."

She shook his hand, not bothering to hide the surprise in her expression. "Your brother."

"Half brother. That's an even longer story."

"Well, Bowie and Milo, it was nice to meet you. I should go finish my shopping."

He didn't want her to leave suddenly. "Thank you for stepping in. Milo can be...difficult." That was an understatement that didn't begin to describe his obstinate sibling.

"No problem. Welcome to Haven Point."

She started to push her cart away, but Milo raced after her and held out the tangled twist tie.

"Thank you," she said, taking it with a soft smile toward the boy. "Goodbye."

Milo didn't return her smile—Bowie would have been shocked if he had, since he rarely did—but he wiggled his fingers in return, which Katrina Bailey seemed to find charming.

She pushed her cart away, reaching for a bag of green onions on her way. As she did, Bowie's brain sifted through the information he had just learned from and about her, and he realized in an instant that she could be exactly what they needed.

If he were the churchgoing sort, he would have called her the answer to his prayers.

"Wait," he exclaimed.

Katrina turned at his overloud call. "Yes?"

"Did I just hear you're only in town for a month?"

"That's right," she said warily. "My sister is getting married in a few weeks."

"I don't suppose there's any chance you might be looking for a temporary job while you're in Haven Point."

She stared at him. "A job."

"I'm in the market for a temporary nanny." He turned around, away from Milo, and lowered his voice. "As you probably figured out, my brother has some issues. He's autistic."

"He has autism."

Right. People first, then the condition. He was working on remembering the correct PC terminology. "That's right. He's on the spectrum, apparently moderate to severe."

"Apparently?" As he might have expected, she keyed in on that single word.

"That's what the test results say, anyway." He didn't want to have this conversation in the middle of the produce section of the grocery store, but here they were and he felt he needed to be honest with her. "I only met Milo less than a month ago and don't know anything about his previous history. He has no medical records, no school records. Nothing."

Her eyebrows rose in clear skepticism. "That's impossible. Was he raised in the jungle?"

"Close enough." How else would a person describe Stella's alternative, nonconformist, substance-loving lifestyle?

"Impossible or not, that's the situation. Though his hearing is fine, Milo is mostly nonverbal, at least as far as we can tell. He can say *no*, but that's it." He didn't tell her *no* was Milo's favorite word and he employed it hundreds of times a day.

"He has obvious behavioral challenges," Bowie went on. "We've seen a couple of specialists over the last three weeks and they place him somewhere on the spectrum, but exactly where is tough to say. I only know he's a difficult kid. I've been through three nannies in three weeks. The last one quit yesterday."

That was why Bowie found himself in the supermarket, dealing with a meltdown he couldn't handle.

"I'm sorry. But I don't see how it concerns me. I'm only home to visit my family."

"I've hired a new nanny who is an autism specialist and is supposed to be the top of her field, but she can't be here for three weeks. I'll be honest with you, Miss Bailey. I can't take three weeks off work right now, and I'm desperate to find someone to help with him."

She arched one of those expressive eyebrows. "So you decided to accost stray women in the supermarket and offer the job to them?"

He had the oddest feeling Katrina Bailey didn't like him, though he couldn't figure out exactly what he had done. "Not just any stranger," he pointed out. "A woman who instinctively knew the right thing to do with Milo, where everyone else seems to flounder—and a schoolteacher who has already been vetted by the school system."

"I haven't taught in the last year," she replied. "How do you know I haven't been in prison during that time?"

"Have you?"

She made a face. "No. But you just met me five minutes ago and have no way of knowing that."

"I saw the way you interacted with that girl. Hannah. She said you were her favorite teacher.

Besides, I watched you with Milo. You're obviously well trained and more patient with him than I can ever be. You knew just what to do during one of his tantrums."

If he hoped to flatter her into taking the job, he was doomed to disappointment. At his words, her features seemed to tighten. "Dealing with a child in the midst of a meltdown can be challenging, but really, you only need a compassionate heart and a willingness to focus on the best interests of the child."

Was she implying he didn't have either of those things? Bowie might have been offended if he wasn't afraid she was right.

He was trying, Bowie reminded himself. Hadn't he immediately flown to Portland, brought the boy back to Haven Point, spent time away from Caine Tech he could ill afford in order to find the best care provider for him?

He didn't need one more thing to feel guilty about.

"I do want the best for Milo. You're the first person in three weeks who instinctively seems to know how to manage him."

"He's a child," she retorted, pitching her voice low, presumably so Milo didn't overhear. He could have told her his brother wasn't paying the least bit of attention to them. He had pulled more twist ties off the roll and was forming them into tangled shapes.

"He's a child," she repeated. "Not some new product under development at Caine Tech. He doesn't need to be *managed*."

He wasn't sure how she knew he worked at Caine Tech or why she reacted so strongly to that particular choice of words. Right now, it didn't matter. The only thing he cared about was convincing her to help him.

"It was only a figure of speech," he said. "Look, I'm desperate here. What am I supposed to do? I can't keep missing work and I also can't take Milo to the office with me. Believe me, I've tried."

She didn't look convinced by his plea. If anything, her features turned even frostier. "I'm sorry. I can't help you."

He felt as if someone had just opened the doorway offering a light at the end of the tunnel and then slammed it shut again in his face.

"Not even for ten thousand dollars?"

She stared at him, her mouth slightly ajar. "Ten thousand dollars? You're willing to pay ten thousand dollars for three weeks' work?"

It probably wouldn't be considered good business practice to admit he would be willing to pay much more than that, if only he could regain some semblance of control in his life.

"Okay. Twelve. But that's my final offer."

She looked dumbfounded, and for a moment he clung to a tiny sliver of hope that he might have a chance. In the end, she shook her head slowly, eyeing him like he had several loose screws.

"I said no," she said. "I appreciate that you're in a tight spot, but I'm sure you'll figure it out."

"You don't have to answer right now. Think about

it overnight. If you change your mind, you can find me at 4211 Lakeview Drive. It's a big cedar-and-stone house right along Serenity Harbor."

"I know where it is. But don't count on me changing my mind, Mr. Callahan. I'm only in town for my sister's wedding and to visit family. I have no intention of taking a temporary job."

"Just think about it," he said.

Before she could respond, a pretty redhead turned the corner of the vegetable aisle. He had met Samantha Fremont a few times since he came to town and found her nice enough, though he always left their interactions wishing he were better at small talk.

She appeared surprised to find him and Katrina talking together, then her carefully made-up features shifted into a bright smile.

"Hi, Bowie," she said, her voice a little breathless, before she turned to Katrina.

"There you are!" she exclaimed. "I've been looking all over the store for you. You're not finished shopping yet? What's taking you so long?"

"I was just about to check out. We had a little… situation, but it seems to be under control now. Sorry about that."

"No worries." She turned back to Bowie. "I don't know if you remember me, but we met a month or so ago at Snow Angel Cove. You work at Caine Tech with Aidan and Ben, right?"

Yes. And they were counting on him to deliver

results, as soon as he figured out what to do with his brother. "I remember. Good to see you again."

"I don't know this little guy, though. Is this your son?"

Milo, who had reacted with uncharacteristic warmth to Katrina, gave Sam his blank, almost empty stare.

"This is my brother, Milo."

"Hi there, Milo. My name is Samantha."

With more of that odd affinity, he sidled closer to Katrina, who gave him a reassuring smile. "Don't worry. Sam is nice. She's my very best friend in the whole wide world and has been since we were just a little older than you."

After a moment, Milo handed over another twist-tie creation. Samantha Fremont blinked in surprise at it for a moment, then accepted it gingerly.

"Um. Thanks," she said, clearly at sea.

Katrina tugged her away.

"We have to go. We're going to be late for a party. It was nice to meet you, Milo."

She hadn't said it was nice to meet *him*. Bowie told himself not to be disappointed by the omission.

"Think about it," he said.

"I gave you my answer, Mr. Callahan. I won't change my mind."

As she walked away with her friend, he had to hope she was wrong about that. If not, he wasn't sure how he would survive the next three weeks until the autism specialist could arrive.

KATRINA'S SHOULDER BLADES itched as she walked away from Bowie and Milo, and she was certain if she turned around, she would find one—or possibly both—of them watching after her.

This was what happened to women who didn't mind their own business. They ended up having to turn down outrageous job offers they couldn't for a *moment* actually be considering.

Sam waited only until they had headed for the checkout line before questions burst out of her. "What was that all about? What are you supposed to think about?"

"Nothing. That looks like the shortest line." She headed for the checkout line closest to the door, waving at one of her mother's friends as she went.

"It didn't seem like nothing." Sam gave a short laugh that didn't sound entirely amused. She shook her head. "I turn my back for five minutes to pick up my mom's blood pressure medication and come back to find you chatting with the hottest guy in town. I should have expected it. Good to see some things don't change. You're still the same flirty Kat."

She wasn't. The last year had changed her profoundly, in ways she couldn't begin to explain to Sam.

"Did he ask you out?" Samantha's voice had a strangely careful quality to it as she started pulling items out of the cart and setting them on the belt.

"No!" Katrina exclaimed, more sharply than she meant to. "No. It wasn't like that at all. He's looking for a temporary caregiver for his younger brother. That's all."

"Like a babysitter?"

"More like a nanny, I guess."

"I still can't believe that's his brother, though I suppose they do look alike."

Katrina wasn't sure she completely agreed. They had the same color hair and eyes, though the boy's skin was a shade or two darker and his mouth was different.

Not that she noticed.

"He seemed like a cute kid, though I don't know what this is about." Sam dangled the little twist-tie sculpture Milo had made for her.

"It's a penguin. Can't you tell?"

"No. Apparently you have to have an elementary education degree to fully appreciate the artistry."

"Apparently."

"No wonder the man wants you to be his kid brother's nanny. You're perfect for it—even though he only met you five minutes ago."

She was still reeling from the dollar signs that had temporarily danced in front of her gaze when he mentioned the amount he was willing to pay. That would more than pay the rest of her legal costs in Colombia from her grasping attorney.

"I said the same thing. He knows absolutely nothing about me, yet he wants to hand over his brother to me."

"How did all that happen in the five minutes I was at the pharmacy?"

She replayed the conversation in her head and still couldn't quite make sense of it. "Milo is on the autism spectrum. He was in the middle of a meltdown in the middle of the produce aisle over some grapes. I was somehow able to divert his attention, and now Bowie Callahan apparently thinks I'm some kind of miracle worker. Anne Sullivan to Milo's Helen Keller. It's ridiculous, really."

But twelve thousand dollars. How could she turn it down?

"You're not taking the job?"

"I'm only here for a few weeks. I don't want to spend my whole time taking care of some rich guy's brother who has autism, no matter how cute he is. The brother, I mean."

"Are you kidding? You should totally take the job. I would jump at the chance to work for Bowie Callahan."

"Too bad he's not in the market to hire a personal shopper or something. Especially one who specializes in women's fashions."

"If he needed my particular skills, I would figure out a way. I'm not the only one. Half the women in town are in love with the man. When Eppie and Hazel saw him for the first time, I was afraid they would go straight into cardiac arrest."

Yet another reason she didn't want to take the job. She'd had enough of good-looking men to last her a lifetime.

She had learned her lesson well after what happened in South America with that idiot Carter Ross.

"You're totally going to do it. I can see you wavering."

"I'm not," she protested.

Before Sam could argue, the shopper ahead of them picked up his receipt and bag from the checker and it was their turn.

"Hey, Katrina!" The checker, an older woman with unnaturally blond hair and nicotine-stained teeth, beamed at her. "I thought that was you when you first came in earlier. My line was backed up and I didn't have time to come find you to say hello."

Her smile felt tight and forced. She genuinely liked Filene Harding, but their encounters were always a bit awkward. Katrina had dated Filene's son a few times in high school, and Filene always acted as if they had a much closer bond than Katrina thought.

"Hi, Filene. How are you?"

"Good. Good. How are you, hon? I heard you've been in Mexico or some crazy thing like that."

"Colombia, actually. A little village about an hour from Barranquilla."

Filene didn't seem to care about the details. "You know, it's the funniest thing that you came in today. I was just looking at a picture of you at the prom with my Bryan the other day. You two were so cute together! I always thought so. I'll have to tell him you're back in town."

Bryan Harding had been renowned for his octopus hands in high school. Once she figured that out after the second date, she tried her best to avoid the guy. "How is Bryan these days?" she asked to be polite, then could have kicked herself for encouraging the woman.

"Good. Good. He's working construction with his brother. He was living with a gal, but they broke up a few weeks ago. She kicked him out, if you want the truth. I don't know why, because they seemed so happy together. So now he's back living in my basement."

"Didn't he have a little boy a few years back with some girl in Boise?" Sam asked.

The red-painted corners of Filene's mouth turned up as she scanned their groceries. "He's got two. Different mamas, of course. Six months apart. They're the cutest little things. Spittin' image of their daddy. You should see them."

She doubted that would happen, since she and Bryan Harding didn't run in the same social circles. They never really had, she supposed.

When she was about thirteen, Bryan had been one of the first guys who noticed she was finally starting to grow into her features and had begun to develop some curves. They had flirted a little, just in fun, and she sneaked out of the house to go to the movies with him a few times, until she figured out he only wanted to see how lucky he could get with StupidKat.

She supposed Bryan was the first in a long line

of dumb decisions she had made when it came to the male of the species. No more. She was done wasting her time and energy on the players of the world.

"I'll be sure to tell Bryan I ran into you," Filene said as she rang up the last of their groceries. "You staying at your mom's place while you're in town?"

"For now," she hedged as she swiped her debit card, ever mindful of the depleting balance in her account. "Thank you. See you."

She scooped up one bag while Samantha grabbed the other and hurried out of the store.

She didn't *want* Bryan to find her. Or any other guy, for that matter.

In a few months, she would have everything she never knew she wanted. Everything else seemed unimportant.

CHAPTER THREE

"THANKS SO MUCH for offering to host the party here, Jules."

Julia Winston smiled, though it didn't quite push away that subtle air of sadness that encircled her. "My pleasure, really. Especially since McKenzie is doing all the work. This house needs more parties."

Julia lived in one of a handful of gorgeous Victorian mansions about a block off the water that had been built by early mining and business magnates, in the days when the area around Lake Haven had been an exclusive retreat renowned for the healing nature of the hot springs in abundance around the area.

Katrina had always loved this neighborhood. Steeped in history and beauty, it always felt graceful and elegant to her, even when she was a girl.

"How are you doing?" her mother, Charlene, asked Julia with a concerned expression. "How's your mom?"

The town librarian gave a smile that didn't quite reach her eyes. She had lived here with her elderly mother until Mariah Winston had a stroke a few months earlier. Mariah was now in a rehab center in

Shelter Springs, the same one where Katrina's father had spent the last few years of his life.

"Fine. Every day she seems to be showing a little improvement. Or at least I would like to think so. It's hard to be sure."

Oh, Katrina remembered those difficult days after her father had suffered a debilitating brain injury after being shot on the job. How many hours had she sat by his bedside, watching for a blink or a facial tic or anything that might indicate the man she adored was still inside the shell lying on that hospital bed?

She squeezed Julia's hand. "I'm sorry. Hosting a bridal shower is probably the last thing you felt like doing."

"Not at all. I wouldn't have offered if I hadn't wanted to do it. I needed the distraction, if you want the truth. The house seems too quiet sometimes."

"It's such a lovely home. Every time I come here, I feel like I'm stepping back into another era," Kat said.

Julia made a face. "Your great-grandma's era, maybe."

"I love it," Sam declared. "You've got that classy, retro vibe going on. That's really in right now."

"There's nothing wrong with old-fashioned," Charlene assured Julia.

"I agree," Kat said. "I wish I had been able to see Haven Point in its heyday."

"Totally," Sam said. "All those rich dudes coming here to soak in the hot springs. I'd be all over that."

Before Julia could answer, Eliza Caine walked into the room. She looked around them as if wondering if someone else was hiding behind the grandfather clock in the entryway. "You don't happen to have brought the guest of honor with you, did you? She's fifteen minutes late, and that's totally not like our Wynona."

"She'll be here," Katrina assured her. "She called us before we left the house and said she had to help Cade with something."

Samantha gave an inelegant snort with a distinctively naughty edge.

"Get your mind out of the gutter, young lady," her mother, Linda, said, glaring at her only daughter.

"What? I didn't even say anything," Sam protested.

"Something at the police station," Charlene said quickly. "I think one of the cases she investigated last summer when she still worked for the police department is going to trial, and he had some questions for her. She'll be here soon. She said she was on her way."

As if on cue, an old-fashioned doorbell chimed through the graceful entryway.

Kat was closest to it. She opened the door and was the first to hug her sister.

"Sorry I'm late," Wynona said. "I didn't mean to keep everyone waiting."

"You didn't," Katrina assured her. "We just arrived ourselves."

"Everyone's in the back, if you'd like to follow me."

Julia led the way through the house, filled with antiques and collectibles. It really was like a museum. How did Julia walk down for a midnight snack without worrying about breaking some sort of priceless family heirloom? she wondered.

This neighborhood was set on a hill some distance from downtown, but the huge screened sunroom Julia led them to offered spectacular views of the lake and the Redemption Mountains.

"Oh, look what you've done to this place," Charlene exclaimed. "It's absolutely stunning, Kenzie."

McKenzie Kilpatrick, the Haven Point mayor and floral shop owner who loved nothing so much as throwing a big party—except maybe her husband, Ben—had pulled out the perfect bridal shower decor for Wynona. Though Wyn had been a police officer, she was a girlie-girl at heart, and the decorations reflected that, with large paper parasols in soft pastel shades hanging from the ceiling and heart-shaped balloons in the same shades in every corner.

"I had a lot of help. Katrina and Sam were here for several hours this afternoon."

As maid of honor, Katrina probably should have handled many of the shower details. She *had* participated in the planning with Julia, Eliza and McKenzie via Skype and email, but it was a little hard to do much more from another country.

"I hope you didn't go up on the ladder to hang those parasols, honey," Charlene said to Katrina.

"With your luck, you'd fall off and break something. Wouldn't that be a sorry state of affairs, if you had a broken arm in a cast to go with your bridesmaid dress?"

She managed to refrain from rolling her eyes—which she wanted to think was a sign that she was indeed maturing at least a little bit. "Yes. Terrible."

"Although, maybe if you had a broken arm," her mother said tartly, "you would have to stick around home longer than a few weeks."

As Katrina was well aware of her mother's negative attitude about her return to Colombia, she opted to ignore that broad hint. "I'm going to go set this salad over on the table and say hello to Hazel and Eppie," she said, then escaped before her mother could call her back.

She adored the two Brewer sisters, sisters ten months apart who had married twin brothers and spent their entire lives living next to each other. She and Samantha often said they wanted to grow up to be just like them, sassy and funny and full of spice.

She set the salad down and hugged each of them in turn. "How are my favorite troublemakers? What have you been up to while I've been gone?"

"Why, there's our favorite world traveler," Hazel said. "It's about time you came back."

"I'm so happy you made it in time for the wedding," Eppie exclaimed.

Surely they knew she wouldn't have missed Wyn and Cade's wedding, no matter what. Even if she had been stuck in a tiny village on the Amazon River without a boat, she would have swum through barracudas to be here if necessary.

"Sit here by us," Hazel insisted. "We want to hear every juicy detail. What sort of hunky guys have you been hanging out with down there?"

"I can picture you now, lounging around on the beaches of Rio or living it up in some penthouse apartment in Bogotá."

For one moment, she could vividly picture Gabriela's orphanage, where she had been spending virtually all of her free time when she wasn't teaching English at the nearby secondary school. She saw the run-down facility as clearly as if she had just left—the peeling paint, the bare mattresses on the floor, the plain, dangling light bulbs overhead.

She had to get Gabi out of that environment, no matter what.

The dedicated staff at the orphanage tried to shower love on the children, but they had limited time and even more limited means to make a real difference.

Her heart ached all over again at the confusion and sadness in Gabi's sweet face when Katrina had hugged her goodbye the week before. Though she wasn't yet four, she had already been disappointed twice when previous adoptions fell through. Children with Down syndrome could be difficult to place in developing countries, especially when they already struggled with complicated medical conditions that could accompany that diagnosis.

Gabi would eventually need heart surgery for a congenital defect, which was highly unlikely in her current circumstances.

"Come back?" Gabi had whispered the plea in Spanish, her brow furrowed and her mouth twisted into a frown.

Katrina had kissed her cheek while running a hand over her dark hair. "I swear it," she had answered, not at all sure how much the girl understood or believed.

She hated to leave her. Under other circumstances, she might have opted to skip the wedding and put the necessary travel expenses toward the ever-rising adoption fees.

But she loved Wyn dearly. Katrina was her maid of honor and couldn't even contemplate missing her wedding to Police Chief Cade Emmett, who had been friends with their older brother Marshall and had been part of their lives as long as Katrina could remember.

She was here, right now, in Haven Point, at Julia Winston's beautiful home celebrating Wynona's upcoming wedding. She needed to be present, she reminded herself. As much as her heart might yearn to be with the child whose generosity and courage had stolen her heart, she wouldn't ruin her sister's wedding celebrations and this gathering with her dear friends of the Haven Point Helping Hands by pining to be somewhere else.

She pushed the ache away. "All right, girls," she said to Eppie and Hazel, who hadn't been girls for about seven decades. "Tell me everything that's been going on around town while I've been gone. You two always know the good dirt."

Eppie giggled. "Oh my. How much time do you have?"

"As long as it takes."

They had only about ten minutes to visit before McKenzie Kilpatrick took charge and told everyone they should eat now so they could save their strength for the games to come.

Katrina suggested the Brewer sisters let her grab plates for them, an offer they accepted with alacrity. After she prepared their plates, she returned to the buffet line for one of her own. While she was chatting with Devin Barrett—McKenzie's sister, whose stepdaughter had been in Katrina's class—Lindy Grace Keegan took her spot next to Hazel and Eppie.

"There's a spot over here," Charlene called.

With a little inward sigh, Katrina manufactured a smile—she was becoming an expert at it—and made her way to the long table where her mother sat with several of their other friends.

"Everything is so delicious, don't you think?" Charlene asked the table at large and received a positive response in return. "I'm especially loving this cheesecake. Who made it?"

Barbara Serrano, whose family owned a restaurant, raised her hand. "It's a new recipe we're trying out."

"I'd say it's a hit," McKenzie said.

"I have *got* to get this recipe," Andie Montgomery said. "Marshall would love it. You know how much he loves sweets."

Andie, a widow with two adorable kids, was marrying Katrina's brother Marshall in the fall. Kat had met her a few times the previous summer and thought her very nice but a little too quiet for the rambunctious Bailey family. She hadn't known about Andie's painful past until pieces of it slithered into town and threatened Andie, those cute kids *and* Wynona.

She still wasn't sure how she felt about Andie becoming her sister-in-law as she didn't know her well yet, but it was obvious Marshall adored her—and vice versa.

"You have to try this," Charlene said, holding her fork just inches away from Katrina's mouth. Her mother never seemed to remember she didn't like cheesecake.

"No, thanks. You have it. I'm good with fruit. Thanks, though."

"Are you sure? It's delicious."

"Positive."

"I don't know why you won't at least have a taste. It's not like you can't afford the calories, unlike some of us. You're so thin," Charlene said with a sigh.

Her mother could win Olympic gold in fussing.

"I'm fine. Really. Look at all this food I've taken."

"But how much of it will you eat?" Charlene countered.

Again, she wondered what her mother would say if she knew some of the interesting meals Katrina had eaten in South America.

"I think you look beautiful," Barbara said with her kind smile. "What have you been up to? You went to South America with that sexy mountain climber who used to come into the restaurant with you, right? What was his name again? How's he doing?"

Her mother's mouth straightened into a thin line, probably from the effort it was taking Charlene not to spill out her own opinions about Carter Ross. Her mother had strongly opposed Katrina's decision to go with him on his quest to climb the highest point in every country in South America.

It's too dangerous. You aren't serious with the man, anyway. Why do you have to go halfway across the world with him?

All valid points, Kat could admit now. At one point, her mother had even sworn she would never speak with her again if she left with him. Obviously, that had been a hollow threat. More's the pity.

To her mother's credit, she hadn't uttered so much as an I-told-you-so after Katrina's tenuous relationship with Carter barely survived two of the countries on the list. That didn't make it any easier for Kat to admit her mother had been right all along.

"No doubt he's fine, but I couldn't say for certain. We went our separate ways several months ago."

That was a polite way of sugarcoating the truth, she supposed. He had been an ass and she had been stupid. Her mistakes still stung, though not with the pain of a broken heart. She hadn't wanted forever, she reminded herself. That didn't prevent her from feeling betrayed when he had basically abandoned her in a foreign country without money, credit cards or her passport.

"I still don't understand why you didn't just pack your bags and come back home after you and he-who-shall-remain-nameless broke up," Sam said.

Funny, how a lack of money, credit cards and passport could impact travel plans. Even after all that had been remedied with help from the embassy in Bogotá, something had kept her there.

"I didn't really go down to South America for him. He was the excuse, not the reason," she said, which had been one of the points of contention between her and Carter. He'd wanted her undivided attention.

"Once I was already there, immersed in other cultures and getting to know the people, I found I really enjoyed the adventure of it. Except for the years I was in college in Boise, I've never lived anywhere else but Haven Point. I decided this was a good chance for me to travel the world a bit, see what might be out there beyond the border of our little town."

"That's easy," Barbara Serrano said with a laugh. "Shelter Springs starts about three miles north of us. But take my advice, don't bother going there unless you absolutely have to. The natives aren't very friendly."

She laughed along with the rest of the Helping Hands. The rivalry between the two towns was ever-present.

"I know what you're talking about," Hazel said after the laughter subsided. "When Donald and I were first married, we spent a year in the Philippines while he was stationed there in the air force. Best year of our marriage, even though we lived in base housing surrounded by mostly Americans. I adored going to the street markets, trying the cuisine, seeing how other people lived. I missed my hometown and my family but loved seeing a different culture. It opens the mind."

"Yes. Exactly."

"I hope, like I did, you've learned a little more about the world and a whole lot more about yourself."

She smiled warmly at Hazel, the first person who seemed to truly understand her experience these last nine months.

"I have," she said.

"Tell them about your latest wild hair," Charlene said, her tone sharp but her eyes filled with concern.

Her mother was strongly against her plans to adopt Gabriela. She thought Katrina was acting on a whim, jumping into something for which she wasn't prepared. Instead of being excited, as Katrina had hoped, her mother was full of dire predictions about how she was limiting her future options by taking on this lifelong responsibility to a stranger at a time when she should be looking to settle down and have children of her own.

She could only hope Charlene's opposition would fade when she had the chance to meet Gabi, to look into those dark eyes and see the life and joy and possibility in them.

"Is this about what happened in the grocery store with Bowie Callahan?" Sam interjected. "That was the craziest thing."

The entire collection of shower guests seemed to perk up, merely at the man's name. She would have found it amusing if she hadn't felt a subtle little shiver rippling through her insides.

"Now, *there's* someone I wouldn't mind packing along in my truck on a world tour," Hazel said with her sly, lascivious grin.

"He is one fine-looking man," Lindy Grace Keegan purred.

Yes. Katrina wholly agreed. Which was all the more reason for her to stay away from him. Her decision-making track record around fine-looking men was dismal at best.

"What happened with Bowie Callahan?" Charlene asked, eyes wide. "I had no idea you even knew the man."

Thanks for that, Sam. She aimed a sharp look at her friend, who gave her an apologetic shrug.

"I don't know him. Not really. I met him today after I had a bit of a situation with his younger brother."

"Bowie Callahan has a younger brother?" Barbara Serrano looked shocked. "Now, there's something *I* didn't know—and here I was under the impression I knew everything that went on around this town."

"He does. His name is Milo and he's very cute. Around five or six years old, I would guess."

"Six," Eliza chimed in.

"He's very cute," Samantha said. "Though he seems like a handful. He was having a fit in the store and Kat headed him off, so now Bowie wants to hire Katrina to be Milo's nanny for a couple of weeks while she's in town. He apparently offered her a boatload of money. Can you believe she said no?"

"Tell him I'll do it for free," Hazel said, with that grin again.

"Why on earth would you turn him down?" Wyn asked.

"I came home for your wedding, not to solve a family crisis for some rich, self-absorbed executive I don't even know."

She instantly regretted her words, spoken more harshly than she really intended. They seemed to fall on the shower guests like a sudden cloudburst.

"You don't have to be rude," Charlene said, clear reprimand in her voice as if Katrina were eight years old again and had eaten something that wasn't on her approved ketogenic, antiseizure diet.

"Bowie is actually a very nice man, which you would know if you'd spent more than a few minutes with him," her mother said. "Why, the very first week he was in town, he stopped to help me load my groceries."

"And he gave a sizable donation to the fund-raiser for a new library," Julia offered in her quiet voice.

"For what it's worth, I've always found him very nice—and Ben and Aidan have nothing but good to say about him," Eliza put in.

"They all went to school together," McKenzie added. "You should hear some of their stories about their time together."

When the entire formidable force that was the Haven Point Helping Hands ganged up on a person, it was like being steamrolled by an avalanche.

"Okay, okay. I get it. The man is a saint. That still doesn't mean I want to spend my limited time home babysitting his kid brother."

Just like with Milo and his behavior issues, sometimes the best strategy was simple diversion, and she quickly changed the subject. "Now, isn't it about time for some delightfully off-color wedding shower games?"

Wynona groaned, but Hazel and Eppie giggled. "Yes," they chimed in unison.

McKenzie jumped up. "You're right. We have tons to do, people. Better get to it."

Katrina managed to avoid the topic of Bowie Callahan and his brother again until the shower was over and she was helping her sister carry presents out to her SUV.

"That was great," she said as they walked out into the sweet-smelling air from the honeysuckle and snowberry that grew in abundance on Julia's property.

"I'm so glad we were able to work it around your schedule so you could make it. It wouldn't have been nearly as much fun without you."

"You're only saying that because Sam and I made the best wedding dress out of toilet paper."

"It was a work of art. I hope my real one looks half that good," Wyn said. "I especially loved the row of toilet paper roses across the shoulders and adorning your veil."

"What can I say? I've always looked good in Charmin."

They both laughed, but Wyn's smile slid away too quickly. "Hey, I hope you're not turning down that nanny gig because of me."

"You mean because I flew six thousand miles to come home and spend a little time with you before your wedding?"

"Yeah. That." Wynona smiled. "I just mean, if you can work around the schedule thing with the wedding, do it. Bowie seems like a nice guy in a tough spot, at least from what everyone said in there.

And the money would definitely come in handy with all your legal expenses, wouldn't it?"

Wynona, at least, supported her efforts to adopt Gabi, and so did Cade. Her brother Marshall hadn't said much about it—but then, he didn't say much about anything.

"The money wouldn't hurt," she admitted. "But I can't just duck out of helping you with wedding prep. I'm the maid of honor!"

"Don't worry about that. McKenzie has whipped all the Helping Hands into a frenzy, getting things ready for the big day. You know how she is. Between her and Mom—and Andie, who did all the wedding invitations—I've hardly lifted a finger for my own wedding. I feel more than a little guilty about it, if you want the truth."

She nudged Wyn with her shoulder, so happy her sister and Cade were ready to start their life together. "You've been a little busy, finishing up your master's program and starting a new job at children's services in Shelter Springs."

"You're right. That's a lot of change in a short time." She paused, clutching her arms as if she were suddenly chilled, though the evening was warm. "What am I doing?"

The sudden panic in her voice shocked Katrina. Her older sister always seemed so together. During those long months after their father was shot on duty and incapacitated, Wyn had been a rock. When Katrina had wanted to quit her last year of college and come home to take care of Charlene, Wyn refused to let her. Instead, Wyn had been the one to move back to Haven Point, taking a job in the Haven Point Police Department.

She might not sew as well as Samantha or be as good as McKenzie at throwing together a beautiful celebration, but she knew her sister and what she needed.

Katrina gripped Wyn's hands tightly, there in the shadow of the beautiful Victorian house, with its gables and turrets.

"Stop it. Right now. You're marrying an absolutely wonderful man—one who adores you and cherishes you. A man you have loved most of your life. You're going to marry him, make a life with him, build a future, and it's going to be beautiful. *That's* what you're doing."

Wyn drew in a shaky breath, then another until the look of panic receded from her gaze.

"You're right. You're right. I don't know what happened there for a moment. I think with the shower and all the gifts and everything tonight, the whole thing suddenly seems more real."

"You haven't had much time to soak in all the changes in your life. Last summer you were a police officer and Cade was your boss. Until a few weeks ago, you were in Boise finishing your degree. Now here you are, about to start the most exciting chapter of your life with your sexy police chief."

"You're right. You're right." Wyn gave a breathy

laugh. "Oh, I can't wait. Thank you for the pep talk. Promise me you won't tell Mom or Cade I needed one."

"Pinkie promise," she said.

"Back to what I was saying about Bowie. I trust you to do what you think is best, but I don't want you to worry a moment that you have to spend every moment that you're home with me. Everything is under control for the wedding, and we'll have plenty of time together after you adopt your sweet Gabi and bring her back to Haven Point. I'll be the best aunt ever. You wait. That girl is going to be so spoiled."

She had no doubt about it. Eventually even Charlene would have to come around and accept Gabi.

How could she not?

CHAPTER FOUR

"ARE YOU SURE you're good for a little while?"

Lizzie Lawson, the teenage neighbor girl who had helped Bowie out a few times in a pinch, nodded and placed a hand on Milo's head.

"We should be fine. Right, Milo?"

His brother didn't pay her any attention. He was too entranced by the big golden retriever that had accompanied Lizzie. The dog—she had called him Jerry Lewis—had a blunt, friendly face and seemed extraordinarily patient as Milo petted him.

"You said you needed about thirty minutes for your conference call, is that right?" she said.

"Give or take a few minutes."

"No problem. We'll go for a little walk on the lakeside trail. Milo, you can hold the leash if you want."

His brother didn't smile, but his eyes did widen with excitement. This was Lizzie's third time keeping an eye on Milo for Bowie when he had work obligations he couldn't escape. She seemed very dependable, and Milo tolerated her as much as he did anyone, especially if she brought the dog along to help entertain him.

If only she could help him out for longer periods of time, but she already had a job working in McKenzie Kilpatrick's store. Besides that, an hour or so with Milo was probably as much as a teenage girl should be expected to handle, no matter how well recommended she came from McKenzie.

He crouched down to Milo's level. As usual, his brother avoided looking straight at him, his attention focused exclusively on the dog.

"Milo. Bud. Look at me." His brother's gaze danced to him for an instant, then quickly away. Bowie supposed he would have to be content with what he could get. "Listen to what Lizzie says. Got it? Nod if you understand me."

Milo nodded, though he didn't stop petting the dog.

"All right, kid," Lizzie said. "Let's do this. Here's the leash. Hold on tight now. Got it?"

Milo clung to the leash handle as if his life depended on it and trotted after the retriever with Lizzie bringing up the rear.

Bowie watched them go, aware of the familiar tangle of his emotions. He was in so far over his head with Milo, all he could see above him was darkness and uncertainty. If this autism specialist didn't work, he wasn't sure what he would do. He hated the idea of putting Milo in some kind of facility somewhere—avoiding that had been the entire reason he had agreed to become his guardian—but he couldn't completely rule out that might be the best option, down the road.

He didn't have to worry about that right now, though, when he had people waiting for him. He tried to shift focus from Milo-worry to work-worry, aware the next few weeks were crucial for several of the projects he was spearheading at Caine Tech.

This conference call with one of their major vendors in Asia was vital. If they didn't iron out some of the problems now, the ripple effect would completely screw their production schedule.

Thanks to the chaos with Milo, it felt like weeks since he had been able to fully focus on work—not a good situation when he was only just finding his way with his team at the new Haven Point facility.

He knew just whom to blame for this frustration. His mother.

An image of Stella the last time he had seen her flashed across his mind. He had been fifteen, almost the same age she had been when she gave birth to him. A child raising a child. The problem was, he eventually grew up. His mother had not.

Growing up with Stella had been tumultuous at best, a nightmare much of the time.

Guilt dug under his skin at the thought. He didn't hate his mother. He never had, even after he had escaped the chaos. Yeah, she had been flighty and irresponsible, self-absorbed, emotional and totally without willpower.

Alcohol, drugs, men. She used all of them with regularity.

Milo's early years apparently hadn't been much different from his own. The social worker who had contacted him about Milo had pieced together enough information on his brother's history to reveal that Stella had never really changed her ways. At the time of her death, she had been destitute, living on the streets of Portland with Milo, begging at street corners and high most of the time. Why his brother hadn't been taken away from her years ago seemed to be a mystery to everybody in the system.

Bo slid into his office chair, catching a view out the floor-to-ceiling windows at the lake in the distance and the soaring mountains beyond.

He thought he had come so far in his own psyche. He hadn't given much thought to his mother in several years, not since the private investigator he sent to find her came back empty-handed years ago.

He should have kept looking.

Again, guilt pinched at him—the familiar guilt of a son who loved his mother despite her failings and wanted more for her than the hardscrabble, free-living, moment-to-moment existence she insisted on.

He had no choice but to think about her now.

Milo—the troubled, silent, *needy* son she had given birth to more than twenty-five years after she had Bowie—was a constant reminder. The boy had his mother's eyes. *Their* mother's eyes. Mysterious, deep, dreamy.

With one last sigh, he shoved away the memories and forced himself to focus on the man he had become, someone far more comfortable in the safe, predictable world of technology than with the murky morass of his past.

"THAT WENT WELL, don't you think?"

Bowie nodded at his personal assistant, the only person still linked into the video conference call. "Excellent. Sounds like with the information we gave them, they can iron out the supplier problems and be set to move into production by next quarter."

Peggy Luchino shifted in her chair. She was plump and pretty, with long curly hair and eyes that always seemed to smile. In the two months since he had come to the Haven Point facility, she had taken him under wing—somewhat like the older sister he never had.

"Good work, Peggy. We never would have made so much progress if you hadn't been there to keep us on track."

"Thanks." She gave a rueful smile. "Even so, it went longer than we anticipated. Sorry about that."

He looked up at the clock above his desk and was shocked to realize he had been on the conference call for two solid hours. Amazing, how fast time went when he was solving a problem, making progress toward a goal. It had always been that way, since his first hacking attempts on a cobbled-together secondhand computer when he was eleven years old.

"Not your fault."

"I'll write up the transcript from the call and send you all salient info by first thing tomorrow."

"Thanks. Talk to you later."

When her image disappeared from the screen in front of him, Bowie stood, feeling a crick in his neck for the first time from being in one position too long. His stomach rumbled, too. He supposed he ought to grab some lunch before he dived in again.

As Bowie tilted his head from side to side to ease some of the tension in his muscles and ligaments, the gleam of sunlight on water caught his gaze, and he looked out the window at the lake rippling in a summer afternoon.

A quick walk out to the terrace would be just the thing to clear some of this murkiness out of his head, he decided.

It was only after he headed out into the hallway that the reminder of his responsibilities suddenly crashed over him.

Milo!

He had told the neighbor girl he would be on the conference call for only thirty minutes or so and it was now more than double that. Shit! He was the worst guardian on the planet. Every time he thought he was starting to figure out this whole being-responsible-for-a-child thing, something like this happened to remind him of his inadequacies.

Where were they? He rushed through the house,

straining to hear any sound that might pinpoint their location, but heard only silence.

Nothing new there. That was one of the toughest things about having a brother who didn't speak. On the numerous occasions when Milo had slipped away, Bowie had discovered it was tough to find him.

After a quick scan of the house didn't reveal Milo *or* Lizzie, he remembered she had planned to take him for a walk on the shoreline trail. Was it possible something had happened to Milo? He had an odd fascination with the water, which scared the hell out of Bowie.

Surely he would have heard from Lizzie if his brother fell in. Someone would have contacted him, right? Unless Lizzie hadn't been able to call for help because she had somehow gone into the water, too…

His mind racing with grim possibilities, he rushed out to the terrace, the last place he had seen them. Relief flooded through him when he spotted Milo at the water's edge, poised to throw a small rock into the water.

Close on its heels was more concern when Bowie realized his brother appeared to be alone, with no sign of Lizzie *or* Jerry Lewis.

Bowie stalked forward and grabbed his brother's arm. "Milo! You know you're not supposed to be near the water by yourself! Where is Lizzie?"

"She left."

He turned around sharply at the voice that most

definitely was *not* the neighbor girl. Instead, he found the lovely Katrina Bailey sitting in one of the Adirondack chairs facing the lake, where she appeared to be keeping an eagle eye on the boy from beneath the shade of an umbrella.

He didn't know how he had missed seeing her in his initial scan of the patio. She had been lost in shadow, he supposed, plus his attention had been focused on Milo.

Now, as she shifted into the sunlight, he couldn't seem to look away. She wore a peach shirt and a pair of khaki shorts that made her legs look long and slim and tanned. All that silky wheat-colored hair was on top of her head in a messy, summery style that tempted a man to pull out the pins and see if it was as soft as it looked.

His heart rate, already high with anxiety over his missing brother, kicked up a notch, a reaction he found as unsettling as it was unwanted.

"What are you doing here?"

"Keeping an eye on your younger brother. Somebody had to."

He knew the quick flash of guilt was completely appropriate. He should have been more aware of the time.

"Where is Lizzie? I thought she was watching him."

Katrina gave him a cool look that left him in no doubt about her feelings toward him, which apparently hadn't miraculously improved overnight. He wasn't at all sure what he had done to deserve her dislike—okay, except maybe completely forget he had a responsibility to something besides his work.

"She left about an hour ago," Katrina said. "She had to go to an orthodontist appointment."

Crap. The girl had told him as much when he asked her to keep an eye on Milo. Like time itself, the memory had slipped his mind. He furrowed his brow. "That still doesn't explain how you ended up here with him. Did she call you or something?"

He thought he saw a tiny hint of color bloom across her cheekbones, though he might have been mistaken.

"No. They bumped into me earlier when I was at McKenzie and Ben's house, working on a few projects with her for my sister's wedding reception."

"Oh. You're friends with McKenzie."

Of course she would be friends with McKenzie Kilpatrick, who was married to his friend and the chief operating officer at Caine Tech. It didn't surprise him a bit. In the short time he'd been in Haven Point, he had already figured out that all the women here seemed to run in one big pack.

They scared the hell out of him, truth be told.

"Yes. She's close to my sister's age and they were friends since school—which means *we* were friends, too."

He liked both of the women Aidan and Ben had recently married. Eliza Caine and McKenzie Kilpatrick both seemed great. More important to him, they made his friends happier than he'd ever known them.

"We happened to be taking a break in the backyard when Milo and Lizzie walked past. He seemed glad to see me, and Lizzie could see that Milo and I knew each other. As we were talking to them, she kept looking at her watch and mentioned her appointment. I offered to keep an eye on him until you finished your call. I didn't think you'd mind. We've been skipping rocks for the last half hour or so."

"Sorry you were dragged into it. I should have kept better track of the time. Lizzie told me she had an appointment, but I was wrapped up in the meeting and it completely slipped my mind. Thanks for helping."

"I'm glad it worked out." She nodded toward Milo, who was paying them no attention. "I do think he's getting a little hungry. I would have fixed him a sandwich or something, but I couldn't figure out how to get in, and I thought you might worry if I took him all the way to my mom's place."

Her words weren't necessarily barbed, but he felt the implicit criticism in them. *What kind of ass locks his kid brother out of the house and then forgets him for hours on end?*

Yeah. Bowie Callahan. That's who.

"I didn't even think about the door being locked. Sorry. Since Milo came to live with me, I've had to buy automatic locks and beef up security. He has a tendency to wander."

That was only one of a million ways his life had completely changed in the last three weeks. He was still trying to process all the changes—and apparently wasn't doing a very good job of it.

"Probably smart. You live on a lake. Anything could happen if he managed to get out."

She didn't have to tell him that. He had the nightmares to prove it.

"I've tried to explain to him that he can't just take off, but I'm not sure how much he internalizes."

As if sensing they were talking about him, Milo wandered over to them, apparently done with throwing rocks.

He barely acknowledged Bo but handed Katrina a rock from the lakeshore with as close to a smile as he ever managed.

She looked confused for a moment, then closed her fingers over it. "Oh, that's a pretty one. Are you giving it to me to keep?"

Milo nodded, though he still didn't smile.

"Thanks. I'll be sure to find a great place for it."

Milo nodded and pantomimed putting something in his mouth.

"You want me to put it in my mouth? I don't think it would taste very good."

That was one particular entry in the Dictionary of Milo that Bowie had figured out. "You hungry, buddy?" he asked.

Milo nodded and Bo felt a rather ridiculous sense of accomplishment.

"Want me to make you a sandwich?" he asked.

This time Milo shook his head vigorously and pointed to Katrina.

"Want me to make Katrina a sandwich?" Bowie tried.

Again Milo shook his head. Okay, so he wasn't completely fluent in Milo-ese yet. He was working on it.

Katrina watched this encounter with an expression he couldn't read on her lovely features. "I think he wants *me* to make him a sandwich."

At this, Milo nodded his head vigorously. The little manipulator.

"Too bad. Guess he'll have to make do with his boring brother. I'm sure you've got other things to do."

"I don't mind. I can make him a sandwich. In fact, if you have more work to do, I'm happy to stick around a little longer."

He blinked in surprise. Now he was quite certain he hadn't mistaken the color on her cheeks. She was blushing. He just couldn't quite figure out why. What was he missing here?

"That's very kind of you," he said. "But you made it quite clear yesterday that you weren't looking for a nanny job."

"Um. About that." She fidgeted. "I was actually glad Milo and Lizzie stopped by while I was at McKenzie's house. I wanted to come over later, anyway, to talk to you."

Bowie felt a tiny flicker of hope. Was it possible? Had she changed her mind? "Oh? Talk to me about what?"

She cleared her throat and looked out at the lake for a second before shifting her gaze back to his. "Um, I was wondering if you were still looking for someone to help you out with Milo for a few weeks."

That flicker grew into a steady flame. He was almost afraid to let himself hope. He had three major projects at critical points in development at Caine Tech, each important to the viability of the new facility in Haven Point. He couldn't continue to split his attention between work and his brother, since he wasn't doing a good job of meeting his responsibilities at either end.

If she could help him over this rough patch until Debra Peters could arrive and start working with Milo, he might have half a chance of making this work.

"Yeah. Desperately. Lizzie is great to help me out in a pinch, but she appears to have a busier social schedule than a Kardashian. Are you really reconsidering?"

She shifted. "Maybe."

Relief flowed through him. "What happened? The last time we spoke, you made it clear you weren't interested in helping me out with Milo."

"Circumstances can change, and so can minds." She shrugged, still looking uncomfortable. "I can't help you longer than a few weeks. You're clear on that, right?"

"Yes. No problem. It will be perfect. The autism specialist I've hired will be here to start around then. If you can fill in the gap until she arrives, you'll be saving my neck."

"I mean it. My time in Haven Point is limited, and then I have…obligations in Colombia."

What sort of obligations? She said she was teaching English down there, but he had somehow gained the impression it was a temporary gig. Maybe she had something more permanent lined up. Or maybe she had a man waiting for her there.

That particular idea didn't sit well with him, for reasons he didn't want to examine too closely. "Not a problem," he answered.

"Good," she said briskly. "Also, I might have errands to run while I help take care of the final touches on the wedding. As long as you don't mind, I probably can take Milo with me on most of them."

Based on his own experience shopping with Milo, he would rather have every single eyebrow hair plucked out one by one than take his brother into a store for any length of time if he didn't have to. The grocery store meltdown the day before had been on the mild end of the scale.

But he would leave her to figure that out for herself. "That should be fine. Do you need a vehicle to drive? I've got several in the garage. You're welcome to use any of them."

"No. I left my car here when I went to South America last year, but it sat over the winter and needs some work. My uncle, er, stepfather has some loaners at his lot and says I can use one of those if I need it."

"Take what you need from the garage. Milo likes the SUV, for what it's worth, since it has a TV in the back. Now, about the salary…"

She blushed again, which he found utterly fascinating. "I'm fine with the amount you mentioned yesterday. More than fine. It's completely ridiculous and entirely too much money for a few weeks' work. But you're desperate and I need the money, so I guess it's a win-win all the way around."

"Absolutely. I can even pay you in advance, if you want."

Surprise flickered in blue eyes he suddenly noticed were the same shade of blue as Lake Haven in afternoon sunlight. "I don't need the money right now, but I will before I go back to Colombia."

Again that curiosity raced through him, along with a little uneasiness. She needed cash and she was going to Colombia. It wasn't hard for his mind to jump to some obvious conclusions. Call him suspicious, but that didn't sound like a great combination.

He had made a few assumptions about the woman, considering she'd taught at the local elementary school. Now he wondered if he should have run some sort of background check on her before he offered her a job caring for a vulnerable child.

After the chaos of his childhood, he had absolutely no tolerance for anyone involved in narcotics in any iteration.

No. He wouldn't believe it. He was going to go with his gut on this one. Her father had been the much-beloved chief of police, and she had a brother who was an FBI agent. He had pieced that together after she told him who she was.

Whatever she was involved with in Colombia, he couldn't imagine it had anything to do with drugs.

She obviously needed the money for *something*, but it wasn't his business. He didn't probe into any of his other employees' personal lives.

"Half now, half when you're done, then. That seems fair. Come inside and I'll write you a check."

Her eyes lit up with a raw sort of relief that she quickly concealed. "That's fine," she said. "Thanks. I appreciate it. And while you do that, I'll make lunch for the hungry kiddo here."

"Sounds good," he said as he led the way into the house. "You should find plenty of options. I have a housekeeper who comes in three times a week to stock the fridge and prep some easy meals I can throw together."

"That's convenient."

"Usually. Until I forget to add things to the list and end up having to go to the grocery store myself for a couple of items when they run out."

He wouldn't be sorry, even though he had been frustrated with himself the day before. If he hadn't gone to the store with Milo, he wouldn't have met Katrina and might be stuck for the next few weeks trying to juggle everything himself.

CHAPTER FIVE

KATRINA OPENED THE subzero refrigerator and took in the bounty of food that was entirely too much for one man and one small boy. "What kind of sandwich do you like?" she asked Milo.

The boy looked at the offerings inside the refrigerator for a long moment, brow furrowed, and finally disregarded the ham and turkey slices, instead pointing to a plain purple jar.

"Grape jelly. Good choice. A personal favorite. Do you want peanut butter with that?"

He nodded with an enthusiasm that made her smile. A boy after her own heart. "What else? You can't have one without the other. Okay, then. Any idea where I could find the peanut butter?"

He nodded again and hurried over to a covered pantry door. Milo tugged on the door but couldn't open it. When she joined him, she noticed the pantry door was fitted with a hook and eye latch that was out of his reach. Another safety precaution, she assumed.

She flipped the hook and opened the door. A quick scan revealed a jar of gourmet peanut butter on one of the shelves, along with an unopened loaf of bread.

There was more food in here than all the children in Gabi's orphanage would eat in a week. Katrina grabbed the bread and the jar, then returned to the kitchen island.

Milo stood watching with interest while she laid out several pieces of bread and started spreading the peanut butter from edge to edge on each piece.

He craned to watch each movement while she finished spreading peanut butter. "Want to help?" she asked. "I would love it. Let's wash your hands first. You always wash your hands when you work in the kitchen."

He obviously wasn't crazy about hand-washing, but he didn't make a fuss when she squirted soap and helped him rub it around on his skin before rinsing while she sang the alphabet song through twice.

"That's what my students at school have to do while they're washing their hands," she told him. "We'll get a timer for you so you know how long to wash your hands."

Something told her he would respond better to numbers than letters.

Milo was a complete puzzle. He obviously understood far more than he could communicate back. He could nod or shake his head to indicate yes or no, and she had watched him employ other rudimentary signs with Bowie to get his point across.

She wished she had more experience with language delays so she might know the best way to tackle his particular issues. If she had been his teacher, speech therapy and some sort of augmentative communication device would have been her first priority. A person had to be able to express his needs and wishes.

In her limited time here, she would have to do some research to figure out if she could help him.

"Okay, now that your hands are clean, I'll grab a chair for you so you can help me with the sandwiches."

He seemed eager to give her a hand—or maybe he was simply hungry and wanted her to get on with it. She couldn't quite tell. But after she scooped out some jam onto the middle of a slice of bread, she handed him another knife and showed him how to spread it across the peanut butter. With his bottom lip tucked between his teeth, he focused on making sure a little purple smear covered the entire peanut butter landscape.

"That's perfect," she said. "Good job. Now, can you do a few more?"

He nodded and turned to the task with gusto after she scooped out more jam and plopped it onto the bread.

"You are one excellent PB&J chef," she told him when they finished. "Now comes the fun part. Now we eat."

She hadn't had lunch either, and the humble sand-

wiches made with so much fierce concentration
looked completely delicious.

To Milo's plate, she added some baked chips she
had found in the pantry and a couple of baby carrots from the vegetable drawer, and he attacked the
food with the same enthusiasm he had thrown into
making the sandwiches.

She was finishing the last bite of hers—every bit
as good as it had looked—when Bowie came back
into the kitchen.

Oh man. If she was going to work here for the
next few weeks, she really needed to do something
about the way her palms started to sweat and her
breath seemed to catch in her chest every time she
was around him.

He was just so darn gorgeous. It wasn't fair that
she should meet him *now*, when she absolutely didn't
have time for men.

"Sorry I took so long. I had four texts and a phone
call from work that needed my attention."

He set a check next to her plate and the amount
still staggered her.

"Thanks," she managed to say without sounding
completely breathless, then folded the check in half
and tucked it into the pocket of her shorts.

"I'm the one in your debt and we both know it,"
he said. "You're doing me a huge favor. I'm more
grateful than I can say."

She wasn't so certain, but she didn't argue with
him. This arrangement would give her a desperately

needed cushion in case her attorney came up with some other expensive fee she needed to pay before she could become Gabi's mother.

He took in their plates and the jars still open on the island "PB&J. Looks delicious."

"Milo and I made you a sandwich, too. That one on the work island is for you."

Surprise flickered in his eyes. "That wasn't necessary. I could have grabbed something. Heaven knows, Mrs. Nielson stocks enough food to feed half the neighborhood."

"We were already making them for us. It was no problem to make one more. Milo spread the jelly, didn't you, bud?"

Milo seemed to have gone somewhere in his head, or at least he wasn't in the mood to respond.

"Thanks," Bowie said after a moment. He looked surprised at the small gesture. Almost…touched, as if the courtesy was out of the norm for him. That was ridiculous. He had a housekeeper who did his shopping, for heaven's sake. Bowie had to be used to women falling all over themselves to take care of him.

She found his reaction absurdly appealing.

Oh, she really hoped she wasn't making a terrible mistake by agreeing to help him out. She couldn't afford the distraction. Money wasn't everything—or so she tried to tell herself, anyway.

She probably would have stuck to her guns and continued to refuse him, if not for the phone call she'd received that morning from Angel Herrera, the inaptly named attorney representing her in the adoption process. She had found nothing angelic about him from the moment they met. Though he had come recommended by the local representative from the Colombia national adoption agency, he was loud, abrasive, and made her feel stupid every time she talked to him, either because of her halting command of the Spanish language or because she struggled to understand the complicated and unwieldy international adoption process.

It didn't help that he constantly seemed to approach her with his hand out.

The latest conversation had been the same. He had insisted he needed an extra two thousand dollars because of unexpected costs associated with filing some of the necessary paperwork.

She didn't understand. How much could it cost to make duplicates of her adoption petition and run them to the adoption office? Did he have to cut down the trees and mill his own paper or something?

After working with him for three months, she was beginning to understand the meaning of the word *extortion*. Angel knew how desperately Katrina wanted to adopt Gabi, knew that she would pay any cost, try to conquer any obstacle.

She felt completely out of her depth, trying to negotiate the complex process and receive approval from two countries to bring Gabi to the United States.

Herrera made her feel like she was eight years old again, forced to repeat the second grade because of a combination of missed classes and the strong medication that mostly controlled her epilepsy making it tough to focus.

StupidKat. TwitchyKat.

The weirdo.

You can't invite her to your birthday party. What if she has a fit or something?

No. I'm sorry. My mom says you can't stay overnight because of your medical condition.

My nana says kids who have seizures shouldn't be allowed in school with normal kids because you could hurt somebody.

She had spent most of her life trying to quiet those damn voices, with varied levels of success.

She didn't want to continue playing Angel Herrera's game, but she didn't know what else to do. At least with Bowie's help, she would feel a little more secure if the attorney came to her again with his hand out.

"Wow, that was a good sandwich," Bowie said, wiping away a little grape jelly at his mouth with a napkin. "I haven't had one of those in years. Thanks."

"See? I told you," she said to Milo. "You've got mad PB&J skills, kiddo."

The boy just gazed at her, obviously not impressed with her assessment. Bowie, on the other hand, smiled for a moment, then looked uncomfortable. "Uh, I know this is a lot to ask, especially on such short notice, but I need to run into the office and sign a few papers that resulted from our meeting today. I was going to take Milo with me, but if I can avoid it, I would rather not. He doesn't like it there."

She thought about the check in her pocket and the peace of mind it provided. "I can stay with him the rest of the afternoon. No problem."

"Are you sure?"

She ought to say no so he didn't completely take advantage of her. *Begin how you want to go on*, right? But Bowie looked so relieved, she didn't have the heart to disappoint him.

"Sure. I can stay until six. After that, I've got a thing." She didn't really. She just didn't want him to think she had nothing better to do than get him out of a bind.

"Thanks. Hey, mind if I take that other sandwich you and Milo made? I'm still hungry, and it tasted delicious."

"It's yours."

His smile was sweetly genuine and made her toes curl inside her sandals.

Oh, she did not want to be attracted to him. That was exactly the sort of thing that always seemed to lead her into trouble.

Something told her it was going to be a long three weeks.

BIG SURPRISE, BOWIE wasn't back by six.

Katrina glanced at her watch for about the twentieth time in the last five minutes and tried not to let her annoyance filter through to Milo.

They sat on the floor of his bedroom with a whole fleet of little cars in every color scattered around them like little shiny insects. They were his favorite toys, apparently, at least judging by the purple race car that was obviously his favorite. Most of them looked shiny and new, but the purple one he pulled out of the pocket of his shorts was battered, dented in places with the paint worn off.

He lined all twenty-five cars on the floor, then drove the purple car through them, scattering the others in all directions.

"That purple car is tough," she observed. "Does it have a name?"

He ignored her, driving it in circles around the carpet mat.

"What other car do you like?" she asked. "Do you like this blue race car or this red pickup truck?"

He looked at them briefly, then continued driving the purple car around the floor with a low humming sound that resembled a car engine.

He could make sounds. The afternoon had amply demonstrated that. So why couldn't he form words? Katrina needed to know his background and any actual diagnoses so she could do a little research to find out the best way to reach him.

Yes, Bowie had hired her simply to be a nanny

to the boy, not come up with an individualized education plan for him, but she was a trained elementary education teacher. It was second nature to her to want to find solutions.

Before taking off with Carter, she had actually been working on her special education certification. Probably because of her own learning difficulties, she had always been drawn to the children who struggled more than their classmates. While she cared for all her students, Katrina found a greater degree of satisfaction in helping those who had to work harder to learn.

It was one of the things that had first drawn her to Gabi when Katrina first decided to volunteer at the orphanage near the school where she found a job teaching English after she had been stranded in Colombia. Some of the children had been apprehensive around Katrina, but Gabi had come right up to her, handed her a flowering weed she'd plucked from the garden and started jabbering away in a combination of Spanish and her own Gabi-speak. Katrina had fallen in love instantly.

Now she watched Milo make sounds with the car, then hold another car, headlight-to-headlight, against the purple one as if they were talking to each other.

He had receptive language skills, he could make sounds and he understood the concept of language. Why didn't he speak? What she really needed was a long conversation with Bowie so she could figure out how best to help his brother during her time with him.

As if her thoughts had conjured him, she suddenly sensed movement by the door, and she glanced up in time to see Bowie walking into the room.

Again, her stupid heart rate kicked up a notch and her palms went clammy with nerves. Her thoughts seemed to scatter like those cars Milo had plowed through.

Her instinctive reaction to him both embarrassed and dismayed her as she rose to her feet, needing to be on a little more equal level.

So the man was gorgeous. She wasn't in the market for gorgeous anymore, especially since it usually came hand in hand with arrogance and conceit.

His mouth twisted into a regretful frown. "I told you six and it's half past. I'm sorry. I was helping one of the software engineers work out a problem and we both lost track of time. It won't happen again, I promise."

Somehow she doubted the veracity of that particular statement. Most gorgeous men of her acquaintance seemed to think the world existed for their convenience—though, okay, that might be a gross generalization. She didn't know Bowie Callahan well enough to automatically make that assumption.

"It was fine *this time*," she said. "We had fun, didn't we, Milo?"

The boy ignored both of them, busy lining up all his cars again in the same carefully ordered row.

"How did it go?" Bowie asked.

With a careful look to make sure Milo was still occupied, she rose and walked out into the hallway, out of earshot.

"Fine, for the most part. He seemed happy to have me there for the first few minutes and then ignored me most of the afternoon. We had one meltdown when I tried to have him leave his car out with the other toys when he had to use the bathroom, but we made it through."

"He doesn't do anything without that stupid, manky purple car. I tried to give him a bunch of new cars with no luck. That's still his favorite. I don't have actual proof of this, but I'm guessing he loves it because Stella gave it to him."

"Stella. Is that your mother?"

"Yeah. That's Mom."

A hundred questions flashed through her mind at his sudden hard tone. Why did merely the mention of his mother's name upset him? And why hadn't he known about his brother until the last few weeks?

"I'm puzzled about why he doesn't speak," she said slowly. "Do you know what sort of speech therapy he's had in the past?"

Bowie shook his head. "That seems to be the big mystery to the specialists we've seen. To be honest, I'm not sure whether he's had *any* therapy. Knowing Stella, I highly doubt it."

Katrina frowned at the bitterness in his tone.

What sort of history did those seemingly casual words conceal?

"What about since you became his guardian?"

"I have an appointment next week with one in Shelter Springs but was thinking about postponing it. I'm thinking maybe we should wait until the autism specialist arrives before we start any intensive therapy, so she can be involved at the outset."

The frustration and weariness in his voice pulled at her. She could only imagine how difficult it must have been for him to take over guardianship of a child with Milo's kind of developmental challenges.

"It makes sense from an outsider's perspective," she assured him.

"Thanks. I appreciate that." He smiled, and she was vaguely aware of her toes curling again.

Oh, good grief. She had to get out of there.

She looked through the doorway at Milo, who was now jumping his purple car over all the others like Evel Knievel was behind the wheel.

"What time do you want me here in the morning?"

"I have a staff meeting first thing. Would eight work?"

She mentally scanned her calendar, which took all of about half a second. "That should work great."

"Thank you." He smiled again. This time she forced her toes to stay firmly planted inside her shoes. "You can't imagine the weight you've lifted from my shoulders."

She thought of Gabi, fragile and needy—and now a few steps closer to their new life together. "This is a mutually beneficial arrangement," she said.

"I hope we can continue to keep it that way."

They could, as long as she managed to hold on to her perspective. She was doing a job here, that was all. She didn't want to become embroiled in their lives, to let herself care for the troubled Callahan brothers.

Keeping both Milo and Bowie at arm's length over the next few weeks just might be the hardest thing she'd ever done.

She made her way past him, back into the boy's bedroom. "I'll see you in the morning, Milo. I have to go home now."

That seemed to catch the boy's attention. He looked up from his cars and she saw confusion flash in his eyes for a moment, followed quickly by disappointment and frustration and what looked like the genesis of a meltdown.

"I'll be back tomorrow to play with you all day," she said quickly in an effort to check the tantrum before it could begin. "I have a job for you while I'm gone. See if you can pick out all the vehicles that are the same color as your favorite."

He looked stymied for a moment, then picked up another purple car and a third one.

"That's an excellent start," she said, pleased. "Good job."

"We'll look for more purple cars in a moment,"

Bowie told him. "We can come back later, but first we have to walk Katrina out to her car and say goodbye to her. That's the polite thing to do when you have a lady over. Come on, Milo."

She thought the boy would ignore him, but after a moment Milo climbed to his feet, tucked his favorite car in the pocket of his cargo shorts and hurried over to them.

When they were nearly to the door, Bowie made a low exclamation. "I totally forgot. You walked over here earlier. We'll give you a ride. Or, as I said earlier, you're more than welcome to use something out of the garage."

"Not necessary," she assured him. "I left my car over at McKenzie's house in Redemption Bay, which is only a five-minute walk from here along the lake trail."

"We really wouldn't mind driving you."

"I'd rather walk. It's a lovely evening and I need to stretch my legs a little."

That answer didn't appear to his liking. To his credit, Bowie didn't argue. "Your choice, I suppose. Have a good evening, then."

"Thank you. I'll see you in the morning. Bye again, Milo."

The boy didn't wave but did appear to nod his head. She decided she would take it. Water lapped against the shore and birds twittered through the branches above her as she hurried along the path that wound through sweet-smelling pine trees. She hadn't lied to him. She did like to walk and she adored these beautiful summer evenings along the lake—with the sun beginning to sink beneath the Redemption Mountain Range, casting long shadows.

Mostly, though, she needed a little distance from the entirely too-attractive Bowie Callahan and his brother.

KATRINA PARALLEL-PARKED about a block away from Point Made Flowers and Gifts—never an easy task, but made much more challenging because the somewhat battered sedan she was borrowing from her stepfather during her stay had a loosey-goosey power steering system that swam a little more than she liked.

"Here we are. Are you excited?"

Milo, fiddling with the strap on his booster seat in the back, didn't answer. Not that she expected him to. Katrina was quickly discovering it was one thing to understand the challenges of autism in academic terms and something else entirely when dealing with it for hours at a time.

She and Milo had been together nonstop for the last three days and had finally settled into a routine of sorts. In the morning, she fixed him breakfast, they did a few basic chores around the house like washing the dishes or emptying the trash, then they took a long walk, either around the lake or along one of her favorite easy trails along the Hell's Fury River.

After lunchtime, she would read to him while he

played cars—though she wasn't entirely certain if he truly enjoyed the stories or merely tuned her out to do his own thing. She insisted he rest in his room for a little quiet time, then they would take another walk or go to a nearby park or merely sit on the patio overlooking the lake and throw pebble after pebble.

He seemed comfortable with their routine, and she was leery about messing it up. This was the first time she had brought him along to a gathering like this, but McKenzie had scheduled a meeting of the Haven Point Helping Hands to finish Wyn's wedding favors, and Katrina didn't know how she could avoid it. She *was* the maid of honor, after all.

"Don't worry. It's going to be fun, especially since there will be other kids your age there."

She crossed her fingers on the steering wheel. She'd yet to see Milo truly interact with others his age. Twice when they had gone to the city park, other children had been playing there, but they seemed much younger than Milo. He had largely ignored them all while he made a road in the sand for his purple car.

As was typical, he didn't respond to her assertion and she couldn't tell how much he understood. She had adopted the philosophy the first day that his level of understanding didn't really matter. She would simply talk to him all the time about everything: her thoughts, concerns, Gabi, the awkward situation at her mom's house. He didn't appear to be bored, and she had to think that exposure to words and more words had to be beneficial.

"I need your help carrying some things in," she told him after she unhooked his booster. It wasn't really true, since she had only one salad and a few stray supplies Kenzie had asked her to grab, but she also had learned early that Milo seemed to like being helpful.

She handed him the small bag of craft supplies, picked up the salad, then took off for McKenzie's store, Point Made Flowers and Gifts.

Downtown Haven Point seemed busier than Katrina had seen it in a while, bustling with tourists and locals alike. Since Ben and Aidan had moved a new Caine Tech facility to town, new stores and restaurants had begun to open up in the previously shuttered businesses in town.

It still wasn't as busy as nearby Shelter Springs, which suited her just fine.

Before they crossed the street, she reached down to take Milo's hand. He tried to wriggle his hand free, but she held fast. "You have to hold my hand while we cross," she told him, her voice firm. "Then you can let go."

He gave a heavy sigh but kept his hand in hers until the moment they reached the sidewalk on the other side, then he yanked it free, though he stayed close to her side.

Despite Bowie's warning that first day, Milo hadn't yet tried to wander away from her.

Bowie.

Katrina tried not to match Milo's heavy sigh of a few moments earlier. She had worked in his house for three days and had seen him maybe a total of thirty minutes that entire time, basically five minutes in the morning as he headed out the door, then five minutes in the evening prior to her leaving for home.

Her face still felt hot and her stomach a tangle of nerves whenever she saw him, but she was working on it. Honestly.

Ten minutes a day didn't give her much time to figure out a guy, which was probably a good thing in this case. She didn't need to know anything about him, other than that he worked hard and wanted the best for his brother— whatever that might be.

When they reached the door of McKenzie's store, Milo hung back a little and seemed wary about going inside. He was nervous, she realized. Had she done that to him, with her talk about other children?

"Hey, buddy," she said softly. "You don't have to play with the other kids if you don't want to. It's just fine if you would rather stay close to me the whole time."

His shoulders seemed to relax at that, and she gave him a reassuring smile. "Let's do this," she said, then pushed open the door.

Inside McKenzie's store, the scent of cinnamon and vanilla swirled around and a furry greeter instantly padded over to them.

"Hey, Rika," she said to the elegant cinnamon-colored standard poodle who came to investigate the newcomers to her domain.

Milo, she saw, did not look nervous around the dog. No surprise there. While he might be apprehensive about children and other humans, he had a deep and abiding love for anything furry or feathered.

"Milo, this is my friend, Paprika. She is McKenzie's dog. Remember McKenzie? You met her the other day over by the lake."

The boy nodded and reached a hand out to pet the dog. He smiled a little when his fingertips found the texture of her curly, wiry hair.

"She feels funny, doesn't she? Poodles don't have hair like other dogs, you know, the long, sheddy sort. They were originally water dogs and the curly hair helps them dry off faster. Just like in people, curly hair has to do with genetics and the shape of the hair shaft opening."

"Do you really think he understands anything about genetics or hair shafts?"

She glanced over to find Linda Fremont watching her from beside the counter, wearing her usual sour expression. She tried reminding herself to be patient with Linda. The woman had things tough after her husband died young. She had raised Samantha while running a small business by herself.

Despite her gruff exterior, she had also been as kind as her nature would allow toward Katrina at a time when other parents in town hadn't been nearly as welcoming. Because of that, Kat generally gained a lot of practice biting her tongue around her.

"I don't know what he understands, so I'll continue telling him anything I think might be interesting."

Linda looked as if she wanted to argue with that philosophy, but McKenzie poked her head out of her large workroom and beamed when she spotted them.

"Hey, Katrina! Hi there, Milo. Everybody is back here. Why don't you bring Rika with you."

Katrina let Milo pet the dog a moment more, then led them both to join McKenzie. Over the years, the long, open workroom at Point Made Flowers and Gifts had turned into the usual meeting spot of the Haven Point Helping Hands, a loosely organized group that tried to improve the town and the lives of the people who lived there—and had lots of fun doing it.

She was gratified when everyone greeted her with enthusiasm.

"All the kids are busy in the other room, Milo," McKenzie said. "I've got a show playing in there and there's a fun art project set up, if you want."

He favored any kind of creative project, from coloring to pipe cleaner sculptures to modeling clay, but right now he simply shook his head, twisting his fingers together and sending a distressed look at Katrina.

"You don't have to go anywhere if you don't want," she assured him, keeping her voice calm.

"You can stay right here with me. Is that what you'd like?"

In answer, he moved closer to her side.

She tried another reassuring smile. "Okay," she said as she found them a couple of empty chairs near one end of the big table. "It might be boring, listening to all of the grown-ups chatter. If you get tired of listening to all of us, you're always welcome to go find the kids."

He plopped into the chair beside her and pulled out his ubiquitous purple car. She handed him one of the coloring books she had packed along and the plastic zipper bag full of crayons.

Devin Barrett, McKenzie's sister, was seated at his other side. She gave him a welcoming smile. "Hi, Milo. Do you remember me? I'm Dr. Barrett. Your brother brought you in to meet me when you first came to Haven Point to live with him."

He looked nervous for a moment, then panto-mimed licking a sucker.

Devin smiled with delight. "That's exactly right. I gave you a sucker. You have an excellent memory."

The interaction seemed to ease his tension. When she felt Milo relax a little beside her, Katrina turned to McKenzie.

"Put me to work. You know I'm lacking in the craftiness department, but I'll do what I can."

"There's not much to it," McKenzie said. "Given that Cade loves gardening, we've got all these herb starts. We just need to tie some pastel raffia around each pot, and then half the crew is making these little garden markers with Cade's and Wyn's names and the date."

"Cute. I think I can tie a bow." She looked around. "Where's the bride?"

"Running late," Andie Montgomery said. "She had a meeting that went long but should be here soon. Didn't she text you?"

"Maybe. My, uh, phone accidentally fell into a sink full of dishwater this morning and is currently drying out in a bag of rice."

"Oh no!"

As the others commiserated with her, she didn't tell them it hadn't really been an accident. Milo had been mad at her when she made him pick up his toys and had picked up her phone from the counter and thrown it into the dishwater on purpose.

Though he could hear their conversation perfectly well, Milo didn't look up from coloring.

"It was old, anyway, and I was due for something new. I'm going to give it a day or two to dry out. If the rice bag doesn't work, I'll run into Shelter Springs and pick up another one."

She didn't really want to take on another expense like a new phone right now when her budget was already cut to the bone. Thanks to Bowie's check, though, she had a little more cushion than she had a few days earlier.

"Still. It's never fun when accidents like that

happen," Devin said. "Doesn't it make you wish you could go back and replay those five seconds?"

Yes. The very next time Milo was mad at her for making him pick up his toys or not allowing him to have ice cream for breakfast or making him take a bath after he jumped in mud puddles outside, she planned to leave her phone safely in her pocket.

Not that there would be too many chances for *next time*. She would be with him for only a few more weeks. The reminder made her a little sad. Milo was a complicated, sometimes frustrating little creature. He could be ferociously stubborn and the smallest thing could set him off. She couldn't always tell how much of what she said might be getting through to him.

He could also be sweet and surprisingly insightful for someone who didn't communicate with words.

She would miss him.

Despite her best efforts to keep a safe distance, after only a few days she could tell she was already falling for this solemn little boy with the big blue eyes and the freckles across his nose and the rare half smile that came out of nowhere and stole her heart every time.

So much for protecting herself. She sighed. This was her whole problem, encapsulated in one little boy. She gave her heart too easily. In a few weeks, she would have to say goodbye to him, and she was already worried about the emotional fallout.

She would simply have to remind herself that sometimes a person had to give up one important thing in order to gain something else.

CHAPTER SIX

ALL IN ALL, she considered it a highly successful afternoon. Milo had no meltdowns, much to her relief. She had become pretty good at coping with them, but that certainly didn't mean she relished them.

While she'd worked on the wedding favors, Milo had colored at her side for about half an hour—mostly scribbles on the page—then eventually wandered over to watch the other children from the doorway of the workroom. He didn't really interact with them in a conventional way but seemed to be interested in their interactions. She thought she had even seen him smile at something Ty Barrett said, but she couldn't be sure.

Eventually he had sat on the floor and pulled out his purple car and seemed content to drive it in circles until she finished.

She studied him walking beside her now as they headed back to her vehicle. "That was fun, wasn't it?"

He didn't say anything, just continued humming to himself, a song with no recognizable melody. The kid was an enigma. Sometimes he wanted her to chat with him, other days he pretended she didn't exist.

"Did you have enough to eat?" she pressed.

He still didn't answer her, which she was going to assume meant yes. If he was hungry, he usually figured out a way to get that point across. She helped him into his booster seat, then climbed behind the wheel. She would have walked to McKenzie's, as the downtown business district wasn't that far from Serenity Harbor, but she hadn't wanted to lug the salad all that way, then the empty bowl home.

She was glad for the decision now when a light rain began to fall as she took off toward Bowie's house. She turned on the stereo to listen to Milo's favorite tape, an old *Sesame Street* collection she remembered listening to when *she* was young.

Just as they walked into the house, the landline phone was ringing. Her heartbeat gave that stupid little hitch when she saw Bowie's name on the caller ID, and she felt ridiculously breathless.

"Hi, Katrina. It's Bowie," he said when she answered. "I tried to call your cell. Is everything okay?"

She decided not to mention her doused phone. "Fine."

"How are things with Milo today?"

The distracted tone of his voice made it obvious the question simply provided an opening to whatever he *truly* wanted to discuss.

"Good. We just got home after having lunch with some friends of mine. The Haven Point Helping Hands. Milo did very well. There were a few other children attending. While he didn't necessarily play directly with them, he played *next* to them."

"That's good, isn't it?"

"I see it as an encouraging sign, especially since your intention is to start him in school as soon as possible. He didn't have a single meltdown either. We've had a great day so far. But I'm sure you didn't really call for a status report."

She didn't possess any miraculous insight into the way Bowie's mind worked, but in the three days she had been caring for Milo—four, counting that first afternoon—he hadn't called to chat one single time. This anomaly must mean something significant.

"You're right," he said, his tone rueful. "I need a huge favor. I've got a bit of an emergency. I know you said you couldn't stay with Milo in the evenings, but I'm wondering if there's any chance you might make an exception tonight. We're in the middle of a major crisis here, and an extra few hours might make all the difference."

She mentally scanned through her social calendar. Again, depressingly blank. Well, not completely— if she counted her plans to hide out in her room all evening while her mother and Uncle Mike entertained friends.

Compared with the alternative, she supposed chilling with Milo in Bowie's beautiful lakeside house wouldn't be much of a sacrifice.

"That should be fine, as far as I know." She paused, making her voice as firm as she did with a misbehaving second-grader. "Just don't make it a habit."

"I'll do my best." She heard relief and a small thread of amusement in his voice.

"So what time can we expect you?" she asked.

"I hope no later than eight. I'll let you know, though. There's plenty of food in the fridge and freezer. You're welcome to eat whatever you want for dinner—or call for pizza, if that sounds better. I don't care."

She was currently stuffed from all the delicious potluck salads provided by the other Helping Hands and wasn't at all ready to think about dinner yet. "We'll figure something out," she answered.

"Thank you. I owe you."

After they exchanged goodbyes and hung up, she turned to Milo. "Well, kid," she said, "I guess it's you and me for a few more hours. What would you like to do?"

She should have predicted when he held his hands up to his chest like they were paws, stuck his tongue out and made a panting sound.

"You want to go see Jerry Lewis?"

He nodded, and she had to smile. Whether he liked it or not, at some point in the not-so-distant future, Bowie would have to consider adding a pet to his household. The kid responded to animals far more than he did to people.

"It's raining right now. Why don't we play for a while until it passes, and then I'll call Lizzie and see if she would let us hang out with Jerry Lewis, maybe take him for a walk. How does that work for you?"

He didn't answer her—but neither did he have a meltdown at the prospect of having to wait for something he wanted. She considered that progress.

HE WAS IN so much trouble. Katrina Bailey was going to kill him.

Bowie pulled into the garage of his house, wincing when he glanced down and caught the time on the digital display on the dashboard. It was after ten, more than two hours past the time he'd told her he would be home. She had been doing him a favor, agreeing to stay past her usual time, and he had abused that favor horribly.

He would be lucky if she stayed in the job at all—and it would be his own damn fault if she quit.

He had no one to blame but himself. When he was focused on solving a problem, figuring out a new angle of attack, he tended to completely lose track of time—and apparently in this case, of his own obligations. He had been in the zone tonight. His team had finally arrowed in on a pesky software glitch, only a few layers of code away from fixing it, and Bowie hadn't wanted to stop.

In some vague corner of his mind, something had tried to remind him he had obligations and responsibilities waiting for him, but he kept telling himself he needed only five more minutes. Then five more minutes and five more minutes. Before he realized it, here he was, two hours past the time he had promised he would be home.

He was fully aware Katrina was doing him a huge favor in the first place by agreeing to help him with Milo. While he was focusing on work again these last few days without that constant nagging worry about his brother, Bowie had felt *centered* for the first time in weeks, and it showed in his job performance.

He didn't know what he was doing when it came to Milo—that was no doubt crystal clear to anyone who might have seen them interact. This, though—combing through code, coming up with solutions—was his wheelhouse.

No matter how good it felt to be back in the groove, he should have been more mindful of time. Now he had to hope to hell he hadn't screwed everything up, sabotaging the best thing that had happened to his crazy world since that unforgettable phone call informing him about his brother.

Katrina was amazing with his brother. Creative, insightful, endlessly patient. He had no idea how she did it, especially when Bowie found himself completely drained from dealing with Milo for only the few hours before bedtime each day.

It was pitiful, really. He thought he was in excellent condition. He hiked, he mountain biked, he could kayak across the lake and back and barely break a sweat. So why did a few hours with one autistic boy leave him feeling as if he had just competed in an Ironman Triathlon?

As if on cue, he suddenly yawned and had a momentary wish that he could sleep right here in the garage for a few hours.

No. He had to go inside and face the music. He slid out of his SUV, a weird mix of apprehension and anticipation rippling through him like the lake against the shore.

The apprehension part he completely understood. The woman was a lifesaver, and he didn't even want to imagine what he would do if she quit, like the other caregivers had.

He understood the anticipation, too—but that didn't necessarily mean he liked it.

He was attracted to Katrina Bailey. Fiercely attracted. Every time he was with her, it swirled through him like the night breeze that rustled the leaves of the aspen trees scattered across his property.

He didn't know what to do about it. He certainly couldn't act on the attraction—not when she was easily the best thing that had happened to Milo in weeks.

Attraction or not, the woman was a mystery to him. What was her story—the reason behind those shadows he had glimpsed in her eyes? Why had she left her teaching job in Haven Point the year before, right before the school year was to begin? What had taken her to South America in the first place?

And what was so important that she intended to hurry right back to Colombia after her sister's wedding?

The questions burned through him. He wanted to ask—but that would require an actual conversation between them, and he had been careful to keep those as brief as possible and focused mostly on Milo and his needs.

With a sigh, he climbed out of his SUV and headed into the house.

The only sound was the quiet hum of the dishwasher in the kitchen and a muted murmur coming from the open-plan family room next to the kitchen.

He followed the sound down the hall and then stopped dead. Milo and Katrina were cuddled up on the sofa, both sound asleep while one of Milo's favorite movies played on the big screen, animated figures flickering in the darkened room.

A weird softness lodged in his chest as he watched them sleep, a nameless…something.

Yearning. That was it.

Assigning a name to it didn't make the feeling any less frightening.

He had never really thought about having a family, too busy trying to prove himself for his whole freaking life, first in school, then at Caine Tech. If he *did* think about it, he quickly shoved aside any inkling that the whole family-life thing might be a good idea for him.

What the hell did he know about being part of a normal family? His childhood had been such chaos. To him, the word *family* held only ugly connotations. His mother used the word when referring to whatever counterculture, free-living, drugged-out group she connected with at the moment.

He had always figured he was better off alone, where he could focus on the things he knew and found comfortable. Mutually satisfying casual relationships filled the void for a little human closeness.

Lately, though, especially since he had come to Haven Point, he wondered. As he watched Aidan and Eliza together with their children or saw Ben and McKenzie laughing together, he had discovered an aching little hollow in his chest, a spot he never realized was empty.

Both Ben and Aidan had been his friends for a long time—the closest thing he had to brothers, really, before Milo came along.

They had worked together in the computer lab at MIT, then all three had been on the ground floor of Caine Tech. Aidan was the idea genius, Ben was the organizational whiz and Bowie liked to think he was the one who really made the magic happen. Without his contribution, working out all the details and fine-tuning the software, none of Aidan's ideas would ever be ready for market.

Both men had changed over the last few years, becoming more *centered* somehow. He thought they would be distracted, splitting their time between their lives in Haven Point and the company's California operations, but that hadn't been the case at all. Both actually seemed more focused.

That was fine for them, Bowie had told himself.

He was happy that *they* were happy. That didn't mean he needed to join their little happily-ever-after club.

He might accept that on an intellectual level. That didn't do jack to fill the stupid little hollow in his chest.

Heartburn, he told himself. Maybe he should have thought to eat something instead of just pounding coffee all afternoon.

Trying to figure out how to tactfully wake her up, he moved closer to the two sleeping figures on the sofa. Maybe she subconsciously heard him or he stirred the air or something. Whatever the reason, Katrina's eyelashes fluttered briefly, then opened. For the space of a heartbeat, he thought he saw something flash in her half-asleep gaze when she first spotted him—something hot and hungry that instantaneously stirred an answering response from him.

Could she be attracted to him, too? The possibility staggered him. She hadn't given any hint of it in their interactions. Instead, she treated him with a polite coolness that always left him wondering if she disliked him.

She quickly closed her stunning blue eyes. When she opened them again, any hint of momentary awareness was gone, replaced by that polite reserve. He might have thought he imagined the whole thing if he didn't see a soft blush climbing her cheeks.

"I didn't realize you were home. How long have you been here?" she asked, her voice low, with a sexy, thready note that she cleared away.

"Only a minute or two. I didn't want to wake you, but I had a feeling you wouldn't be very happy with me in the morning when you woke up on my sofa with a stiff neck."

"You would be right," she murmured, looking down at his sleeping brother. "I can't believe I fell asleep."

"You don't have to tell *me* how tiring Milo can be."

She stood and stretched a little, arms stretched above her head, with probably no idea how the movement accentuated her curves and made him suddenly ache.

He should get out of here before he embarrassed both of them. "I'll take Milo to his room. Do you mind waiting?"

He owed her an apology, one he didn't want to have to deliver in these same hushed tones they were using so they didn't wake up Milo.

Besides, a few moments away from her should give him a chance to regain a little control over his wayward thoughts.

She nodded. "I can wait a few minutes."

"Thanks." Bo carefully scooped Milo up, aware as he did of how small the boy was for his age.

As always, the boy's small size left him feeling frustrated and guilty. Bowie should have tried harder to find Stella. If he had, he would have discovered she'd had another child and could have stepped in earlier to protect Milo from the chronic malnutrition he had suffered during his early years.

Bowie knew what hunger pangs could be like. He had always been small for his age, until he received a full-ride scholarship to MIT that included a meal plan and access to workout facilities at school.

When he wasn't in the computer lab in college, he could usually be found in the cafeteria—and then in the gym, trying to add muscle tone. He wasn't the scrawny nerd anymore, but no matter what he ate or how much he worked out, he still suffered from fifteen years of scrambling to have enough to eat.

That was one reason his charitable foundation's primary focus was on eliminating child hunger.

His brother would never know hunger again. Yeah, Bowie wasn't great at most of the whole family thing and was struggling to know how to deal with Milo's autism. But at least he would always be able to provide well for his brother.

As Bowie set him down in the bed, Milo opened his eyes. They were bleary and unfocused, but Bowie wanted to think they lit up a little when Milo spotted him. When his brother first came to live with him, he had looked around his world with a resigned sort of insecurity, ready for his circumstances to change again at a moment's notice.

Milo was beginning to seem more settled than he had at first. Bowie wanted to think his brother was beginning to accept that he intended to be a permanent fixture in his life. Who knew what was really going on inside his head, though?

"Good night, partner. Time to ride the rainbow to

dreamland." He spoke the words by rote, then had to stop as the echo of them sounded in his head. That was something his mother used to say to him, one of the few maternal-type memories he had.

It was good for him to remember Stella wasn't completely terrible. She had loved him, in her way. She just had no business being responsible for another human being. Not when she wasn't at all competent to take care of herself.

Milo gave him a sweet, sleepy smile, rolled over and closed his eyes. Bowie tucked the purple car on his pillow next to him, pulled the blanket up, then went down to face the music with Katrina.

He found her in the kitchen, putting away the dishes from the dishwasher that must have finished its cycle.

"You don't have to do that," he said. "The housekeeper can do it tomorrow when she comes."

Katrina shrugged. "I don't mind. Mrs. Nielson has osteoarthritis in her back, and sometimes it can be tough for her to reach down to the bottom rack."

That was news to him. Mrs. Nielson hadn't said a word to him about arthritis, and he'd never noticed any hitch in her step.

Then again, he wasn't always the most observant of men. Just today, he had congratulated one of the team members he saw on a daily basis for having a cast removed from the guy's broken wrist—only to be informed it had actually been off for a month.

Sometimes Bowie wondered if *he* was on the

spectrum. Every once in a while the thought would poke at him like a sore tooth. Some of the signs fit, he had to admit. Since Milo had come to live with him, he had read numerous books on autism and had wondered if he would have been diagnosed as having a mild form of Asperger's.

He had always preferred safe, reliable computers to dealing with the whims and vagaries of people. He knew he could be brusque and impatient and wasn't always aware of the mood and underlying emotion behind a comment.

Just because he preferred to make decisions using his higher brain function and not his emotional reactions didn't necessarily mean he had Asperger's, he reminded himself. In his situation, his behavior was only logical. He had spent his childhood with a parent who let her emotions do all her thinking for her. If she wanted something, Stella wouldn't let little things like reason or common sense get in the way.

And that was enough thinking about Stella *or* autism for the night, Bowie decided.

"Did he stay asleep?" Katrina asked.

"Yes. He opened his eyes for about half a second, but that was it."

"That's good."

"Thanks for helping Mrs. Nielson," he said. "And I owe you an even bigger debt of gratitude—not to mention a deep apology—for keeping you here later than I promised. I don't really have an excuse, other than that time slipped away from me."

"Time has a way of doing that," she said, reaching high to put a wineglass on the top shelf. The movement elongated her slender form, making her tawny legs look about a mile long below her shorts. Just like that, the awareness he thought he had wrestled into submission jumped back, raring to go.

He frowned. No. He absolutely would *not* go there. So he was attracted to her. Big deal. He had been attracted to plenty of women before without trying to pursue anything with them, unless they indicated it was a mutual thing.

Even if he *did* think he saw that moment of awareness when she awoke, he wasn't about to screw up the best thing that had happened to him in a long time because he wanted something he couldn't have.

"How did things go today?"

She went to work putting away utensils. "Busy but fun. He's a sweet boy."

"Barring his epic tantrums."

"Even those aren't happening as often. I think his meltdowns usually come when he's frustrated that he can't communicate. I would probably have a tantrum, too, if I couldn't understand why people weren't listening to me."

He studied her, struck again by her compassion and kindness for a child she hadn't even known existed a week earlier. "You genuinely enjoy being with him," he said.

"Why wouldn't I? He's a sweet boy ninety-five percent of the time. I want to think I'm making prog-

ress with him, too. He seems calmer, and he's starting to make a few more noises that almost sound
like words."

"I've seen improvement in these last few days,"
he said. "Our evenings together have been much
easier than they were before. He's sleeping like a
rock, too, so you must be tiring him out. Thanks for
that. I don't have to stay up all night worrying that
he might wander."

She gave a soft, lovely smile, and Bowie had to
swallow the sudden urge to kiss the corner of her
mouth where her lips lifted.

His heartbeat seemed unnaturally loud in his
ears, which annoyed the hell out of him. She was so
darn beautiful. Somehow she made him feel like that
awkward kid in college in those tough first months
when all the pretty coeds at MIT made it clear they
thought he was too scrawny, too serious and especially too young.

He had dated plenty of beautiful women since
then who didn't spark this restless, achy reaction
in him. What was different about Katrina Bailey?

"You're welcome," she said. "Today he helped me
make wedding favors. Tomorrow we're going to buy
some things for the bachelorette party. I thought he
would be bored to tears, running all over and helping
me with my wedding errands, but he actually seems
to be enjoying himself."

"Glad to hear it."

"Oh," she suddenly exclaimed. "I almost forgot

to tell you. We made pasta for dinner. Chicken and broccoli. It was very tasty, if I do say so myself. Milo even had seconds. We had plenty of leftovers, so we fixed you a plate and left it in the refrigerator, if you'd like it."

"Did you?" Warmth unfurled inside him at her thoughtfulness. "Sounds delicious. I didn't realize I was hungry until right this moment."

He decided it probably wouldn't be wise to add that not all of his hunger was necessarily for food right now.

"Would you like me to heat it up for you?"

Given that he'd mostly taken care of himself throughout his childhood, he probably had been punching buttons on a microwave for longer than she had been alive, but he didn't tell her that.

The truth was, he was touched that she wanted to take care of him. It wouldn't take an advanced degree or months of psychoanalysis to figure out why.

That was probably the reason why he should decline her offer. "Thanks, but I can heat it up," he said.

She opened the refrigerator and pulled out a plate covered in plastic wrap and mounded over with thick, creamy-looking pasta with bright green broccoli.

"Wow. That looks delicious."

"There was nothing to it. You had all the ingredients. All we did was throw them together."

She didn't make a move to leave while he slid the plate into the microwave and hit a couple of buttons to reheat it, making him wonder if she was waiting for something else from him. For the life of him, he couldn't think what that might be.

"I should go home, I guess," she finally said.

"You don't sound particularly enthusiastic about that."

"Is it that obvious?"

Considering he had just been thinking he was the most unobservant man on the planet, it must be. "A little," he admitted.

"My mother and stepfather are having a gathering," she said. "Dinner and board games with a few friends. Even though it's late, I doubt they're finished yet."

"You don't like parties? That surprises me."

Her gaze narrowed. "What is that supposed to mean?"

"Nothing," he said quickly, sensing he had pissed her off somehow. "You just seem to have so many friends in Haven Point. I assumed you would enjoy socializing with them while you're here."

"Not this particular gathering. My mom is trying to set me up with one of her friend's sons. She confessed after I called to tell her I was working late."

The microwave signaled his food was ready. He pulled it out and set it on the kitchen island. To his delight, she poured a glass of water and sat down across from him.

"And you don't want to be set up."

She sighed. "Something I have told her again and again. She refuses to get the message."

"Some moms can be pushy." So he had heard, anyway.

"If there were Olympic competitions for stubborn, interfering mothers, mine would win a medal without question. Charlene can't get it through her head that I'm no longer the same old flighty Katrina, willing to forget everything important to me, everything I've worked for, because some cute guy smiled at me."

"Flighty? *You?* Are you serious?"

He had a hard time imagining it. The woman he had met was loyal and dedicated, patient to a fault and endlessly kind.

She looked gratified by the doubt in his voice, and he wanted to think some of her coolness warmed up a bit. "Yes. Unfortunately. I love my mother, but when she looks at me, she only sees what she wants to see. What she's *always* seen. She expects me to be distracted by the next good-looking guy to come along. I think that's what she's praying for—what she's counting on—so she's doing everything possible to throw every available guy in town at me. And some who aren't even available."

The mystery of Katrina Bailey deepened every time he talked to her. She painted a picture of a lighthearted, flirty woman only out for a good time, but that didn't resemble the woman he had entrusted with his brother.

And what was her mother trying to distract her *from*?

If he kept her talking, perhaps he might finally begin to find out a few answers. "Why would she think that?" he asked.

"I'm not saying she doesn't have some basis for that. I haven't, um, always made the best decisions when it comes to men." Her color heightened a little, and she looked down at the table. "That's in the past, though, and my mom refuses to see that I've changed. That *everything* has changed."

"Because of what waits for you in Colombia."

"Yes. Exactly!" she exclaimed. "I never would have guessed you would be one of the few people in Haven Point who seems to understand and appreciate that. Thank you!"

"You may wait to hold your applause," he protested. "I was only making an observation. I never said a word about understanding and appreciating anything. How can I, when I don't even know what you're talking about. I have no idea what waits for you in Colombia."

She studied him, her blue eyes glittering. "Do you really want to know?"

Yes. Hell yes.

"You're caring for my brother. Of course I want to know. What is so important in Colombia that you can't wait to leave your family and your life here in Haven Point?"

Her soft, pretty features twisted with indecision

for a long moment, then she picked up her tablet and scrolled through it.

"This," she finally said, holding out the tablet. Bowie reached for it, wondering if he was going to be forced to look at some beefy South American dude.

The display didn't show a photo of a man. Instead, a little girl about three with long dark braids and the familiar features of someone with the extra chromosome he knew led to Down syndrome smiled back at him.

"Wasn't expecting that," he said truthfully. He studied the picture, struck by the sweetness of the little girl's smile and the light in her eyes. "Who is she?"

"Her name is Gabriela Campos. She's my daughter."

CHAPTER SEVEN

BOWIE STARED AT her in shock for a full twenty seconds before he could manage to string together his fragmented thoughts enough to come up with a coherent response.

"Your...daughter. Who lives in Colombia."

"For now. Only until the adoption is finalized and I can bring her back home with me."

Adoption. Of course! All the pieces fell into place, leaving him feeling supremely foolish at the direction his thoughts had taken. For a minute there, he thought she actually had given birth to the girl, but that would have made no sense. Not that this explanation was much more rational.

"You, a young single woman, want to adopt this little girl with Down syndrome from Colombia and bring her back here."

"No. I *have* to adopt her. She's mine and I'm hers."

She spoke with a quiet simplicity that struck straight to his heart, dredging up an ache from somewhere deep inside. Every mother should feel that way, adoptive or not. They didn't always, as he knew too well.

Had Stella wanted Milo that way? For his brother's sake, he had to hope so.

"And you're going to bring her back to Haven Point and return to teaching?"

"I would like to. That's the plan, anyway. The school system and medical services here would be so much better than what is available to her now, living in a cash-poor orphanage in a small village. She could find somewhat comparable services in one of the larger cities but not where she lives."

"That makes sense."

"Gabi is such a smart girl. Yes, she has some problems with her hearing and she will face heart surgery at some point, but she already knows the alphabet and she can count to fifty in Spanish and twelve in English. She's not even four yet!"

She flipped through the photo album on her tablet and held up another image, this one of the two of them laughing together. The sheer joy on both faces made his chest ache again.

"She loves to hear me read stories to her, and she can pick out a few written words she recognizes, especially her name," Katrina went on, with clear pride in her voice. "I know I can give her a good life, one filled with laughter and joy and possibilities, if I only have the chance. I have to make it happen, no matter what it takes."

Bowie gazed at her, entranced not only by her words but by the passion behind them. She had a goal and was doing everything she could to make it come to fruition, trying to provide a loving home to a girl who faced some of the same challenges Milo did.

He admired Katrina's determination, especially since it sounded as if her family wasn't totally supportive. That had to make everything much tougher.

"She's a very lucky girl," he said gruffly. "You'll be a great mom."

At his words, her eyes softened and her lips parted slightly. "Oh," she said, sounding a little breathless. "Thank you, Bowie. That's a lovely thing to say."

"It's the truth. I've seen how patient you are with Milo when he's in a mood. If you can spend ten hours with him and not end the day wanting to bang your head against the wall, you've obviously got the necessary patience to do whatever it takes to help your daughter. She's a lucky girl," he repeated.

"You and my sister are the only ones who seem to understand how important this is to me. I... That means a lot."

When she spoke about this little orphaned girl in Colombia, she glowed with life and light and warmth and was so lovely he couldn't seem to look away.

Awareness shivered through him, heady and thick. The air in his kitchen buzzed with sudden tension, like fireflies sparkling on a summer evening.

He wanted to kiss her, more than he had wanted anything else in a long, long time. As the tension heightened, he saw the softness in her eyes shift to something else—a reprisal of that heat and hunger he thought he had glimpsed when she awoke and found him watching her.

She wanted him to kiss her, too.

It sounded arrogant as hell to think that and he tried to push the thought away, but it clung on with a surety he couldn't deny. Somehow he knew that if he kissed her, she wouldn't push him away.

He couldn't do it, for a hundred reasons.

He had zero time for a relationship right now, between his new job and new responsibilities, as well as trying to find his way with his needy brother. Besides, whatever she might want in this moment, she had other goals and plans that didn't include a brief fling with him.

Most important, he needed her. She was working wonders for his brother, and he couldn't afford to screw that up.

Not to mention that he knew he wouldn't want to stop with just a kiss—and anything more was completely impossible with his brother sleeping upstairs.

All those reasons made sense yet somehow didn't make it any easier for him to break the connection and force himself to take a long drink of water. Katrina Bailey wasn't for him, and he had to burn that reminder into his mind, no matter how tough.

"When will the adoption be finalized?" he asked, hoping that might distract both of them from this awareness that seethed and sizzled like rain on a sun-warmed sidewalk.

She blinked a little, as if disoriented by the sudden

question. "I wish I knew," she finally said. "International adoptions are much more difficult than they used to be, for many good reasons. The Hague Adoption Convention has tightened rules in most countries. I've been jumping through hoop after hoop for weeks because of the complicated circumstances—mainly, as you said, I'm a single woman trying to adopt a child with special needs and take her out of the country. I also don't have a permanent home and I went on sabbatical when I left for South America, with no guarantee I can return to it, although I've had promises from the school district."

She sighed. "All of that puts me at a huge disadvantage. Gabriela has serious medical needs that will require expensive therapies and treatments when we return here. The process of obtaining approval through the Colombian national adoption agency has been difficult enough—and that's not factoring in the process to legally travel with her to the United States."

From his own experience with his brother, he knew how complicated guardianship issues could be. He couldn't imagine trying to navigate that process between two countries.

"That's why you agreed to take the job helping me with Milo, even though you came home to be with your family."

Color rose on her features. "My savings are starting to run out. I'd been working in Colombia while I was there, but English teachers in small villages don't earn that much. What you're paying is a huge buffer."

For a moment, he was tempted to tell her he would make up any difference between what she had in savings and what she needed to complete the adoption. It would be easy enough for him to do, but he had a feeling she wouldn't welcome that blanket offer, no matter how well-intentioned it might be. Perhaps he could figure out a creative way to give her some kind of adoption bonus.

"Who's taking care of her while you're here?"

"She's been in the same orphanage since she was born, and the nuns who run it adore her. Apparently her mother was a very young girl herself in a tough situation and couldn't handle the extra responsibilities of a child with disabilities. The nuns are very kind to her and do their best to give her extra attention, but the orphanage is crowded and there are other children who need them, too. I've Skyped with her twice since I've been home. I wish I could do it every day, but the sisters are too busy to arrange it more often."

"Does she understand why you came back to the States?"

"Oh, yes. I showed her pictures of Wyn and Cade. She knows I'm here for a wedding. She thought for a minute it was my own wedding and that she'd have a father, too, when the adoption was final." Her blush intensified. "Sorry. I'm talking your leg off. And look, you've worked your way through dinner and dessert."

He hadn't even realized he'd cleared everything off his plate, even the slice of chocolate cake she had unearthed from the refrigerator. Now he wiped his mouth with his napkin and set it beside the plate. "That was truly delicious. Thank you again."

Her smile was sweeter than the cake. "You're welcome."

"If you want the truth, I enjoyed the company even more than the food." He spoke before he really thought through his words.

In reaction, she looked first startled, then amused. "Are you flirting with me, Bowie Callahan?"

"No. That was completely sincere."

"Good. Because I wouldn't want you to waste either of our time. I'm only home for a few more weeks, and I have absolutely no intention of wasting any of that precious time with a go-nowhere fling."

Though he had been thinking roughly the same thing about ten minutes earlier, he didn't like hearing her make such a stark declaration.

"I can guarantee you this," he said, unable to resist. "If we had a fling, you would not consider a moment of it wasted."

She gazed at him, pupils dilating slightly for a moment before laughter rippled out of her. "Full of ourselves, are we?"

Her laughter was infectious, and he couldn't help joining in.

"Just stating a fact," he drawled.

Her laughter faded into a sigh. "I wish I could take you up on that, Bowie, I really do. A year ago, I would have been on you so fast your head would spin."

He had to swallow down a moan at the image her words conjured.

"Is that right?"

"Are you kidding? Eligible men aren't exactly thick on the ground in Haven Point. You are eligible, aren't you? No wife or girlfriend hidden away back in California?"

Who had time for a wife or a girlfriend? He had been too busy trying to prove he wasn't the punk self-taught hacker who had lied his way into MIT. "None. I have enough complications in my life right now, suddenly being forced to become guardian of a younger brother I didn't know about a month ago. I can promise there's no wife or girlfriend waiting to come creeping out of the woodwork, too."

"That's something, at least." She gave a smile he wanted to think held a shadow of regret. "My point is, a year ago a great-looking single guy like you moving in would have been the most exciting thing to happen around here in forever. Trust me. I would have camped out on your doorstep until you noticed me. But I'm not the same woman I was then. My priorities have changed."

"Gabi."

"Exactly. I need to focus all my energies and

resources on the adoption—and you're helping me do that by paying me an exorbitant amount to hang around with your brother."

"Glad I could help," he said drily. He was aware of a thick regret that circumstances hadn't been different between them. What if he had moved here last summer, as Ben had wanted him to—before Milo burst into his life, before she left for her adventure in South America and found a child who needed her?

I would have been on you so fast your head would spin. He had a feeling that particular thought would haunt his dreams for weeks.

She glanced at the clock. "Oh. It's late. I should probably go."

She slid her chair away from the table and rose, and he followed suit.

"I'll walk you out," he said.

"I would tell you it's not necessary—that I've lived in Haven Point my whole life and it's perfectly safe—but I'm fairly certain you would only argue with me and walk me out anyway."

He couldn't help smiling, completely charmed by her. "That's me. Boring and predictable."

She made a low, rumbly sound in the back of her throat but didn't comment. Instead, she grabbed a slouchy woven bag from the counter and headed for the door.

When Bowie followed her outside, he saw the rain clouds of earlier in the day had blown away, leaving the night air cool and sweet and the sky a vivid scatter of stars.

"Wow. Beautiful night," she said. "You've sure got a view here."

"I'm convinced there aren't very many houses in Haven Point that *don't* have a view, either of the mountains or the water."

"True enough. What was your house in Silicon Valley like?"

He pictured the small condo he still owned in San Jose. When he paid cash for it after his first big dividend check at Caine Tech, he had felt completely empowered. This was his and no one could take it away. Nobody could wake him in the middle of the night saying it was time to move on.

His.

The condo had represented *everything* to him— safety, security, roots. All the impossible things he had craved as a child.

"Nothing special," he answered, which was a bald-faced lie. "A town house with three bedrooms and a little backyard that was barely big enough for a grill and a patio table."

He could have purchased something far more grand after their risky start-up took off in a huge way none of them had expected, but he hadn't been able to bring himself to part with the first thing he had ever owned outright.

He wasn't sure he would *ever* be able to sell the condo and tried to justify that reluctance by telling himself owning a place in San Jose made perfect sense when Caine Tech still had significant facilities there.

"It was just right for a bachelor," he went on. "I didn't have to mow the grass or worry about maintenance."

"There are a couple of new condo developments here in town and several more in Shelter Springs. I know, because I was looking around a little last summer before I took off. If you enjoyed the condo life in California, why not move into one of those after you came out to Lake Haven?"

"That was the plan," he admitted. "I was checking out a few possibilities with my real estate agent when she had to stop here to drop something off for an open house the next day. Since the house was empty, she asked if I wanted to take a look around instead of waiting in the car."

She snorted, reinforcing his vague suspicion that he'd been conned. He had a feeling his agent had dropped by the house only because she fully expected him to fall in love with it.

"Let me guess." A thread of amusement curled through her voice. "Roxy Nash was your real estate agent."

"Yeah. Do you know her?"

"In case it's escaped your notice, Haven Point is a small town, Bowie. Everybody knows everybody. Roxy is sort of a friend of mine, and she's excellent at her job."

"One look at this view and I didn't see any point in looking elsewhere."

"Like I said. She's excellent at her job."

He didn't care and figured she deserved props for doing her job well and understanding what her client needed even if it hadn't necessarily been what he thought he wanted. "It worked out. I love the house—and it turned out to be for the best, since I'm not sure a condo situation would have worked out after Milo came into the picture."

"Good point. It's nice you have all this space for him to run. Now you just need to add a swingset for him. And a dog."

"A dog."

She laughed. "You know you're going to have to eventually. He loves them too much. You might as well surrender to the inevitable."

She didn't give him time to respond. "I really do need to go. The dinner party should be wrapping up by now. It ought to be safe for me to go home— for tonight, anyway, until my mom tries to set me up with her friend's cousin's son from Bozeman."

"If you really want to avoid your mother's match-making, you could always stay here while you're in town."

The words spilled out of nowhere, and he had to wonder just how long his subconscious had been mulling over that particular idea.

While he might have been a little surprised by them, she looked completely gob-smacked.

"Here?"

Maybe his subconscious was smarter than he gave it credit. The more he thought about it, the more he loved the idea. "Sure. I've got plenty of extra bedrooms, and that way I wouldn't have to worry about keeping you after hours when I have to stay late on a project."

"You want me to move in with you," she said, her voice curiously flat.

"Why not? It would only be for a few weeks while you're in town and would be a huge help to me. I'll even add to the Adopt Gabi fund by paying you double our agreed-upon rate, since you'll basically be on call twenty-four hours a day."

There. That was a subtle way to help her meet her Adopt Gabi goal while at the same time giving himself a little breathing room on nights like tonight when he had to work late.

"Double," she repeated. In the moonlight, her eyes looked huge, shocked.

"Look at it this way, if you're not staying with your mom and stepfather, you won't have to worry about your mom's matchmaking while you're home. Out of sight, out of mind, right?"

She stared at him for a long moment, and then she burst into laughter that had an edge of hysteria.

"You are delusional, Bowie Callahan," she said when she caught her breath. "What do you think will happen if I move in with the most eligible bachelor in Haven Point? My mother will think she just won the matchmaking lottery."

"You can explain it's merely a business arrangement."

"Oh, I can explain until I'm blue in the face. Remember what I said earlier? She thinks she knows me and what I want. She can't see me as anything but silly, flirty, man-hungry Katrina. If I move in here for the few weeks I'll be in town, somehow Charlene will think I engineered the whole thing to be closer to you. I have a feeling she already believes our encounter at the grocery store that first day was deliberate on my part, just a way of meeting the sexy new guy in town."

He could only wish—both that he were the slightest bit sexy and that she might want to arrange things to meet him.

"So what? Let her think what she wants. You and I will both know there's nothing between us, and that's the only thing that matters, isn't it?"

He could tell she was wavering.

"We could always prove it."

"What did you have in mind?" she asked, eyes suddenly wary in the moonlight.

The same thing that had been on his mind since he walked into his house and found her sleeping on the sofa.

Kissing her.

He ached to taste her soft mouth, to pull her close and run his fingers through that silky hair. It probably wouldn't prove a damn thing except that he was stupid and crazy and reckless, but he had resisted her as long as humanly possible.

"Bowie?"

"This," he finally said. Tossing the rest of his common sense to the wind, he edged forward, slid a hand behind her head and lowered his mouth to hers.

She froze for a moment, her breath caught between them, long enough for him to be certain he had just made a terrible miscalculation. Then her mouth softened under his and she pressed that slender, luscious body against him and returned the kiss.

CHAPTER EIGHT

THE ONLY THING they were proving by this kiss was that they were both out of their freaking minds.

Katrina knew it even as she kissed Bowie, as his hard mouth on hers tangled the breath in her lungs and scattered her thoughts like October leaves in a hard wind.

They should *not* be doing this. It would now be that much harder not to kiss him again. How would she possibly be able to live in his house and share the same space when she was afraid she would constantly be remembering the delicious way he smelled, masculine and earthy and outdoorsy?

Or that he tasted even better, like chocolate cake and heaven?

She was vaguely aware of the slow, sluggish churn of her blood, the heady excitement, the butterflies twirling in her stomach. She wanted to stand here all night and savor every second—or, better still, to tug him over to those chaise lounges, where they could both *really* prove there was nothing between them.

All night long, if that was what it took.

She swallowed a moan. No. That was the sort of

thing the old Katrina would do, let her decisions be ruled by something—okay, some*one*—she wanted in the moment.

She was trying to become more than that, a woman of substance and strength and determination.

The only thing she needed to prove here was that she had the strength to walk away from something she wanted with every single aching beat of her heart.

It required every ounce of strength inside her to slide her mouth away from his and suck in a greedy breath. That gave her a little more clarity and strengthened her resolve enough that she could lower her hands from around his neck—oh, he smelled so good—and step back a pace.

"Okay. There," she said, her voice raspy in the quiet night. "Now we both have that out of our systems."

"Do we?" he murmured. His eyes were heavy-lidded, aroused, and the corner of his mouth quirked up into a sexy half smile that made her want to grab his shirtfront, yank him toward her and explore that hard, delicious mouth again.

She drew in a shaky breath, reminding herself of all the reasons why kissing him was disastrous. "Yes. Like you said, there's nothing between us. We have a business arrangement, one that has worked out well for both of us up to now. You want me to continue helping you with Milo, and I need the outrageous amount of money you're willing to pay me. Let's not complicate things unnecessarily."

She tried to sound casual, unaffected, though it was a serious struggle when she felt as if she had just been kicked in the head—when her entire being wanted nothing more than to stretch and purr like a cat in a sunbeam and keep on kissing him forever.

Her words had the intended effect. As he gazed at her, she could almost see his control click back into place, inch by slow inch. After a long, charged moment, he nodded. "Sound advice. Neither of us needs unnecessary complications."

"Right?!" Her hands shook a little as she tucked her hair behind her ear, but she hoped it was too dark for him to notice. "You want me to stay here. I get that. It's not a bad idea, and I can't say I want to turn down an increase in salary. I'll do it, but only if we both agree there won't be more of this kind of nonsense."

He arched an eyebrow, eyes still blazing with heat and hunger. "Define *nonsense*."

How about kissing me until I can't think straight, throwing all my plans and intentions into Lake Haven while you do?

She released a shaky breath. "I'll leave that to your imagination."

"Thanks for that, at least," he said.

He spoke in such a deadpan voice, it took her a moment to realize he was making a joke.

The last few moments left her disoriented, as if she had fallen asleep in one location and awakened somewhere completely different. He had a subtle, sly sense of humor—a fairly acute one, by all indications. She wasn't sure she wanted to know that. Somehow it seemed easier to think of him as the serious—albeit gorgeous—one-dimensional computer geek.

She liked him. It was a rather surprising discovery. He was devoted to his brother, he was passionate about his work, he was clever and funny.

She was aware of the vague, unsettling sensation that something significant had shifted and her life would never be the same. As soon as it registered, Katrina pushed the strange feeling away.

It was just a kiss, for heaven's sake, no different from all the others she had known.

The assurance rang hollow, somehow. She sensed this man saw her as no one else did, that he could devastate her in ways she hadn't begun to imagine.

"I really do need to go," she said. That was the absolute truth. She needed to get away from him, where she could breathe and think again. So what was stopping her? Only her own inaction. With a deep breath, she forced herself to slide into her car.

"Good night."

He leaned into the vehicle, one hand on the frame, the other on the door. "Thank you again for helping me out tonight with Milo."

"You're welcome."

"So you'll stay?"

She was so stupid to agree to this, given these fragile new feelings bursting to life. "Yes. I'll stay. I'll bring my things with me tomorrow morning."

He must have sensed her conflicted feelings. He leaned in, his eyes serious and intent. "You don't have to worry about a repeat of what just happened. You're saving my ass, helping me out with Milo until the autism specialist can arrive. I know what a huge favor you're doing me and that it means you won't be able to spend as much time as you intended with your family. Believe me, I fully understand what's at stake, and I won't jeopardize that again. I would be stupid to screw things up between us simply because I'm attracted to you."

"Good night, Bowie," she said, then pulled away, wondering why his firm assurance left her feeling vaguely depressed.

By the time she made the ten-minute drive between Serenity Harbor and her childhood home, her heartbeat had almost returned to its normal rhythm and the butterflies in her stomach had quieted down for the night.

Her thoughts continued to race, though, after she pulled into the driveway and turned off the engine.

That kiss.

When she closed her eyes, she relived every heavenly moment of it. Who would have guessed that a computer geek would be so tightly muscled or that he would know just how to kiss a woman to make her feel like she was some kind of priceless gift?

It would be entirely too easy to fall for Bowie. Staying in his house might be the hardest thing she ever had to do. How would she do it, manage to keep her head *and* her heart when she wanted to surrender both to him?

I would be stupid to screw things up between us simply because I'm attracted to you.

His words rang through her head again, and she had to close her eyes. She didn't want to *know* he shared this low hum of awareness that seemed to sizzle through her veins whenever they were together. Now that she knew, how on earth was she going to focus on her job, on taking care of Milo and keeping focused on her goal of adopting Gabi and making a new life for her child?

It would be so much like the same old Katrina to throw away everything important to her because she was weak. She wasn't proud of her track record when it came to men. When she looked back now, she was mostly embarrassed that she had dated so many different guys and typically lost interest after a month or so.

Contrary to what some of the old biddies in town might think, she wasn't promiscuous. Yes, she liked to flirt and have fun, to tease and flatter a guy, but that was about as far as it went, for the most part.

She had kissed more than a few, but she had slept with only three guys—her first boyfriend in high school, her college boyfriend whom she had dated for a year, the standing record, and then stupid Carter Ross.

After giving it considerable thought these last eight months when she had been focused on everything *but* having a man in her life, she thought she finally understood why she thrived on the attention.

When a guy was smiling at her—totally focused on her—she didn't feel stupid, weird, *wrong*.

That was just one of the repercussions of the epilepsy she had suffered as a kid, that constant awareness that she was different, that at any moment she could totally lose it and have another stupid seizure.

Limbs thrashing, teeth grinding, head flung back, out of control.

Having an overprotective mother hadn't helped her fit in at all. Charlene hadn't allowed Katrina to play sports or even go out on the lake with other kids. She hadn't been allowed to go to sleepovers either—not that many of the kids' parents wanted her.

Because she missed so much school, she had been behind everyone else—and the medication she took in an attempt to control the seizures left her fuzzy-headed and sleepy, with a hard time focusing on schoolwork.

StupidKat. TwitchyKat.

She had hated both nicknames. Kids had said them to her out loud on the playground, but she had also felt the implication from their parents, with their whispers and their pitying looks.

Her seizures made her different—and when you're a kid and you're different from everyone else, you can't help but feel it.

Like a miracle, the best possible answer to all her

prayers, the seizures started to taper off as she grew older and then stopped completely around the time she hit puberty. Her doctors said that wasn't uncommon, for kids to grow out of seizures.

As the months went on without seizure activity, she had begun to feel unrestrained by her physical condition for the first time in her life. Charlene, of course, had still been inclined to hover over her and keep her wrapped tightly in her warm arms at home, but her dad had finally put his foot down, one of the rare times she had seen her parents argue.

Around the same time the stranglehold eased a little at home, Katrina had started to develop curves and grew into her features. Some of the tourist boys coming to the lake for the summer started to notice her, which made the local boys suddenly wake up and really see her for the first time.

Heady stuff for a girl who had always felt *wrong* somehow.

She wasn't that girl anymore, she reminded herself now. She was a grown woman with a college degree, a career, and hopes and dreams that didn't leave time for her to heedlessly throw her heart at the next gorgeous guy who smiled at her.

While she lived in Bowie's house, she simply had to keep her attention focused on those dreams. To remind herself of them now, she pulled out her tablet and clicked to the images of Gabi.

This little girl loved her and was counting on her

to provide a better life for her, and she couldn't afford to let anything distract her from that.

Not even a man who smelled like sin and kissed like salvation.

"YOU'RE MOVING *IN* with the man? Seriously?"

Katrina had to hold the phone away from her ear a moment at Samantha's shriek.

"It's not like that," Katrina answered, though she had a feeling Sam didn't hear her. Her friend's words confirmed the suspicion.

"How do you do it?" Sam asked, clear admiration in her voice, though Kat thought she detected something else there, too.

"Do what?"

"You've been in town less than a week, yet you've managed to get closer to Bowie than any of the rest of us could even dream."

Katrina closed her eyes, wincing. Crap. She had totally forgotten that Sam had a bit of a crush on the town's newcomer. That first day in the supermarket, she had all but put a "hands off" on him.

The memory of her mistake of a kiss suddenly flashed through her mind, surrounded by big flashing uh-oh lights. She could never tell Sam about that. Her friend would definitely see it as a betrayal. Yes, it was junior high of them, but they had an unspoken pact that anytime one of them showed interest in a guy, the other one would back down. No exceptions.

Maybe she shouldn't move in. Maybe she ought

to call Bowie right this moment and tell him she had changed her mind. All night long, she had gone back and forth, wondering the right thing to do.

Double what was already an exorbitant salary, though. How could she in good conscience say no to that?

"I barely know him, Sam. I'm helping him with Milo. That's it."

"What does your mom think?"

She didn't want to think about her mother's reaction. As she had predicted to Bowie, Charlene had been over the moon. Oh, she had made a big show of saying she would miss having Katrina in the house to talk to and how she hoped she knew what she was doing, but Kat hadn't missed the anticipatory gleam in her eyes.

"She's fine with it, especially after I promised her that Milo and I will still be around during the day all week leading up to the wedding to help her out with whatever she needs."

As she hoped, Samantha allowed herself to be distracted from talking about Bowie. "I can't believe it's almost here. That's why I called, actually. My mom wants to know if you can come in today for your last fitting. She's all stressed that we're down to the wire on your particular dress. It's been a little tough to get this one fitted, with you being out of the country for the last year."

While Linda's taste in clothing was about twenty years out of date, she was an excellent seamstress who had made all of Kat's and Sam's dresses for school dances.

"Yes. I can come in anytime, as long as you don't mind me bringing Milo."

"I don't mind at all, but I can't promise the same about my mom. You know how she can be."

"It shouldn't take long, though, right? I'll bring a DVD for him to watch or something."

"Sounds good." When Samantha spoke again, her voice had a wistful tone that worried Katrina. "When are you moving in with Bowie?"

"Today. Right now. I'm zipping up my suitcase as we speak."

"I can't believe you," Sam said again. "At least I'll have a good excuse now to drop by, right?"

"Sure," she said. "But he works a lot. That's the whole reason he hired me to live in, because of his long hours. It's not like we're going to be hanging out together in the hot tub all day."

It was the wrong thing to say, on several levels—mostly because Katrina suddenly had an entirely too vivid image of that particular picture in her head, of hard muscles and sun-bronzed skin and Bowie with that sleepy, sexy look in his eyes again.

"Oh man," Sam said, sounding breathless.

"What time works best for the fitting?" she asked, hoping to distract both of them.

"How about eleven? Then maybe we can grab lunch after—if you're not too busy hanging out in the hot tub, anyway."

"Sounds good."

She ended the call shortly after, unsettled by the worry that her friendship with Sam might grow even more strained than it had become after Katrina took off with Carter.

Her worry didn't solve anything, she told herself, especially when she should be focusing on the job and on helping Milo.

She picked up her laptop bag and her battered suitcase with the broken zipper and headed for the stairs.

When she walked into the kitchen, she found her mother and Mike wrapped together in an embrace that raised the temperature in the room about thirty degrees.

Yeah, she wasn't too broken up about moving out.

She cleared her throat and set the suitcase down with a bang. "Don't mind me. I'm just going to grab some coffee."

Charlene jerked away, hot color flooding her plump, still-pretty features. "Oh. We didn't hear you come down."

Maybe because Mike's tongue was in your ear? she thought, then wanted to cringe at her bitchy thoughts.

She was thrilled for both of them, honestly. Mike, her late father's younger brother, had been divorced and had lived alone for years. He and his wife had never had kids, so after she moved out, Mike had spent holidays and many Sunday dinners with his brother's family.

He had been a quiet, steady force in their lives forever, and she had always adored him.

Charlene, on the other hand, had been a devoted wife, even after John Bailey's severe head injury from a police shooting that left him unable to walk, talk or feed himself. For years she drove to the care center in Shelter Springs every single day to sit beside him even though he hadn't known her name or why she showed up in his room every day.

Yes, Charlene could be frustrating at times, but Katrina loved her and wanted nothing more than for her to be happy.

She didn't necessarily want to have that happiness shoved in her face, though——especially when she still missed her beloved father with a fierce ache.

"It's fine," she assured them. "I'm sorry to interrupt. I was just heading out and wanted to say goodbye."

"I'll make you some toast," Charlene said instantly. "Do you want scrambled eggs to go with it? You need some protein, honey."

"No. I'm fine. Just toast and coffee."

Wishing she had just skipped breakfast altogether, she poured a cup, stuck a couple slices of bread in the toaster and then sat at the table, since she didn't know what else to do.

After a moment, Uncle Mike joined her, his features troubled.

"Are you sure about this Callahan guy?" Uncle Mike asked, his eyes dark with concern and his mouth set in a frown. Somehow she had the feeling he had been gearing up for exactly this conversation.

"What do we know about him, really?" he went on. "I'm not sure I'm completely comfortable with you moving into his house after only knowing him for a few days. I was watching a show about human trafficking the other day. It was very upsetting and a good reminder that you can't be too careful."

Katrina smiled a little, touched at his concern. She found it very sweet that Mike was trying to stand in and be a protective father figure. Good thing he hadn't seen the neighborhood where she lived in Colombia and the buses she rode through even scarier parts of town.

If she were ever in danger of human trafficking, being snatched off a dodgy bus in South America would be a much more likely scenario than encountering a trafficker at the luxurious home of a computer company executive in a small town in Idaho.

But then, one never knew.

"Bowie is a very nice man, Uncle Mike. You don't need to worry. I'll be fine."

"I hope so." He didn't look convinced, and she couldn't resist touching his arm.

"I can take care of myself, you know. And I promise, if anything feels weird, I'll call you. Who would dare to mess with me, when I have one brother who's an FBI agent and another who's the county sheriff?"

He smiled back at her. "Not to mention a sister who's tougher than either of them."

Katrina would forever regret not inheriting the badass gene in her family. Of her four siblings—including Wyatt, Wyn's twin, who had died several years earlier—Kat was the only one who hadn't gone into law enforcement. Wynona had left the Haven Point Police Department the previous summer to pursue her master's degree in social work, but she still taught self-defense classes at the community center.

"Exactly. He'd have to be stupid to mess with the Bailey clan. I promise, Bowie Callahan is far from stupid."

"She'll be fine. You watch too many of those crime documentaries," Charlene said with an exasperated look at him as she pulled Katrina's toast out of the toaster and started buttering it for her before Kat had the chance. "He is a nice man. I knew it the first time we met him. Handsome, well-mannered, personable. And he's *loaded*. You could do much worse."

She sighed. So much for all her good intentions about not being frustrated with her mother.

"That is all true," she said. "But I'm not interested in Bowie. I don't know how many times I need to tell you that."

Perhaps the one she really needed to be telling was herself. She thought of those moments the night before in his arms and the heat and magic that swirled around them and did her best to fight back a shiver.

"Just keep an open mind. That's all I'm saying. When you do that, you never know what might happen. Why, if I hadn't been willing to keep an open mind, I never would've given Mike a chance. I never would have seen him as anything other than my former brother-in-law."

Mike sipped at his coffee, color crawling up his cheeks above his beard.

"And look at you now," Katrina said.

"Exactly! Both of us would have been alone and miserable. Instead, here we are looking at the rest of our lives together, and we couldn't be happier."

"Not everybody is as lucky as you two," she murmured. Especially not when they waste time on guys like Carter Ross when they know from the beginning they're completely wrong for them.

"Look at your sister and Cade," Charlene protested. "And Marshall and Andie. It's your turn, wouldn't you say?"

Katrina had a daughter to worry about now, but she knew Charlene wouldn't want to hear that. She probably wouldn't listen to anything Kat had to say, anyway. Her mother's mind had been made up before Katrina even came back to town.

Frustrated and a little sad, she took a bite of the toast, then dumped the rest of her coffee in the sink. "Thanks for the toast. I'll eat it on the way."

"You can't take five minutes?" Her mother looked disappointed, though Katrina had a feeling that was only because Charlene was gearing up to offer more *advice*.

"I need to hurry or I'll be late. I'll see you guys later."

"Just be careful," Mike said.

"And don't forget to smile," Charlene added. "You have such a pretty smile."

She pasted on a fake smile, picked up her laptop bag and suitcase, and headed for the door.

CHAPTER NINE

BOWIE HAD NEVER been so close to pulling out his hair—and that even counted the time he spent thirty-six hours straight, back-to-back with Aidan on their respective computers, trying to fix a critical software glitch in one of the early Caine Tech apps.

He sucked in a breath and tried not to let the frustration trickle into his voice. "You made the mess, you're going to clean it up," he said calmly, doing his best not to step into the ever-widening puddle of milk and Cheerios beside the kitchen table.

In answer, Milo crossed his arms defiantly over his chest, chin screwed up and eyes narrowed to slits.

Bowie tried to count backward from ten. He made it to three before the tenuous hold on his temper started to fray. The entire past two hours had been a series of confrontations—made even more frustrating because Milo did all his arguing without words.

"You wouldn't tell me what kind of cereal you wanted, remember? I asked you four times, and you were too busy playing with your toys to answer me. New rule. When you refuse to tell me what you want, you aren't allowed to complain at what you get—and you're absolutely not allowed to throw your bowl of cereal on the floor because you're mad about what I gave you. Got it?"

He couldn't tell whether Milo was listening or not. His brother continued giving him that same snake-eyed stare. What was spinning around inside the boy's mind? Bowie would give anything to know.

"Come on. Help me clean it up or you won't see your purple car for the rest of the day." Autism or not, Milo needed to learn his actions had consequences.

They continued their silent battle of wills for a full ninety seconds. He was asking himself how the hell he was going to follow through on his threat and wrestle a beloved toy away from a six-year-old with autism when, without warning, Milo dropped to the ground and started wiping at the spill with the paper towels Bowie had pulled from the roll.

Bowie sat back on his heels, watching his brother. This little interaction was even more proof that Milo understood far more than he could communicate back. Not that he needed more evidence. From the beginning, he could tell Milo's delays probably had as much to do with neglect than from severe cognitive deficits.

Guilt, his constant companion, churned through him. His brother's rough start in life wasn't his fault. He knew it. He couldn't change the past. All he could focus on now was providing his brother the best possible future, one where Milo could have friends and a purpose, where he could communicate what he wanted.

"You're doing a great job so far," he said after a moment, when Milo tried to hand him the soggy paper towel. "Looks like there's a little more cereal under the table. Would you like me to help you reach it?"

Milo nodded and the two of them worked together, with Milo cleaning up the milk and cereal and Bowie going along behind him with a wet cloth so Mrs. Nielson didn't get too mad at them for leaving another mess for her to mop. They were nearly finished with the job when he heard someone punching in the code for the door, and a moment later Katrina walked in looking fresh and sweet and lovely in a peach flowered skirt, white T-shirt and strappy sandals.

He was both astonished and dismayed at the way his heart seemed to kick in his chest like a rabbit in a cage.

He had dreamed of her all night, a tangle of skin and heat and madness, and had awakened hard and aching. He hadn't been able to shake the memories of their kiss—the taste of her, the sexy little breath she sighed against his mouth, the softness of her curves pressed to his chest.

His body stirred to life again, making him glad his position on the floor helped him conceal that fact.

She took in the scene at a glance and came to the correct conclusion.

"Apparently Cheerios wasn't the preferred menu choice today."

"Who knew?" he drawled. "Certainly not me."

Her smile was not without sympathy. "This week it's been Cinnamon Toast Crunch and scrambled eggs every morning. Nothing else will do."

How had she figured Milo out so well after less than a week, when he had spent three times that with his brother and still considered him an unfathomable mystery?

Again, he couldn't help wondering if he had been wrong to categorically dismiss the various professionals who had suggested a school that specialized in helping autistic children might be the best placement for Milo.

His brother had spent his first six years in chaos. Bowie couldn't bring himself to go that route, though he hadn't completely ruled out the possibility.

The sense of his own inadequacy sharpened his tone more than he intended.

"It might help if you bothered to share that particular info with me. Milo's being his usual loquacious self."

"I'll write a sticky about the day's menu preferences and put it on the refrigerator for you," she answered in a cool voice that made him feel like a jerk.

"Sorry. It's already been a long morning. He's been up since five."

"Ouch. I'm the one who should apologize for

being late. I can finish up here, if you need to head into Caine Tech."

He glanced at the clock and saw she was only a few minutes late. "We're almost finished. I told him he'll lose his purple car if he doesn't help me clean up the mess he made. So far he's doing a great job. That's it, Milo. Almost there. I only see one more little puddle of cereal."

Milo didn't acknowledge him or meet his gaze, but he moved the towel to the spot Bowie indicated and wiped until it was gone.

"That should do it." He wiped the wet cloth across the floor one more time behind him, then rose. "You brought a suitcase. Do I dare hope this means you haven't changed your mind about staying here while you're in town?"

A host of emotions chased themselves across her expressive features before she sighed. "I've changed it a hundred times since last night."

"Still, here you are, suitcase in hand."

Only now did he fully understand how apprehensive he had been since that ill-considered kiss—worried that she would not only refuse to stay in his house but would stop helping him with Milo altogether.

He didn't want to think about how depressing that would have been—especially when he would have had no one else to blame but himself.

"You're a tough man to say no to," she murmured.

Not true. She certainly had found a way to do it the night before.

Eventually.

Against his will, his stomach muscles clenched with the echo of desire as he tried not to remember the sweetness of her mouth, the soft curves pressed against him, the hunger that had swirled around them.

"In that case," he said, yanking his mind away, "let me introduce you to my brother, Milo Callahan. He can teach you all you ever imagined about that particular topic. Saying no to me, I mean."

Her laughter rippled through the kitchen, and even Milo seemed affected by it. He looked up, and Bowie could swear his brother almost smiled.

The day that had started out rough suddenly took a brighter turn. The sunlight streaming in through the windows seemed more intense, and the world seemed beautiful and rich and full of promise.

He needed to get out of there. Quick.

"So," she said after a moment, "where do you want me?"

She did *not* want to hear the answer to that. He gazed blankly at her for about two seconds before he realized she was gesturing to the suitcase at her feet.

"Oh. Right. In between nannies, I've been sleeping in the room next to his down here so I can hear him if he wakes up and starts wandering in the night. With you here, I'll move back upstairs to the master bedroom."

"I don't want to kick you out of your bed," she protested.

What about yours?

Yeah. He needed to get out of here before he said or did something stupid that he couldn't take back. "The master bedroom upstairs is bigger, with a nice balcony overlooking the lake. It's the room I prefer, actually."

"There are plenty of bedrooms up there. Why didn't you move him up near you instead of vice versa?"

"The first week or so, I was worried enough about him slipping out without me knowing and didn't want to have to worry he might fall out of a second-story window, too."

"Good thinking."

"I changed the sheets for you and cleared out the few belongings I've been keeping in there."

"Thanks."

"Milo," he called to get his brother's attention, "let's help Katrina with her bags."

His brother didn't hesitate. He shoved his toy into his pocket and picked up her laptop bag. Bowie picked up the suitcase, and all three of them made their way to the hallway on this level that contained two bedrooms and his home office.

He opened the door and carried her suitcase inside. "Will this work? Sorry it's not very big."

She looked around at the bedroom that did have a lovely view out over the patio to the lake's edge.

"Trust me, it's just fine. Great, actually. I've got a bed with an actual mattress and an en suite bathroom. Compared to some of the places where I've slept the last year, this is like a five-star hotel."

He could only imagine. Given that he once spent six months when he was thirteen sleeping in the back seat of an Oldsmobile, it wasn't that tough to picture.

He didn't like thinking of her in primitive, dangerous conditions. "What did your family think about your taking off to a bunch of Third World countries?"

Her features grew pensive. "About what you might expect. My mother wasn't thrilled. She thought I was going to be kidnapped and held for ransom. She had Marsh, my brother who's the sheriff, recount all the bad things that might happen to me and she made Elliot, my brother the FBI agent, send me a list of every government travel warning in the region. Wynona didn't understand why I couldn't just take a sabbatical and hike across the country or something."

"Despite their objections, you did it anyway. Were you at all anxious about traveling alone?"

"I wasn't alone," she said after an awkward moment. "Not at first, anyway. I went with…a friend."

"A friend."

More than that, he suspected, judging by the color soaking her cheeks. "Carter was a climber trying to summit the highest points in every country in South America. I was part of his support crew."

"Wow. I thought you said you'd been teaching English in Colombia."

"I have been, for most of the time I've been gone. The climber thing didn't work out and we...parted ways."

She said nothing more and he didn't press, sensing she didn't want to talk about it. He couldn't help wondering, though. What kind of idiot would drag her to South America and then walk away from her? Or had she been the one doing the walking?

"Why didn't you come back after things ended?" he couldn't resist asking.

"You sound like my mom. Because I met Gabi. I already loved her and knew I couldn't simply leave her there. Could you have left Milo in another country and gone on to merrily live your life without him?"

"Not a chance," he answered without hesitation. The moment he found out about his little brother, Bowie knew his life was about to change. He owed Milo the sort of childhood Bowie had always wanted, no matter how difficult it might prove to deliver.

At his answer, her expression softened. "I know it's not the same. Gabi isn't my blood, but I loved her from the beginning. Even if I hadn't met Gabi, though, I wouldn't have come home right away."

"Why not?"

"And prove everybody right? Not a chance."

That he could understand completely. He had spent his whole life feeling like he needed to prove something, the brainiac runt in the secondhand clothes and the shaggy hair he had to cut himself, when he bothered.

In each new school, he had to prove he could handle the work—a challenge magnified a thousand times after he conned his way into MIT.

About a month after he started school, he had almost been thrown out after the burden of his guilt had become too great and he confessed the truth to the department head of the computer program. He might have been ousted, if the dean of the department had been a stuffy ass.

Instead, Monte Lewis had been flabbergasted to learn Bowie had been able to pull off a monumental hack that could fool the entire admissions department. He had insisted on a demonstration—yet another time when Bowie had to prove himself.

When Bowie confessed the reason for the deception, that he had earned his GED a few months before because he moved around with his mother too much to attend high school, Dean Lewis had taken him under his considerable wing and cleared his way to stay in college.

He had met Ben and Aidan there. While Aidan's ideas had started Caine Tech, Bowie had been there from the beginning. He hadn't even been old enough to vote when he helped Aidan perfect the software that had been the cornerstone of the business.

How successful did a guy have to be before he

lost the feeling that he had to face the world with his chin out and his fists raised?

"This room should work fine," Katrina said, distracting him from the rhetorical question.

"Good," he said. "I need to take off. Milo, I'll see you later, okay?"

His brother ignored him, apparently still holding a grudge over the cereal thing.

Bowie swallowed his sigh. "Thank you. If you have any questions or problems, you know where to find me."

"We're going to have a great day. Don't spare us a thought."

Given that he hadn't been able to *stop* thinking about her since the night before— even in his dreams—he didn't hold out much hope for that.

"You want me to read to you from the book about the true story of the Big Bad Wolf, is that right?"

Milo nodded vigorously, holding up the funny book that made him smile no matter how many times she read it to him.

She wanted nothing more than to curl up beside him on the bed and read the story, since it was one of her own favorites, but she wasn't a second-grade teacher for nothing. When necessary, she had become pretty good at channeling her inner hard-ass.

"I would be happy to read. You know I love that story, too. But I need you to do something for me first."

The noise he made sounded remarkably like a wordless question, complete with the raised inflection at the end.

"We need to practice what the speech therapist told us today. I need you to practice the *B* sound. *B* for book. Can you do it?"

He shook his head vigorously, and she sighed. She had been trying all afternoon since their appointment, with various other incentives but roughly the same result. "Well," she said, her voice shaded with regret, "I guess you can look at the pictures by yourself. Maybe you can find the letter *B* I showed you. *Big* and *bad* both start with the letter *B*."

He thrust the book at her stubbornly, and just as stubbornly, she shook her head. "Sorry, kiddo. I'll read to you when you practice what you learned today from the speech therapist. Book. *B*. Buh. Remember that boat ride we were talking about? *Boat* also starts with *B*."

Milo's eyebrows lowered with his frustration, but he must have sensed she was serious. He looked at the book, then back at her, and finally repeated the sound. "Buh. Buh. Ba-oo."

She figured it was as close as he could come, since the *K* sound at the end of the word was tough.

Delighted, she couldn't resist pulling him into a hug that she knew he merely tolerated. "Milo, that's fantastic! I'm so proud of you. You said *book*! Great job! Wait until Bowie hears you. That's another *B* word. *Brother. Bowie. Bo.*"

"Bu-o."

Oh, she hoped he would be able to replicate the sound the next morning when he saw Bowie again at breakfast. Milo could learn to use words to communicate. She knew it. Yes, he was six years old and had a long way to go, but she wanted to believe the boy was on the verge of a big speech breakthrough.

"You earned the story for sure. Maybe I'll even read it twice!"

He offered the small half smile that indicated he was pleased and then settled into his bed, pulling the blankets up to his chin. She sat beside him and started to read. By the time she finished the last page, his eyelids drooped and he struggled to keep them open.

"There you go. Sleep well, little bug. That's another *B* word. Buh-ug."

He didn't try to tackle that one, because he was already mostly asleep.

She tucked him in, setting the purple car in his hand on the bedside table, where he would be sure to see it first thing, then smoothed a hand over his hair, aware of a soft tenderness settling around her heart.

Oh, this was exactly what she had been afraid would happen. Despite her best efforts to steel her emotions, she deeply cared for this cute little boy.

Leaving him would gouge away a little corner of her heart.

It wasn't like she would never see him again. If all went well with the adoption, she would be back in Haven Point by Christmas. Still, she knew it wouldn't be the same. She wouldn't be a regular part of his life, only someone he might remember and wave to when she saw him at school or if they bumped into each other in a store.

At least she would have the chance to watch him soar from afar. That would have to be enough.

She arched her neck from side to side, aware of the ache in tendons and muscles that spread from her neck to her shoulders.

Milo might be cute, but he was also a handful. Teaching twenty-four six- and seven-year-olds in her classroom had kept her on her toes every day, constantly alert to head off trouble. One would think being responsible for only one child would be easier. Not when that child was Milo Callahan. Spending hours at a time alone with him was the very definition of exhausting.

Through the open window, a soft breeze whispered through the curtains, tantalizing, beckoning, scented with pine and the lake.

She and Milo had spent a good portion of the evening outside when they ate dinner out on the patio, then took a walk over to the Lawsons' house to play with Jerry Lewis, but she still wanted to be out there. She couldn't seem to get enough of the long, balmy Haven Point evenings, where the sun didn't completely sink behind the Redemptions until nine thirty, still an hour or so away.

Unable to resist the temptation, she grabbed the

video monitor into Milo's room off the table and walked outside.

This was her favorite part of the day, when the shadows were long and the air was starting to hum and peep with night creatures. The lake still buzzed with activity as people enjoyed the glorious summer evening by whatever means they could—kayaks, stand-up paddleboards, inflatable rafts.

When a power fishing boat trawled past, close to the shore, she recognized her friend Lindy Grace and her husband, Ron, and two young sons.

The boys spotted her first and waved with an enthusiasm that drew their mother's attention. Lindy Grace waved and mouthed something Katrina couldn't understand. Probably, *What are you doing at Bowie Callahan's house so late?* Or maybe not. The way word spread in Haven Point, everybody in the Helping Hands probably already knew she had moved into Bowie's house.

Certain tongues were probably already wagging.

She couldn't let it bother her. She was making a difference to Milo, and that was the important thing.

She remembered his painstaking effort that evening to squeeze out the word *book*. His brother would be thrilled at his progress. Before they knew it, Milo would be chattering Bowie's ears off.

Thoroughly enjoying the mental picture, she settled into one of the loungers overlooking the lake and propped the video monitor on the table next to her, where she would hear the slightest peep out of Milo.

She tilted her face to the dying sun, enjoying the warmth on her skin and listening to the buzz of activity out on the lake and the soft wind murmuring in the treetops.

Not a bad way to spend a summer evening. Not bad at all.

It was her last conscious thought for some time.

CHAPTER TEN

SHE AWOKE TO the vague, unsettling sensation of being watched.

For an instant, she was disoriented, caught up in the dregs of a nightmare where someone who looked like Angel Herrera was dressed in a suit that appeared to have been fashioned out of filled-out adoption forms. The man held Gabi in his arms and walked briskly away from Katrina. No matter how quickly she ran to catch up, he and the precious cargo in his arms stayed several paces ahead of her, just out of reach.

She understood the dream perfectly. She was deeply afraid something would go wrong with the adoption and she and Gabi would be forever separated.

Milo. An instant later, she remembered her charge, and her gaze shifted instinctively to the monitor, where she saw the boy sleeping peacefully.

With that worry gone, she could focus on her surroundings and the unsettling feeling of being watched. The sun had set, and though it wasn't fully dark yet, everything seemed in shadows. She could just make out a shape about six feet away, big and somehow menacing.

As her sleepiness receded, panic washed in to take its place, acrid and hot. She instinctively reached for the pepper spray she always carried in her pocket while traveling by herself, but her hand came up empty.

Haven Point was a safe town, for the most part. But not always. She wasn't the daughter of a police chief for nothing. She knew the lake attracted boaters and tourists—and alcohol. The sleepy calm of the community could quickly become an illusion.

"You're awake."

At the voice she sagged back against the lounger. Bowie. Of course. At least he wasn't some crazed, drunken boater out to cause trouble, yet somehow knowing the identity of that dark shape did nothing to ease her jumpiness.

"I'm awake now!" she finally said. "You scared the wits out of me."

"Sorry about that. You were sleeping so peacefully, I didn't want to wake you, but I was afraid if I didn't, the mosquitoes would probably carry you away."

She was mortified suddenly. How long had he been standing there? Had she been snoring? Or, worse, drooling? She wiped at her mouth and was relieved when it was dry. Whether she was snoring or not would probably have to remain a mystery, unless she worked up the nerve to ask him.

"I can't believe I fell asleep on the job again. This is becoming a habit. I'm sorry."

"No apologies necessary. You don't have to explain it to me. Milo can be exhausting. I spend an hour with him and I'm more tired than when I used to pull all-nighters in school."

She tried to picture a younger version of Bowie walking across a college campus with his backpack and a bunch of giggling coeds and couldn't quite make the image stick. "What time is it?"

"Not that late. Nine thirty or so. Later than I should be coming home, that's for sure. I meant to be back before Milo went to bed, to at least give you a break. Despite what I said last night, you shouldn't have to feel as if you're on duty twenty-four hours a day."

"I don't mind. It's good training for after I adopt Gabriela, right? Moms don't take evenings and weekends off."

An odd expression slid across his face like the clouds drifting across the moon. "The good ones, anyway."

She wondered again about his life, about the mother he and Milo shared, but didn't have the nerve to ask about that either.

"Did you get dinner? We had grilled ham-and-cheese sandwiches. I thought about making an extra for you but figured it would be easier—and taste better—if I fixed you a fresh one when you came home."

"That's very kind of you," he said, his expression a little shocked. She had the feeling he wasn't used to people taking care of him and didn't quite know how to respond. "I sent an intern for takeout earlier. But thank you."

He smiled, but she didn't miss the weary lines around the edges of his mouth. He seemed even more tired than she was.

"Those mosquitoes you were worrying about aren't too bad yet. This isn't a bad place to unwind after a tough day." She gestured to the chair beside her.

When he didn't immediately sit down, she pressed a little harder. "What's the use in buying a spectacular house on a lake if you never take a moment to enjoy it?"

He looked out at the lake, then back at the chair. She thought he was going to refuse, but after a moment, he eased into the lounger next to hers and stretched his long legs out.

He gave a heavy exhale and then another one. Instantly, he seemed more relaxed.

"There. What did I tell you?"

He smiled a little, and the butterflies seemed to be doing kung fu against her insides. "This is good. You're right. It's nice to sit still for a moment."

Maybe it was a mistake to invite him to sit beside her. She was intensely aware of him, unable to shake the memory of that heated embrace.

Little night creatures peeped and hooted as the

water lapped softly at the shore, with the occasional muted splash out on the lake as a fish flopped out after a bug.

She couldn't exactly call herself a world traveler, but she had seen a bit more of the planet the last year than she could have said the previous summer. No matter where she traveled, she had a feeling she would still consider Lake Haven on a summer night as close to paradise as her feeble brain could imagine. These priceless evenings were made all the sweeter by the memory of how harsh and cold the winters could be around here.

"Tell me about your day," he said after a moment. "What was Milo's final meltdown tally?"

She looked back over her day, which in retrospect didn't seem all that bad. "A few minor skirmishes, but only two big meltdowns, if you can believe that. He went with me to my friend Samantha's boutique for my final bridesmaid dress fitting and decided it was taking too long."

"Can't really blame him for that. I might have had a meltdown, too, if I had to be stuck there for longer than ten minutes," Bowie said with a half smile that made all her girlie parts shiver.

Yes. This was definitely a mistake, sitting alone with him here while the stars popped out one by one and the moonlight wrapped them in an intimate cocoon.

She should jump up right now and go inside to her room. That was exactly what any smart woman would do—especially a smart woman who told herself she was done playing the game.

Somehow Katrina couldn't seem to make herself move.

"A man who hates shopping," she said instead. "How unoriginal."

"I don't hate shopping," he protested. "I could spend hours in an electronics store and be perfectly happy. But a women's clothing store would hold about as much interest and appeal to me as it probably does to a six-year-old boy."

"Okay. I'll give you that." She smiled. "Milo actually did okay, until Sam's mom got after him for playing around inside the dress racks. He was only exploring the different textures of fabric, but she didn't want him to get greasy fingerprints all over the dresses. We were able to distract him by asking his help to untangle a box of hangers they had in the back. It worked pretty well."

"Smart. How was the rest of your day?"

"Oh! I have news!" she exclaimed. What was *wrong* with her? She couldn't believe she hadn't told him first thing!

"Is it about your adoption?"

The interest in his voice warmed her, but she didn't let it distract her. "No. Nothing has changed there, unfortunately. Still waiting to hear from the attorney working with me there. This is about Milo."

She paused for dramatic effect until he finally

huffed out an exasperated breath. "What is it? Don't tell me, he met another dog he loved."

She laughed. "No. But I'll just remind you that therapy dogs can do amazing things for children with autism."

"Yeah, yeah. If not a dog, then what?"

Suddenly, she wasn't sure how he would feel about their progress that day, since he hadn't sanctioned their visit with Jane McMillan, the speech-language pathologist at the elementary school, who had agreed to take a look at Milo.

He hadn't *unsanctioned* it either, she rationalized.

"This is bigger than a dog. It's huge."

"A horse? A giraffe? An elephant?"

"Okay, not *literally* bigger. Conceptually bigger. Drumroll, please. He said your name!"

He jerked his head toward her abruptly, his eyes clearly reflecting shock. "Really?"

"Well, not completely. He said ba-oo for *book* and then Bu-o for *Bo*. I didn't try to have him tackle *Bowie*, but I'm sure that won't take long."

"That's incredible! How did that happen? I haven't been able to get anything but *no* out of him."

She beamed, thrilled all over again at Milo's accomplishment. "I knew he could say certain sounds, and I knew he was capable of far more than anyone has expected from him. Today we made a visit to a friend of mine who is also the speech-language pathologist at the elementary school."

"You did what?"

She was almost positive his tone was more confused than annoyed, but it was hard to read his expression accurately in the dim light.

"It was a casual visit only. She couldn't do an official assessment of him, nor would I ask that of her,
since you—as his legal guardian—weren't present to
give consent. But she did give me a few exercises I
might hypothetically want to use if I knew of any hypothetical boys who had hypothetical speech delays."

"Which you do. Hypothetically."

"Exactly! The *B* sound was the only one we
worked on this afternoon. It wasn't easy and I had
to offer an incentive you might not like."

"Dare I ask what kind of incentive?"

She hesitated again, again not sure how he would
respond. She couldn't help thinking about Charlene
and all her rules. Her mother would have been livid
if someone had promised her what she had promised Milo.

"I told him you would take him on a boat ride."

He didn't say anything for a long moment. When
he did, he sounded bemused. "You told him I would
take him on a boat ride."

"He's fascinated by the water but a little afraid
of it. I thought it would be good for him to have the
chance to go out and explore how much fun it can
be."

"Makes sense. One problem, though. I don't happen to have a boat."

"No. But we both have friends who do. I thought

maybe we could even ask Ben to take us out in his Killy one evening next week, after the wedding. It's a gorgeous wooden boat made by Kilpatrick Boatworks, back in the day. His family really knew how to craft beautiful boats."

"I've seen the Killy. It is a thing of art."

"If Ben is too busy, I have plenty of other friends who have boats. I knew it was nervy to offer him a ride, but it seemed to motivate him. He tried pretty hard after I suggested we could do it, though he didn't speak until later in the evening."

"He really said my name?"

"Wait until morning and I'll see if I can get him to say it directly to you. By this time tomorrow, you just might be as sick of *Bu-o* as you are of *no*."

"Impossible," he declared.

She smiled. Oh, he was a tough man to resist. "You're a nice man and a good brother, Bowie Callahan. Milo is very lucky."

He made a disbelieving sound low in his throat.

"It's true! You have the resources and the connections to help him reach his highest potential. If he had been sucked into the foster care system, his situation might have ended up very differently."

"Yeah. But he also might have ended up with a decent family—a mother and father who know what the hell to do with him. Who don't lose their tempers when he dumps his cereal on the kitchen floor."

At the bleak frustration in his voice, she reached a hand out and rested her fingers on his forearm. His skin was warm, covered in crisp hair, and she had to resist caressing her hand up and down. Instead, she gave a reassuring squeeze and quickly withdrew her fingers. "You're doing great with him. Get off your own back. Milo can sense you care about him. That might be one of the reasons he tests you so much, to make sure you're really going to stick."

"I'm sticking," he said. "But I have no idea how to reinforce that to him."

"Just continue loving him," she said simply. "That's the only thing you can do until he begins to believe it for himself."

Had she really once thought he was an arrogant jerk? Katrina couldn't help thinking back to that first day in the store and her initial impression of him. Bowie was about as far from that image as she could imagine.

She would have to tread carefully here or she might be in danger of losing her heart to Bowie as easily as she had to his little brother.

She was living in his house, sleeping in the bed he had used until that very morning. The scent of him still clung to the room, a masculine, woodsy soap, laundry detergent and something else that seemed essential Bowie.

While in his house, his presence seemed to surround her all day long—as if his shadow walked beside her. After their heated kiss the night before, it would be entirely too easy to surrender to the attraction along with the soft tenderness beginning to take root.

She let out a breath and shifted the conversation to something safer than his insecurities about his brother. "While we're speaking of boats and water, I wanted to talk to you about something else."

"That sounds ominous."

She made a face. "It's not, I promise. What do you think about swimming lessons?"

"I think I'm too old and the little plastic floaty things won't fit on my arms," he said instantly.

She couldn't hold back her laughter. "Ha ha. For Milo," she said, wondering if anyone else had the chance to see this lighthearted side of him. Maybe he could relax his tight control only here, amid the peace of the lake and the intimacy of the night.

"Given his fascination with the water, he should really have some basic survival skills," she went on. "You live on a lake and you have a hot tub. It's disaster waiting to happen—and you can't keep him under twenty-four-hour surveillance, try as you might."

"I agree. It's a great idea. I had it on my list, along with a dozen other things. Every kid should learn how to swim."

She again felt the sting of being the weird one out. "I wish you had been here to tell my mother that. She never let me have lessons, and it's still one of my deepest regrets."

"Why?"

"Because you're right. Everybody should know

how to keep themselves afloat and at least do the dog paddle. Like many things, it's easier to pick up that skill when you're a child. I took lessons later in life but still don't feel like the greatest swimmer."

"I meant, why didn't your mother let you have lessons."

With that simple question, she flashed back to summers when she was around Milo's age, watching Wyatt and Wynona splash around with Elliot and Marshall while she was forced to sit on the bank—or, worse, in the house, where she couldn't even feel the warm sunshine or smell the pines or listen to the laughter of her siblings.

Oh, how she had envied them their freedom.

"It was for my own safety," she finally said.

"Not learning how to swim was for your own safety?"

Why had she opened her big mouth? She wished she had never started on the topic. Since she had opened the door, she didn't know how to avoid telling him about the whole StupidKat thing.

As soon as she did, everything would change. She had seen it too many times before.

Might as well get it over with.

She looked out at the lake, one hand clenched into a fist on her leg. "I had a seizure disorder when I was a kid. It was mostly controlled by medication and diet, but occasionally I would have a breakthrough seizure. Once when I was about five or so, it happened while I was on a boat in the middle of the

lake with my uncle Mike and his wife at the time.
I had a seizure out of nowhere and ended up falling overboard."

"Scary," he murmured.

She avoided his gaze. "For them, definitely. Not
so much for me. I didn't know what was happening,
if you want the truth. When a seizure hit, I would
check out. Apparently that particular time, I had a
life jacket on but wasn't cognizant enough to turn
myself over so I could keep my face out of the water.
My uncle managed to fish me out and did mouth-to-
mouth until his wife could motor back to shore and
call an ambulance."

That had been a critical moment for her family—
one she didn't even remember. Through family lore,
she had always seemed to know Uncle Mike had
saved her life that day and there had been a special
bond between them ever since.

After that day, Charlene's protective gene had
gone into hyperdrive. On some level, Katrina
couldn't blame her. Now that she knew a little about
that maternal love, she understood the desire to protect, no matter the cost.

"I'm glad you didn't," he said, his voice gruff.
"Drown, I mean."

She finally glanced over at him, wishing she
could read his features better in the gathering darkness. To her relief, she didn't sense any shift in his
voice that might indicate his perception of her had
changed.

Did he feel the awareness shivering between them, the sudden seductive tug?

"Me, too," she said.

"Do you still have seizures?"

"No. I was lucky. They started to trickle down in frequency when I was about eleven and seemed to shut off altogether a few years later. That's not uncommon, apparently, when hormones change and nervous systems mature."

What a weird time that had been. For her entire childhood, her condition had completely defined her. Then, suddenly, she was someone else.

"That couldn't have been easy to deal with as a kid."

She shrugged. "Everybody has something. I try not to throw too many pity parties for myself. I had a medical condition that limited my activities somewhat when I was a kid, but it's since resolved itself, allowing me to live a normal life as an adult. Not a bad trade-off. I'm fully aware I could have been dealt a far worse hand."

She had been raised by two parents who had adored her. Maybe Charlene had loved her a little *too* much, but her intentions had been good and Katrina had never doubted she was loved.

"Anyway. Enough about me. We were talking about swim lessons for Milo. I suspect he would do best in a one-on-one situation, without the distraction of other children. There's a woman in Shelter Springs who teaches lessons in her home pool. I've heard good things. Do you mind if I give her a call and talk to her about enrolling Milo?"

"Go ahead. It's a good idea."

"If the swim teacher has room for him in her schedule, the autism specialist you've hired will have to continue with the lessons after I'm gone."

"I'll make sure of it," he promised. "I don't see a problem."

He was the only one, then. As she sat in the dark next to Bowie, listening to his commitment to his little brother and fighting the tug of attraction seething between them with everything inside her, Katrina saw a problem so slippery and so big she didn't know what to do with it.

How on earth would she be able to spend the next few weeks in his house and not completely fall for this man who had opened his heart and his life to his troubled brother?

CHAPTER ELEVEN

"I DO HAVE one question for you," Bowie said when Katrina didn't immediately answer.

"Oh?" she said, her voice sounding oddly breathless.

"Yes." Bowie kept his gaze on Katrina as he asked the question—or the shape of her, anyway, since he couldn't make out the fine details of her features in the darkness. "How are we going to get along without you?"

He didn't even want to think about her leaving. She had been working with Milo for less than a week and she had already made incredible progress with his brother. Milo was saying words! He couldn't quite believe it.

Was it really possible that his brother might be able to eventually say more than *no*? The implications boggled his mind.

"You'll figure it out," she answered after a moment. "I'm sure the autism specialist you've hired will be amazing with him."

"She does come highly recommended. But she's not you. You've got him saying words. That's amazing!"

"I'm not some kind of miracle worker, Bowie. The words are in there. He just needs a little extra help getting them out. Every child should be able to communicate his or her wants and needs."

He thought of what she had told him, about the seizures that had been part of her early childhood. Had she struggled to communicate? He wanted to ask, but it seemed presumptuous, so he tried to keep focused on his brother.

"Not many people have cared enough to see past all his behavioral problems."

"I'm starting to wonder how many of those problems stem from frustration at his inability to communicate effectively."

Again, did she know that from experience? "You could be right. Whatever the reason, you at least have given me hope. I can't tell you how grateful I am to you for everything you're doing to help him. I don't know how I can ever repay you."

"You are paying me an outrageous amount, which is making it possible for me to adopt Gabi. That's more than enough."

"You won't persuade me the only reason you're working with Milo is because I'm paying you. It's much more than that. Helping children is in your nature or you wouldn't have become a teacher—and a wonderful one, judging by what I've seen and the reaction of that girl in the store the other day. It's part of you, as much as your blue eyes and that dimple that occasionally peeks out when you smile a certain way."

She gaped at him for a long, rather awkward moment while he asked himself what the hell had come over him, why he was waxing almost poetic about her dimple.

Bowie was shocked by the fierce urge to pull her from her chair into his lap so he could point out which dimple he was talking about by pressing his mouth to the exact spot.

Memories of that heated kiss the night before had been playing through his head on an endless loop all day. He wanted to taste her again, the heady sweetness of her mouth, those delicious little breathy sighs.

"That's a very nice thing to say," she finally said, her voice a little strangled.

He shrugged. "It's the truth. I'm only pointing out what I've seen."

She didn't seem to know how to answer him, and they sat quietly for a few moments in a silence that wasn't at all uncomfortable—until she suddenly slapped her leg, making him jump. "There's one of those mosquitoes we were talking about earlier."

Even as she spoke, he felt a similar sting. "One just got me, too. I guess it's time to go inside. That's a shame. It's a lovely evening. You're right. I need to take advantage of it more often."

"Next time I'll bring the bug spray."

She grabbed the video monitor where they could

both see Milo sleeping soundly and they headed into the house.

It was one thing to be alone with Katrina outside in the dark with the vast lake beside them. Their conversation had been easy and comfortable, for the most part. So why did walking inside to his kitchen heighten the intimacy between them?

Without warning, he felt awkward suddenly, tongue-tied and unsure, and could feel his shoulders tighten with tension.

The attraction that simmered between them didn't help matters.

What should he say to her? Should he bid her good-night? Ask her if she would like a glass of wine? He was suddenly aware, as he hadn't been before, that she would be sleeping here in his house, just a few steps away from him.

She spoke before he had a chance to find the right words. "It's been a long day and tomorrow will likely be more of the same. I should turn in, if I hope to have any chance of keeping up with Milo."

He tried not to let his regret show on his features. "I know you've only been staying here less than twenty-four hours, but are you comfortable here? Do you have everything you need?"

"I can't imagine what that might be. The house is lovely and my bedroom is bigger than most multi-family houses in the village where I've been living the last few months."

"If you don't like the sheets or the towels are too

scratchy or whatever, just say the word and I can have Mrs. Nielson take care of it."

"Everything seems fine. Don't worry."

"You'll have to forgive me, but I'm a little new at this. Until the last few weeks when I had to hire a nanny for Milo, I had never lived with a woman who wasn't related to me."

As an adult, anyway. His childhood was another story. Stella was always picking up a roommate here or there, when she wasn't moving them into another "family."

"Never? You've never had a live-in relationship?" She looked shocked, making him wish he hadn't said anything. "And according to the generally reliable Haven Point grapevine, you haven't dated in the two months you've been in town."

He could feel his face heat and wasn't sure how to feel at the idea of somebody gossiping to Katrina about him. The women in this town were a formidable lot, with more influence than Caine Tech— contrary to what Aidan and Ben might think.

The first few weeks after he came to Haven Point, he had tried to get a feel for his new town by hitting up the local watering hole, going to a couple of outdoor summer concerts at the park, eating with Aidan and Ben and their wives at the favorite local restaurant, Serrano's.

That had all ended abruptly the moment he found out about Milo. Since then, his life had completely shifted, and his brother and work had filled up all his free time.

"Yeah. I've been a little busy."

"You should make time. You're not getting any younger, you know."

"I'm not quite ancient yet," he protested.

"What you need, Mr. Callahan, is a wife."

Okay. That was random. He blinked away his shock and gave her a long look. "Do tell."

"I'm just saying. That might seem old-fashioned in this day and age, but your situation has changed. Now you have Milo to think about."

"As I'm well aware."

"Hired help like me is fine, but Milo will need a solid, steady mother figure in his life. Yang to your yin. There are some fantastic prospects right under your nose here in Haven Point. If you want, I could make you a list."

"A list," he said faintly. "Of possible wives. So I can provide a mother figure to my younger brother."

"Possible women to *date*," she corrected. "From there, who knows?"

She wanted to offer him a list of other women, when all he could think about right now was pressing her against those kitchen cabinets and tasting that mouth that had been tantalizing him since they met.

"At the top of that list," she went on, "I would put my friend Sam. Samantha Fremont. She's funny and smart and kindhearted, not to mention absolutely lovely."

"She is," he agreed.

"And she runs a moderately successful boutique in Haven Point, which is good. You're going to want a potential wife who has her own interests, especially if you plan to continue the kind of crazy schedule you've worked this week."

"This week is an anomaly. But I see what you're saying."

He pictured Samantha Fremont, the pretty redhead he had met at Snow Angel Cove and then seen a few times around town—including that first day with Katrina, he remembered. She seemed nice enough…but she didn't make his heart race like he'd just run full tilt up a mountain trail and now stood on the precipice of something he couldn't name.

"Another possibility you could consider asking out is my friend Julia Winston, who works at the library. She's a bit older than Sam and me and also kind of on the quiet side—I know, cliché, right? A quiet librarian—but she's absolutely lovely."

"We've met. Long brown hair, right?"

"That's her. She is one of the most caring people you will ever meet, and she's fantastic with children. Milo really warmed up to her when we stopped in for story hour a few days ago."

"That's nice, but—"

She cut him off. "Oh, and I can't forget Megan Hamilton. She's the owner of the newly remodeled Haven Point Inn, and she's an incredibly gifted artist as well, not to mention beautiful enough to be a model. Make sure you add her to your list."

"Okay, while I appreciate the thought, I'm not making a list. Don't you think I have enough on my plate without adding a girlfriend into the mix? A new house, a new job, Milo? When am I supposed to find time to date?"

"If it's a priority, you make time."

He raised an eyebrow. "What about you? You're trying to adopt a kid. Don't you think Gabi deserves to have a father? Maybe you should make a list of your own."

"That's different."

"How is it different? Because I have a Y chromosome?"

"Among other things," she answered tartly, surprising a laugh out of him.

"You don't think Gabi needs a father?"

Her light smile seemed to slip a bit. "I don't have a good track record when it comes to men," she admitted. "I've wasted entirely too much time on losers and deadbeats, simply because they were cute and available and interested in me."

"Like the guy who took you to South America with him."

"Carter is the perfect example. Immature and self-absorbed and also not the brightest tool in the shed, as Wyn said to me once. I knew exactly what he was, but I still gave him three months of my life."

Immature and self-absorbed or not, the guy had

hurt her, Bowie could tell. He didn't consider himself a violent man—he had absorbed a *few* things during his unconventional childhood being raised by a hippie pacifist, after all—but he suddenly wanted to find this Carter Ross dude and toss him into the nearest crevasse.

"Considering I don't make the best choices with men, I've decided it's best if I stay single. I have Gabi to think about now. I'm planning to raise Gabi on my own, without the distraction of guys coming in and out of our lives."

"That's a big sacrifice. Choosing to spend the rest of your life alone."

A shadow drifted across her eyes, a momentary sadness, but she seemed to shake it off. "I know what I'm giving up. I think I'll survive. Think of all the energy I'll have to be Gabi's mom when I don't have to constantly cater to a man's ego."

"Wow. Surprisingly jaded attitude from one so young."

"I'm not that young. I'm twenty-seven years old. And I've spent at least half of those years chasing one male after another. I'm done."

"That mountain climber really did a number on you."

"No. He only forced me to see that I had spent so many years trying to mold myself into whatever the guy I was dating wanted me to be, trying to impress guy after guy, that I never bothered to take the time to impress *myself.* I had no respect for myself.

What sort of woman leaves a good job doing something with meaning that she loves so she can chase after a guy she's only known a few weeks, simply because he crooks his little finger and it sounds like fun? I didn't really care that Carter abandoned me in a foreign country. I did, however, care that I'd put myself in a position where he could."

Yeah. The guy had hurt her. A crevasse wasn't good enough for him. How about a crevasse with a polar bear in it?

"You made a mistake. That doesn't mean you have to slam the door on finding something better."

She had so much love inside her, as he had already seen with Milo. He didn't like thinking of her tucking away her heart in a drawer somewhere because of some jerk.

"Once I worked through the anger, I decided it was past time for me to stop acting like I'm a silly fourteen-year-old girl. I'm making progress to become someone I can like and respect again, but I still have a long way to go."

"I don't think you have as far as you think," he murmured.

"That's nice of you to say," she said. "But you barely know me."

"I know enough. I've seen your compassion with my brother and heard nothing but strength and determination in your voice when you talk about Gabi. You're someone *I* like and respect. Maybe you should cut yourself a break."

"Oh."

She gazed at him, awareness blooming in her blue eyes. He might have been able to ignore it, to shove down his own awareness back to the little corner of his psyche he'd been trying to wrestle it into all day, but then her gaze flickered to his mouth, and he knew she was remembering their kiss, too.

Instantly, that awareness flared hot and fast into something more. Bowie drew in a breath. He was about to do something monumentally stupid, but he couldn't stop himself from taking a step forward.

He hesitated, trying to hold on to a little bit of sanity, but she snatched that right out of his grasp when she breathed his name.

With a sigh, he did what he'd been thinking about nonstop for the last twenty-four hours and lowered his mouth to hers again.

He knew the taste of her now, but it still jolted through him, the shock of skin against skin, mouth against mouth. Her hands trembled between them, but then, as she had the night before, she wrapped them around his neck and held on tight.

He wanted to devour her, to lick and taste and explore until he knew exactly what would leave her as breathless and achy as he was. Instead, he purposely held back, deliberately keeping the kiss slow and sensual.

He pressed her back against the kitchen counter, exulting in her soft curves and the sexy little sounds she made as his hands explored her back.

She sighed and pressed those curves against him, her hands playing in his hair and her tongue sliding across his.

He wanted to stay here all night, but he knew it wouldn't be enough. Something told him he would never get enough of Katrina Bailey. Closer. He needed to be closer. Where was the nearest flat surface? The table? The sofa in the family room? Her bed was just down the hall…

The moment the thought flashed across his brain, reality followed right behind, smacking him hard.

He had no business thinking about taking her to bed, slipping her out of those shorts and exploring all that luscious tawny skin.

Hell, he shouldn't even be *kissing* her. Twenty-four hours ago, he had promised her he wouldn't do this again.

Bowie liked to think he was a man of his word, one who could be trusted not to take advantage of a seductive moment of weakness when she had specifically asked him not to the night before.

Though every base, hungry instinct howled in protest, he eased his mouth away.

"I'm sorry. This is the part where you slap me."

She stared at him, eyes wide and her breathing uneven.

"Where I…what?"

"I obviously don't have very much self-control around you. I'm sorry," he said again. "You asked me not to kiss you again, and I completely disregarded the request. You haven't even been staying here twenty-four hours. I wouldn't blame you for quitting."

"You wouldn't?"

"I would beg you to reconsider, if that's the direction you're leaning. You're reaching Milo in a way I suspect no one else has. Please don't make him suffer because of my mistake."

She stared at him for a long moment, several emotions he couldn't identify passing in quick succession across her expression.

"Let's just consider this a mistake on both our parts," she finally said, avoiding his gaze. "I already told you I'm weak when it comes to great-looking guys. I guess I just made that abundantly clear."

"It wasn't your fault."

She didn't look as if she believed him. "If we're going to make this work for the next few weeks, we should probably avoid these late-night rendezvous, when we're both tired and our judgment is questionable."

"Agreed."

"I'm going to bed," she said, still avoiding his gaze. "Good night."

She hurried from the room before he could say good-night in return, leaving him alone with his aching regret.

WHEN SHE WAS safely in her bedroom next to Milo's, she closed to the door with great care, then sank onto the wide bed.

Holy freaking cow.

With fingers that trembled, she touched her lips, where she could still taste him there. With a single kiss, he had completely smashed all her good intentions.

She wanted so much to open that door, wander through the house until she found him and jump back into his arms. It would be so easy. He had wanted her, too, which made her light-headed, stunned.

But not so distracted that she would forget her responsibilities. Needing to strengthen her resolve, she pulled out her tablet and flipped to the photo album, scrolling through her many pictures of Gabi.

The girl's adorable smile beamed out at her, and Katrina's racing heartbeat began to calm.

This.

She refused to let anything derail her from her goal of adopting this child, helping her obtain the medical care she needed for a long and meaningful life.

For once in her life, she had to focus on something bigger than what she wanted *right now*. She had to think about her daughter.

Needing a shower to clear her head—a cool one— she hurried into her en suite bathroom and turned on the water. As she shrugged out of her shorts and T-shirt, she caught a glimpse of herself in the mirror, the full breasts that had developed around the time her seizures stopped.

Sometimes she wondered how differently she

might have turned out if she'd stayed flat-chested and boyish, with freckles and hair she didn't know how to tame.

She could still remember the first boy who had noticed her. Lance Goodwin. He looked just like Jake Gyllenhaal. In fact, every time she saw Jake in a movie, she thought of Lance.

She had been just a few months shy of her fifteenth birthday and he had been a year older, a summer visitor to Haven Point and grandson of McKenzie's neighbor Darwin Twitchell.

At the time, Charlene still wasn't crazy about the idea of Katrina swimming, but she used to tell her mother she and Sam were only going to get some sun and play volleyball at Lakeside Park in town, the narrow beach in downtown Haven Point where most of the teenagers in town liked to hang out.

Lance didn't know anything about StupidKat— and the absence of that baggage between them had been heady and exciting. *Freeing,* somehow. With him, Katrina could be someone different, someone flirty and teasing and fun.

They had gone to the movies with a carefully selected group of her friends. When he held her hand, she felt like the luckiest girl in the theater, and later when he walked her home, he had kissed her awkwardly outside her door.

It had all been magic, and for the first time in her life, she hadn't felt stupid or weird or different.

He was in town for two more weeks. Lance had

been enraptured by her the whole time and asked her to keep in touch when he returned to Seattle after his visit.

They emailed back and forth for a few months… until another cute guy moved to Haven Point with his family and started coming around.

She dated Jason for a month or so, until he started wanting to get too serious and take their relationship to a much more physical level than she was comfortable with, then she broke things off. Another guy followed and the pattern was set, one that seemed to follow her through high school and college—and after.

Though she had worked hard in school, she never quite recovered from those difficult early years, when she had missed so much school and struggled to focus. She always felt a little lost in her classes, especially when the assignment involved anything to do with math or science. As a result, her grades had been mediocre at best.

In order to earn her associate degree, she attended a community college right out of high school and managed to get into Boise State to finish her elementary ed degree.

She wanted to think she had been a good, dedicated teacher. She had worked hard to teach her students—harder than her fellow teachers because she thought she had to. Still, some part of her had always been distracted, looking for the next guy, that undeniable thrill of falling in love. The best two semesters she had were in the year she had a steady boyfriend.

She was tired of it—and she finally had something more important. She scrolled to another picture of Gabi, this one when they were throwing a ball back and forth on the grounds of the orphanage.

She would be staying in Bowie's house for only a few weeks. Surely she could control herself for that long.

"Oh, you look stunning, Wynnie," Katrina exclaimed as she took in her sister's reflection in the full-length mirror of Wyn's old room at their mother's house.

"The dress is absolute perfection," Andie Montgomery, her future sister-in-law, agreed with a dreamy smile. "I love the off-the-shoulder look and the full-length lace sleeves. It's completely you."

"You look like a fairy princess, Auntie Wyn." Andie's seven-year-old daughter, Chloe, gazed at the bride, her eyes huge and glittery with excitement.

"Oh. I think I'm going to cry." Charlene gazed raptly into the mirror. "Turn around and let's see the whole thing."

Wyn turned this way and that, displaying the exquisite dress in all its glory. The gown was slim and formfitting, clinging to Wyn's slim, athletic frame perfectly. This was Kat's first glimpse of the entire finished product, though she had seen plenty of pictures of the work in progress emailed to her by Wynona while she was in Colombia.

"It's a great dress," Wyn said, looking over her shoulder at her reflection. "Sam did an amazing job. I should have known."

"*I* knew she would," Katrina said. "And you were so nervous about having Sam's shop handle the wedding dress!"

Her sister's shrug accentuated the lovely floral lace around the low neckline. "You can't blame me for worrying. I was afraid Linda would throw in a hoop skirt, lamb-chop sleeves and fifty pounds of beading."

"Sam has good taste, even if Linda is a little stuck in the eighties," Katrina said. "It's stunning on you."

She hugged her sister, careful not to mess up Wyn's elaborate updo. When she glanced over at Charlene, she saw their mother wiping tears away on a lacy handkerchief she pulled from her cleavage.

"I can't believe the first of my children is finally getting married," Charlene breathed.

"And one more in just a few months," Katrina said, nodding her head toward Andie.

Kat never would have picked Andie Montgomery for her brother Marshall, but now that she'd seen them together, she had to admit that they were perfect for each other. Marsh's life had always revolved around his job, until Andie and her kids came along. Now he was far more relaxed and fun to be around—and obviously crazy about Andie *and* her two kids.

"And isn't it nice of Andie to provide your most

cherished dream? Ready-made grandbabies," Wyn said with an impish grin.

"It's about time *somebody* did," Charlene said in an exasperated tone, which made all of them smile.

Marsh, who had always seemed the most remote and self-contained among them, was now going to be a family man with Andie, Will and Chloe—as well as his own teenage son, Christopher.

"You really do look beautiful, my dear," Charlene said. "Cade is a lucky, lucky man."

"I'm the lucky one," Wyn murmured with a dreamy look.

Charlene nodded. "He's a good man. You know how much your father loved him."

"He did," Wyn agreed, with a smile that trembled a little around the edges.

"Oh, I wish John and Wyatt could be here to celebrate this day," Charlene said, her voice rough.

Katrina tried to swallow down the emotion frothing up in her throat. It wasn't easy, especially when Charlene dabbed at her eyes again and gripped Wyn's hand.

A wave of loss washed over her like it sometimes did, stealing her breath with the pain of it. She missed her father desperately. John Bailey had been the best man she knew, a devoted husband, dedicated lawman and patient, loving father.

He had been a frequent intercessor between Kat and her mother, often sneaking Katrina off to do things both of them knew Charlene never would have allowed if she'd known. Horseback rides and sledding runs and teaching her how to pedal a two-wheeled bike.

She knew John had loved all his children, but she had always felt a special bond with him.

She had deeply held memories of a few of her frequent hospitalizations when he would trade off with her mother staying overnight so Charlene could get some rest. She remembered more than once waking up afraid and disoriented, only to find instant calm when she would see her father sitting at her bedside.

And Wyatt. Wyatt had been Wyn's twin and partner in crime. He had been a rookie highway patrol officer, killed in the line of duty after being hit by a car while trying to help a stranded motorist during a snowstorm. She mourned him deeply, but she knew her loss couldn't begin to compare to Wynona's. Her sister had never been the same after he died.

"It doesn't quite feel right without them both," Wyn said, her ragged smile slipping away and her eyes brimming with tears.

This wouldn't do. Today was Wyn's wedding day. As maid of honor, it was Katrina's job to keep her sister focused on joy, not the sadness of celebrating this day without Wyn's beloved twin and their father.

She ran a hand down her sister's lace-covered arm and gripped her fingers. "We might not see them, but Dad and Wyatt will both be here. I know they will. You think either of them would miss your wedding? Forget it. Dad would move heaven and earth to watch his Wynnie marry Cade Emmett, a man he already loved like a son. And Wyatt would never let you go through this on your own. I imagine right at this very moment, they're both busting through Saint Peter and his gate with a battering ram if they have to. No way would Dad and Wyatt let a little thing like mortality get in the way of something so important."

Some of the sadness lifted from Wyn's eyes, and after a few more loud sniffles, Charlene tucked her handkerchief back in her bra. "Katrina's right. I'm sure they'll both be standing right beside you, beaming from ear to ear. It was lovely of you to ask Mike to walk you down the aisle. I can't tell you how much it means to him."

Wynona raised an eyebrow. "Who else would I ask but my stepfather-slash-uncle?" she asked ruefully, which made Kat laugh.

They fussed around Wyn a little more, adjusting a strand of hair here, a fold of the dress there.

Katrina tried to push down a little niggle of envy that made her feel small and selfish. Her sister was about to marry a great guy who loved her with all his heart. She was happy for Wyn. After everything her sister had been through—not only losing her twin and their father but other traumas she had endured alone and only recently told her family about—she deserved everything good coming her way and more.

Katrina didn't want to take this moment away from her sister, yet helping Wyn prepare for the giddy excitement of her wedding only seemed a reminder of everything Katrina had decided to give up.

"Perfect," Charlene breathed after a moment.

"You know we're going to have to do all this over again when we get to the church," Wyn said.

"It won't be as hard when we're there because we'll know how perfection is supposed to look," Charlene declared.

"Are you ladies about ready?" Her oldest brother, Elliot, asked from the doorway. He looked handsome, if a little stiff, in his groomsman tux. "I'm one of your designated drivers. When you're ready, come on down. Uncle Mike has a surprise for you."

"Oh no," Charlene said with a look of trepidation.

"Don't worry," Elliot said. "I think you'll like it. No rush, though. We still have time. We don't have to be at the church for half an hour."

Wynona and Cade had chosen to be married at the little church in town that Katrina's family had attended her whole life, with a reception and party to follow in the beautifully landscaped backyard of Cade's log home on Riverbend Road.

"It never hurts to be early," Charlene said. "That will give us plenty of time to primp again at the chapel. If everybody's ready, we can go now."

After grabbing last-minute necessities, they all headed down the stairs in a flurry of hair spray and perfume. Katrina was one of the last outside, and she stopped short when she spotted two gleaming black Rolls-Royces in the driveway.

"Where on earth did these come from?" Charlene exclaimed.

Uncle Mike stood beside the closest one, beaming from ear to ear. "I did some bodywork for a collector in Stanley. We hashed out a deal, and he loaned them to me for the weekend."

"How did you keep this a secret from me?" Charlene asked, looking both stunned and pleased.

"Mad skills, babe," Mike said, winking at Katrina and Wynona. "I have to return them in pristine condition, so just be careful getting in."

"He is barely letting me drive one, even though I've passed all the Bureau's driving courses with top grades," Elliot grumbled.

"I'm riding with you," Katrina said loyally. Elliot had always been a hero of hers, even though seven years separated them.

"Aunt Jennie already claimed the front seat. You'll have to sit in the back."

"I don't care. I'll just pretend you're my chauffeur," she responded. "Let me put this box in the car, and then I have to grab my shoes. I don't think Wyn will want me to walk down the aisle with her in my flip-flops."

After greeting her great-aunt, who must have arrived while they were all upstairs, she set the box holding the veil in the back seat of the Rolls-Royce and hurried back into the house. She had brought all of her things here that morning so she could get ready after she and the other Helping Hands took Wynona out for an early breakfast.

She thought she had packed her shoes on top of the bag with all her makeup and hair accessories, but suddenly she couldn't remember seeing them when she'd been digging through the bag earlier as she had dressed.

Was it possible that in her flurry to be ready she might have pulled them out and left them somewhere? She searched around her bedroom but could find no sign of them. After a frantic five minutes, she came to one grim conclusion.

"You ready, Kat?" Elliot called from the front door. "How long does it take to put on a pair of shoes?"

"I don't have them," she exclaimed, feeling increasingly distraught. "I must have left them at the house where I'm staying."

"This Callahan guy's place?"

"Yes. I don't know where else they might be." She could picture the shoes in her closet and visualize herself picking them up and putting them in the bag, but try as she might, she couldn't remember if they had been inside when she closed it.

Maybe she had taken them out for some reason, then forgot to put them back in. It had been a little crazy when she left, with Milo upset that she was going without him. In between trying to calm him while making sure she had all she needed to be ready for the wedding, anything was possible.

"Don't you have another pair here you could wear?" Elliot asked.

She barely refrained from rolling her eyes. Typical male, thinking she could grab any old shoes for a wedding to replace the custom-dyed, carefully chosen heels that matched her bridesmaid dress to perfection.

"It has to be these. Go ahead. I'll grab them and meet you at the church. I'll still make it in plenty of time."

Elliot looked conflicted. "Why don't we just swing by on the way to the church?"

"You've got the veil plus Aunt Jennie. No sense all of us arriving flustered and late. Go ahead. I'll be there in fifteen minutes."

Elliot looked as if he wanted to argue, but their aunt called to him from the Rolls-Royce and he sighed. "All right. I'll see you at the church."

She nodded and hurried to her car, hoping this was the only thing that would go wrong that day.

"Now, *THAT* IS an impressive decahedron," Bowie said, admiring the creation Milo was forming.

They sat at the kitchen table with a bowl full of mini marshmallows in front of them and another full of thin pretzel sticks. Milo was shoving the pretzel sticks into the mini marshmallows at various angles to create geometric shapes.

What had started out as an impulse to distract his brother—an activity Bowie vaguely remembered enjoying during one of his rare, brief stints at an actual school—had turned into a big hit.

To his great surprise, Milo picked up on it quickly. At first his brother had been making weird abstract creations with no form or function, but after a few moments of playing around, he started building geometric shapes. First he had made a basic square, then a cube, a triangle, then a pyramid and finally increasing in sophistication to the ten-sided shape he was making now, which was technically a square cupola.

Milo had skills. No getting around it. Yes, he was definitely on the autism spectrum with serious language delays and behavior problems, but Bowie suspected his brother had the potential to do great things if his abilities could be channeled in the right direction.

They had been at this for at least an hour, and his little brother showed no signs of flagging interest in the activity—a big benefit to Bowie as he sat beside him, using his laptop to try catching up on emails.

Every few moments, his brother would hold up another creation, eyes expectant as he waited for Bowie's approval.

Bowie had to say, this was probably one of the more enjoyable hours he had spent with his brother. He still felt completely overwhelmed with the responsibility of caring for a special needs brother, but he was beginning to hope that maybe, just maybe, there was some chance they could build a future together.

"Kat?" Milo said suddenly, out of the blue. Okay, not really out of the blue, since he had brought up Katrina's name at least every fifteen or twenty minutes.

From those first fledgling sounds the week before, Milo now had a vocabulary of about fifteen words. Katrina had also taught him a few basic sign language signs, such as "more" and "all done."

"She's not here, remember?" Bowie said, giving him a patient smile. "She had to go to her sister's wedding, but we'll see her later tonight when we go to the reception. The party afterward," he explained.

He suspected Milo wouldn't have any frame of reference to understand what a wedding or a reception might be.

"Kat," Milo repeated.

Bowie sighed, wondering how many times today he was going to have to explain the situation to his brother. "She's not here," he repeated. "She should be back tomorrow morning, after the wedding."

In answer, his brother pointed to the door just seconds before it opened and Katrina rushed inside, all pink and glowing and luscious in a plum-colored dress that swirled with every step.

She stopped short when she spotted them both at the table. "Oh. Hi."

"Aren't you supposed to be somewhere right about now?" he asked.

"Yes, but I'm an idiot. I must have left my shoes

here this morning when I was in such a rush to get out the door. If I had my choice, I would wear my flip-flops, but I doubt Charlene would approve."

She extended one foot wearing sparkly nail polish and a silvery flip-flop. Bowie's sudden wild desire to grab her foot and kiss each glittering toe seemed wholly inappropriate with his brother sitting next to him.

He and Katrina had taken great care to stay out of each other's way the previous week, since that stunning kiss in this very kitchen.

Though he tried to convince himself of all the reasons he shouldn't be attracted to her, he still went to sleep each night aching with desire and haunted by the knowledge that she was sleeping only steps away. He had grown to crave the few moments in the morning and evening when he could see her and talk to her before one or the other of them would find a reason to escape.

"Shoes. Right," he managed to say now. "I can grab them for you."

She shook her head. "I'm going to have to find them, since I can't tell you exactly where they might be. I thought they were in my bag, but somehow they didn't make it to my mom's house. I must have left them in my room."

She hurried down the hall, and Milo, clearly delighted to see her, jumped up and raced after her. Though he still didn't give a full-fledged smile, his eyes had a brightness to them that hadn't been there since she left that morning, even when he was busy with the marshmallow and pretzel stick creations.

Bowie was aware of a pang of misgiving as he slid his chair away from the table and followed after the two of them. He wasn't the only Callahan who was crazy about Katrina. Milo adored her. He hung on her every word and had worked incredibly hard at whatever she asked of him.

Katrina had been tireless in working with him, with a deep patience Bowie could only envy, and she deserved every bit of credit for any progress Milo might have made over the last week.

What would his brother do when Katrina returned to South America to finalize her adoption? Her time in Haven Point was drawing to a close. She was supposed to be leaving in only a little more than a week, and the thought of her leaving filled him with dread.

Bowie worried that Milo had become so attached to Katrina that he would revert back to his old withdrawn self after she left. He had to hope his brother would respond just as favorably to the autism specialist Debra Peters when she arrived a few days before Katrina was set to leave Haven Point.

He had a few days to worry about that, Bowie decided. Better to focus now on the problem at hand. He followed after both of them, on the off chance that he might be of some help finding her shoes. When he reached the doorway, he spotted Katrina bent down, shapely rear end in the air as she dug through her closet.

"They were here," she wailed. "I swear they were right here! I picked them up out of the closet and placed them in the bag. So why weren't they inside when I got to my mom's place?"

"Are you sure? Maybe you set them down somewhere there."

"I looked everywhere. And to be honest, I have no memory of seeing them again after I set them inside the bag this morning." Her eyes were wide with panic. "Where can they be?"

"They've got to be here somewhere. Milo, help us look. Katrina needs her shoes. Shoes." To reinforce the point, he pointed to her flip-flops.

If he hadn't happened to glance at his brother at that moment, he might have missed the odd look that flashed in Milo's eyes, a mixture of understanding, wariness and something that looked suspiciously like guilt.

Bowie suddenly had a random memory of something that had happened earlier in the day, before he had come up with the marshmallow construction idea, when he had gone looking for a too-quiet Milo. He had walked into his brother's bedroom in time to see Milo shove something under his bed.

He should have investigated then.

"Milo," he pressed, "do you know anything about Katrina's shoes?"

His brother looked down at the floor and refused to meet his gaze. That was nothing unusual, but there was something different in this particular evasion.

"What would he know about them?" Katrina asked, looking as if she were about to cry.

Bowie decided to go with his sudden hunch. "You're not in trouble, Milo, but if you know where they are, you need to tell us," he said firmly. "It's important. She needs her shoes so she can go to her sister's wedding. Can you help her find them?"

Milo looked down at the floor for a moment, then at Katrina in her flouncy, swirly plum dress. Bowie briefly thought maybe he had been imagining his brother's initial reaction until Milo brushed past him through the doorway and went into his own room.

Bowie followed him and entered the room in time to see Milo pull a bundle the same color as Katrina's dress from under the bed.

Her shoes!

That must have been what he shoved down there when Bowie came in first thing that morning.

"You knew those weren't yours, kiddo. Go give them to Katrina."

Milo looked reluctant, but he slowly walked over to her and held out the shoes. Katrina took them, her expression baffled but grateful. "Thank you so much, Milo."

She grabbed the shoes from him and kissed the boy on the top of his head. "I'll see you later tonight, okay? Promise you'll save me a dance."

He didn't say anything, just headed back toward the kitchen. By tacit agreement, Bowie and Katrina both followed him and found Milo back at the table with the marshmallows and pretzels, acting as if the last few moments hadn't happened.

"That was odd," she said, brows furrowed as she gazed at the boy.

"Not really." He didn't want to tell her that *this* he understood too well, the chaos of not knowing what or who might be a constant in his life and what might be gone the next day. "This is a kid who has lost everything, who has never had a single safe, secure thing to hold on to. Stella isn't the mother I would have chosen for him, but she was all he had, and now she's gone, too. I would guess he wasn't sure you were coming back. Maybe tucking your shoes under his bed was simply his way of hanging on to a piece of you."

She gave him a careful look, and he instantly regretted saying anything. He should have kept his big mouth shut. Would she guess that Bowie also had been a pack rat when he was a kid, had cached everything from flashlight batteries to quarters to sleeves of saltine crackers, just in case he needed them?

"You should probably slip those on your feet now, Cinderella, and hurry to the ball," he said quickly. "You don't want to be late for your sister's wedding."

It was true, but he was also hoping to divert her attention. To his relief, the transparent tactic worked.

"You're right. Wyn would kill me if I made everybody wait for me." She looked over at Milo, who wasn't paying them any attention. "I guess I'll see you later, then. You're still coming to the reception?"

"We'll stop there, but I doubt we'll stay long," he said. This probably wasn't wise either, but he couldn't resist adding it anyway. "Save me a dance, too, would you?"

Her gaze met his, and he saw heated awareness flash in her eyes before she looked away.

"I don't know," she murmured. "My dance card is already pretty full, what with two older brothers and uncles and assorted preadolescent cousins vying for my hand. But I'll see what I can do."

Shoes dangling from one hand, she wiggled the fingers of her other hand in farewell and hurried out of the room. As soon as he heard the outside door close, he let out a breath, feeling as if she had sucked all the oxygen from the room with her.

"Kat," Milo said. He pointed to the flat creation he was making, a smiling face with pretzels laid end to end for the face and hair, marshmallows for eyes and more stick pretzels for the mouth.

Milo never gave a full-fledged smile, but he lifted his mouth in as close an approximation as he could manage.

"Yes. Kat," Bowie answered as worry pinched at him again. His brother adored Katrina. She had brought laughter and joy and *fun* to his world, and Bowie didn't want to think about how empty and colorless it would seem when she left.

CHAPTER TWELVE

"YOU'RE POSITIVE HE'S COMING?" Samantha kept her gaze glued to the garden gate on the side of the house that had been festooned with flowers and ribbons by McKenzie and her little squadron of decorators armed with florist wires and ribbons.

Katrina really didn't want to talk to Sam about Bowie, but she didn't know how to tell her friend the topic made her uncomfortable. She shifted, searching her mind for a way to change the subject, but nothing came to her. She didn't know how to avoid answering a direct question, anyway.

The awkwardness of it was becoming overwhelming. Sam had a serious thing for Bowie, which left Katrina with a hollow feeling in her gut she wasn't sure she wanted to examine too closely.

She had *told* him he should date Samantha, had extolled her friend's many virtues to him. How would Katrina react if Bowie actually took her up on that suggestion? Would she be able to bear seeing the two of them dating?

She wasn't sure she wanted to examine the answer to that too closely.

"He said he would stop in briefly," she finally answered, "but maybe he changed his mind. Maybe Milo wasn't feeling well. Or maybe he was having a bad evening and Bo didn't want to risk behavior issues in the middle of a crowd."

Sam's features fell. "Oh, I hope he makes it—for Wyn and Cade's sake, I mean."

"Of course you do," Katrina murmured. "Oh, look. There's my cousin Josh from Idaho Falls. You had such a crush on him in junior high, remember?"

Sam whirled around to where Kat's tall, good-looking cousin on her mother's side was talking to Marshall and Andie. "Is he still dating that dental hygienist?"

"Last I heard from my mom, they broke up. I think he was ready to settle down and she wasn't. I know he didn't bring a date to the wedding. Let's go talk to him."

It was a fairly obvious ploy, but Sam didn't seem to notice. "How's my breath?" her friend asked.

Katrina sniffed the air when Sam breathed in her face. "Fine."

"I'd better pop a mint anyway."

She opened the tiny jeweled purse that dangled from her wrist and pulled out a Tic Tac container, then shook out a couple of mints and handed one to Katrina.

When she reached in again to pull out a compact and started rubbing her tongue over her teeth to clear away any stray lipstick stains that might dare cling,

Katrina had to roll her eyes. "You look beautiful, as usual. Let's hurry before my mom matches him up with one of Barbara Serrano's nieces who are in town to work the restaurant summer crowds."

As she hoped, Sam let herself be distracted. They went over and struck up a conversation with Josh, who ran a fairly lucrative outdoor clothing store, and within a few moments, Josh was asking Sam to dance.

When he led her out to the dance floor set up on Cade's large patio, Katrina sighed with relief—and maybe a little sadness. Sam could be exhausting. She adored her friend, but it was becoming painfully clear that their paths in life had begun to diverge.

With Samantha busy for now, Katrina grabbed a little cheesecake bite from a passing waiter and a flute of champagne from another and made her way under the globe lights strung across the backyard. As maid of honor, she should probably check to see if the bride needed her for anything.

Her sister stood beside a gloriously gorgeous Cade, dressed more formally than Katrina had ever seen him in a black tux he wore with polished cowboy boots.

Wyn looked radiant as the two of them talked and laughed with guests, and the happy glow surrounding them made Katrina feel almost weepy.

Wynnie didn't need her. Why would she? Her sister had Cade at her side now.

Oh, that sounded pitiful. She was a terrible person, Kat decided. Bad enough that she was being dishonest with her best friend by withholding the fairly pertinent information that she had kissed the guy Sam had a crush on—twice—and desperately ached to do it again.

Now she was feeling sorry for herself that her sister had found love with her onetime boss and best friend.

Needing to distract *herself* now, she spotted McKenzie talking to her sister Devin and Dev's family—her husband, Cole, and his two children.

On impulse, Katrina set her half-empty flute on a tray and hurried over to their group. "You have completely outdone yourself, my dear," she said, hugging the mayor hard. "I don't know how you've managed it, but you and the Helping Hands have taken a lovely but average backyard and made it spectacular. Magical. I want to kiss every last one of you."

McKenzie puckered her lips up and made a smacking noise that made Cole—an ex-con former rodeo star—give that slow, sexy cowboy smile that once had the power to make Katrina's knees wobble.

"It's beautiful out here, that's for sure," he said.

Yes, Katrina once had a crush on Devin's husband. And she'd had a crush on Eliza Caine's husband, Aidan. *And* she'd once had a crush on Ben Kilpatrick, McKenzie's husband.

Probably about the only male not related to her in town she *hadn't* had a crush on was Cade, but that was because unlike Wynona, Kat had considered him in the same category as their brothers.

"You look like a princess, Miss Bailey," Cole's daughter, Jazmyn, exclaimed. She had been in Katrina's class when she first came to Haven Point a few years earlier, after her father obtained custody of his two children, Jazmyn and her brother, Ty.

"Why thank you, Jaz. I could say the exact same thing to you."

The girl twirled around, showing off an adorable sleeveless pink dress embroidered with white daisies. "My grandma Anita sewed me this dress. She's teaching me how to sew pillowcases, too."

Anita, Cole and Devin's onetime housekeeper and nanny, had married Cole's father the previous year and lived in a lovely house they had built just down the road from Evergreen Springs, Cole's ranch.

"Sewing is an excellent skill that will definitely come in handy, trust me. Just ask my friend Samantha. She sewed Wynona's beautiful wedding dress *and* the bridesmaids' dresses, too."

"She's really good," Jaz said, eyes wide as she looked more closely at Wyn's elegant dress.

"She is, indeed." Katrina was horrible at sewing. Maybe *she* could take sewing lessons together with Gabi once they moved back to town for good.

"Hey, are you coming back to school this year?" Jazmyn asked. "Ty really, really, *really* wants you to be his teacher when *he's* in second grade."

Her brother nodded his head with all the energy

and enthusiasm of a bobblehead stuck to the dashboard of a pickup going down a bumpy mountain road. She had to smile. "Not this year, but maybe the one after that."

He pouted with gratifying disappointment. "By then it will be too late! I'll be in third grade. I won't *need* a second-grade teacher."

She smiled. "Sorry, kiddo. I'm sure you'll have a great teacher and a great year anyway."

He didn't look convinced, but Devin distracted her stepson by asking if he wanted to dance with her.

Katrina was chatting with McKenzie and Cole, shifting her weight in the beautiful but uncomfortable shoes and wishing she still had on her flip-flops, when Charlene hurried over with a hot guy in a well-tailored gray suit.

"Katrina, darling, you remember Jamie Caine, Aidan's brother."

How could any woman who had ever met Jamie Caine possibly forget him? "Of course. Hey, Jamie."

Aidan's brother, a former military pilot who now owned his own corporate charter business, gave his charmer of a grin and leaned in to kiss her cheek.

"You look stunning, as always," he said, which made Charlene beam.

"I was just telling Jamie what a great dancer you are," her mother said. "Two seconds later we saw you standing here alone. The opportunity was just too good to pass up."

"No doubt," she said drily, which made Jamie grin.

"May I have the pleasure?"

She wanted to tell him her feet hurt too much, but her mother was looking so pleased with herself that Katrina didn't have the heart to disappoint her.

"Sure," she answered and let him lead her out to the dance floor.

The band chose that moment to shift to a slow song, naturally. The year before, she would have considered this the luckiest night of her life, the chance to be this close to one of Haven Point's sexiest and most eligible bachelors. Now she just wanted to kick off her shoes somewhere and eat a little more bacon-wrapped shrimp.

"How is my favorite elementary teacher?" Jamie asked. "Eliza tells me you've been teaching English in Colombia. That must be incredibly rewarding."

One thing about Jamie, he knew how to make every woman he talked to feel like the most important one in the room.

"It is," she answered. She launched into a story about a couple of her students, happy she could make him laugh in all the right places.

Why couldn't she feel all the feels for somebody like Jamie? He was sexy and funny and gratifyingly attentive—but even as she flirted right back, she thought he could tell that her heart wasn't in it.

The song was drawing to a close when she suddenly heard a loud "Kat. Kat. *Kat.*"

She turned just in time to see Milo barreling toward her. He didn't slow his momentum, crashing into her at full speed and throwing his arms around her waist, which pushed her back into Jamie's muscled chest. His arms tightened around her to steady her until she could regain her balance. "You made it! Hi, Milo."

The boy hugged her tightly, resting his cheek against her, and Katrina's chest was suddenly tight and achy with emotion. So much for keeping a professional distance.

Warning bells clanged in her head, but she could barely hear them over the pounding of her heart, especially when she spotted Bowie making his way through the crowd in search of his younger brother.

She had just been dancing with the biggest charmer in Haven Point and hadn't been fazed at all. So why did her heartbeat suddenly skip and her breath catch in her chest at the sight of Bowie moving toward them in a coal-colored suit that showed off his slim hips and the breadth of his shoulders?

She couldn't seem to take her gaze off him and was vaguely aware she felt a little light-headed, then realized that was probably because she was holding her breath.

Right. She wasn't keeping much of a professional distance from him either.

"Ah. I see how it is," Jamie murmured in her ear.

She turned to give him a slit-eyed look. "Whatever you think you see, you're imagining things," she snapped.

"If you say so, darling." He leaned down to Milo's level. "Hello there. I'm Jamie. You must be Milo."

The boy nodded but kept his arms around Katrina's waist.

"It appears you want to dance with Katrina. Is that right?"

Milo continued gazing up at him, clearly not sure how to respond.

"You might not know this," Jamie said, "but when you want to dance with another guy's partner, next time you can tap them on the shoulder. Like this."

He demonstrated by shifting slightly and drumming his index finger on the shoulder of a passing male—who just happened to be his brother, Aidan. Aidan turned around with an annoyed look and gave a heavy sigh as he relinquished his stepdaughter, Maddie, who twirled with a giggle into her uncle's arms.

Milo watched this interaction with wide eyes, still looking confused.

"Do you want to dance?" Katrina asked. "Here. Put your hand right here on my waist, and then we hold hands like this."

She put her hand on his shoulder and they stood for a moment, moving in a rather herky-jerky rhythm in a little circle. When she turned with the movement of the dance, she caught sight of Bowie standing at the edge of the plywood dance floor. He was talking to McKenzie and seemed to be listening intently to her but still didn't take his gaze off her and Milo, which left her breathless and achy.

"Thank you for the dance, sir," Katrina said to Milo the moment the music stopped. He broke away from her and headed toward his brother, leaving her little choice but to follow.

"Sorry about that," Bowie said with an apologetic look when they reached him. "He slipped away from me."

"It was fun. He's a great dancer," she said with a smile to Milo.

"I could see that. You've got the moves, kid."

"I'll say," McKenzie said. "Any chance you might want to dance with me? Maybe some of that dance skill will rub off."

She held an arm out. Milo looked from Katrina to Bowie and back to McKenzie, then hooked his arm through hers as the band struck up a faster dance number.

Only after they left did Katrina realize she was now alone with Bowie. Or as alone as she could be in a backyard filled with two hundred of her closest friends and family members.

"That surprises me," Bowie said, looking after Kenz and Milo. "I thought he would stick pretty close to me tonight. He doesn't like crowds or strangers much."

"McKenzie's not a stranger. We've spent a great deal of time with her over the last few weeks, helping to get things ready for the wedding. Milo likes her—and he absolutely adores her dogs. And speaking of dogs of a different sort, I have to get out of these shoes. My feet are killing me."

She slipped them off and tucked them under the nearest table, where she conveniently had stowed her flip-flops for just this eventuality.

"Emergency shoe storage. That's handy," he said.

"Can I borrow your arm for a moment?"

He held it out and she grabbed his biceps—purely for balance, she told herself—while she slipped the flip-flops onto her bare feet.

"There. Much better," she said, trying not to notice that delicious, woodsy scent of his aftershave that made her want to snuggle against his neck and inhale.

She forced herself to drop her arm and step away. When she lifted her gaze to his, she thought she saw something hot and glittery flash in his eyes for just a moment—but that might have been a trick of the spotty light out here on the moonlit grass.

"All that dancing. Can't be easy on your feet," he murmured.

"Jamie was the first person I've danced with all night. It's not the dancing, it's the standing and walking, anyway. Have you ever tried to walk in high heels on grass?"

"Can't say I have." His mouth twisted into a half smile. "I was going to ask you to dance, but if your feet need a rest, I totally understand."

"They're fine now. I could go all night in flip-flops or barefoot," she said, breathless all over again.

He paused, with an endearing hesitancy in his eyes. "I don't know, though. Without shoes, you might end up with broken toes. I'll warn you ahead of time I'm a lousy dancer. I didn't go to much high school—certainly not in one place long enough to go to any school dances—so I never really had the chance to learn."

"I'm willing to risk it," she said softly, unable to tell him how touched she was by the confession she sensed didn't come easily to him. "Though as an educator, I feel it's my obligation to point out there are plenty of dance classes around, if you feel that strongly about it. We even have a free one here in Haven Point. Wilma Searle teaches ballroom dance every Tuesday night at the community center."

"Good to know. I'll keep it in mind. I understand if you'd like me to take a few lessons first before you dance with me."

She wasn't going to let him weasel out that easily. "Devin is a doctor. She can fix me up if I need first aid."

"Let's both hope it doesn't come to that." He took her hand and led her out to the floor. She felt ridiculously light-headed again and sucked in a few deep breaths, but that only made her more aware of that delectable aftershave.

His hand was warm in hers, his body tightly

muscled, and she again had to fight the urge to throw her arms around his neck and hold on.

After only a few turns around the dance floor, she drew away and gave him a mock glare. "You are such a liar!" she exclaimed. "You're a great dancer. Apparently you've been taking advantage of Wilma's ballroom dance lessons already."

He gave a rueful smile. "One of my college roommates had a thing for a salsa instructor, so he dragged me along to a couple of classes. Apparently a few things stuck, all these years later."

"In my neck of the woods, that's what we call a con."

He laughed and spun her into a twirl. "Maybe a little one. I'm afraid I still won't win any dance competitions."

"If it's a life goal, Wilma probably can help you out with that," she offered, which made him laugh again.

"No, thanks. My need for fancy footwork is limited to the occasional wedding. And I'm good with that."

She was, too, she decided. It was close to perfect, with the sprawl of stars overhead and the music playing softly over the sound of the river rolling past at the edge of Cade's lawn. She could see Wynnie and Cade dancing nearby, heads close together, and her mom dancing with Uncle Mike.

Katrina relaxed a little more and gave herself up to the moment.

"Has it been a good day?"

"The best. Wyn is so happy, my heart wants to burst with joy for her."

He smiled a little. "That's nice. You have a pretty tight family, don't you?"

"Yes. We've always been close."

"I met your brother Elliot when we first arrived. He was talking to Ben and Marshall. FBI, right?"

"That's right."

"One brother who's a sheriff, one who is an FBI agent, and Wynona used to be a police officer. Now you've got a police chief in the family. Nobody better mess with the Bailey family."

"Not if they know what's good for them."

She smiled, though it was tinged with sadness. Her family had a long and storied history in law enforcement, but it had come at a terrible cost. "Law enforcement is something of a family tradition," she told him. "There have been Baileys protecting the people around Lake Haven since the first European settlers came here more than a hundred and fifty years ago."

"You decided to break the mold, hmm?"

"We each have our strengths," she murmured. Law enforcement had never appealed to her in the slightest, something else that set her apart from the rest of her family.

"Looks like Milo has a new partner," she said to change the subject.

He followed her gaze to where Lizzie Lawson,

Milo's teenage babysitter, had just tapped McKenzie on the shoulder so she could dance with him.

"Man, how does he do it?" Bowie said. "I'm over here trying to keep from crushing your toes and he's moving through all the other pretty girls at the wedding. It's obvious which Callahan brother ended up with all the mojo."

"I think you do all right in the mojo department," she murmured, then could have kicked herself when his gaze caught hers.

For one intoxicating moment, she saw that heat glitter in his gaze and knew he wanted to kiss her again.

The worst thing was, she wanted him, too, with a hunger that bordered on desperation. And wouldn't that be a disaster?

CHAPTER THIRTEEN

THIS WAS A MISTAKE.

He should have stayed home on Serenity Harbor, where it was safe. He didn't need the memory of Kat in that soft swirl of a dress, her eyes that were the same color of Lake Haven in the morning reflecting the globe lights and her lovely features bright with pleasure.

Her words seemed to echo through him. *I think you do all right in the mojo department.*

He didn't. When it came to Katrina, he felt tongue-tied and awkward, like he was sixteen again, thrust onto a college campus with coeds who scared the hell out of him.

"While Milo is busy ripping up the dance floor, you ought to use this as a chance to get to know some of the eligible women in town," she said briskly. "My friend Samantha, for instance. She was dancing with my cousin, but it looks like she's available now. She's a fantastic dancer, too. She could give you a few pointers—not that you need any, as we've already established."

He followed her gaze to her friend, leaning down

to talk to a pair of older women who seemed to be holding court at a table in the corner.

He didn't want to dance with Samantha. He didn't want to dance with anyone except the woman in his arms—the same one now trying to throw him at her friend. He said nothing, though, and Katrina apparently took his silence as assent. In midsong, she slipped her arm through his and tugged him to the table in the corner.

"Hi, Eppie. Hi, Hazel. Have you met Bowie Cullahan yet? He works with Aidan at Caine Tech. Bowie, these beautiful ladies are my friends Eppie and Hazel Brewer."

"It's a pleasure," Bowie said to the women, who had to be in their eighties.

The one who looked like the older of the two winked at him. "We haven't officially met, but we know who you are. We've seen you around town."

Bowie wasn't sure how to respond to that. "Uh, next time I'll know to say hello," he finally said.

"You bought that big house on Serenity Harbor, didn't you?" the other woman said.

"I did."

"How do you like Haven Point so far?" she pressed.

"It's a lovely town. I'm enjoying it so far." What else was he supposed to say?

"I was just telling Bowie that Sam is the best dancer I know," Katrina said. "Sam, would you care to show him a few moves while I go take care of a few bridesmaidy things?"

"Sure," Samantha Fremont said, jumping up from her chair so quickly she almost knocked it backward. He wanted to tell her he had to find his brother, but it wouldn't have been true, since he could clearly see Lizzie had the Milo situation well in hand.

He didn't *mind* dancing with Sam Fremont. She was pretty and vivacious and seemed nice enough every time he talked to her. He just didn't like Katrina cornering him into it. With few options available to him that wouldn't seem rude, he held out a hand and led the other woman out to the dance floor.

"I understand you made the bride's dress and her bridesmaids' dresses," he said. "They're lovely."

She gave him a bright smile. "I didn't make them on my own. I designed them, piecing together a couple of patterns we saw in magazines, but my mother did most of the sewing."

"How long have you been a dressmaker?"

That was apparently exactly the right question because she launched into what was basically a soliloquy about studying business and textile design in college, rooming with Katrina at Boise State, then coming home to take over her mother's struggling boutique in town.

He liked the woman, but he was aware the entire time he danced with her that he didn't feel any kind of spark—certainly not when compared with the inferno that threatened to consume him when he had Katrina in his arms.

"I don't know what Kat was talking about. You

don't need any dance lessons," she said in an exasperated voice.

He managed a smile, but before he could answer, Milo hurried over to him and hovered at his side.

"Done dancing, kiddo?" he asked his brother. Bowie thought of what a strain it must be on Milo to tolerate being touched as long as he had managed.

His brother nodded and pointed to his throat.

"I get it," Bowie said. "All that dancing made you thirsty. Should we grab a drink and a piece of cake and then head home?"

Milo nodded vigorously, so he excused himself from Samantha and led his brother to the lace-covered tables where various beverages and an assortment of delicacies had been laid out.

They picked a few pieces of cake and some punch and headed to an empty table in the corner. Several people he had met around town stopped to say hello as they went, and a couple of them even greeted Milo by name, though Bowie had no idea how his brother might have met so many people.

Katrina probably deserved the credit. She had done a good job of introducing his brother around, which would certainly help pave Milo's way in the future.

Haven Point was a nice place. Bowie was gradually coming to see exactly how nice. What would it have been like to grow up in a community like this, somewhere caring and decent and *normal*?

"Are you about finished?" he asked Milo a short

time later. The boy had a trail of chocolate frosting from his mouth nearly to his ear. Bowie picked up a napkin and dabbed at it. "There. Much better. Let's go give our best wishes to the bride and groom again and then head home."

"Kat?" Milo asked.

It was rapidly becoming his brother's favorite word. Bowie didn't want to think about how it was becoming his own, too.

"We can say goodbye to her, too."

That task was made easier when he found Katrina in a small group that included the bride and groom and her mother and stepfather/uncle.

"Thank you for a lovely evening," Bowie said. "Milo, what do you say?"

His brother did the ASL sign for *thank you*, tapping his flat hand to his chin and moving it straight down—something Katrina had taught him.

She gave a soft laugh and made the sign in return, which she had informed Bowie was one way of also saying *you're welcome*.

"You're leaving?" Charlene Bailey exclaimed in a disappointed voice. "It seems like you only arrived."

"Yes. We only planned to stop for a moment, but we ended up having so much fun, we stayed longer than we intended to enjoy the dancing."

"Thanks so much for coming, Bowie." Wynona Bailey—now Emmett, he remembered—gave him a broad smile.

"You're welcome. Congratulations again to both of you. Thank you for inviting us."

"You're welcome. Good night."

His wave encompassed all of them—though he didn't miss the way Katrina seemed to be avoiding his gaze.

His brother reached for Katrina's hand and started tugging, pulling her along with them.

"I'm not going with you right now," she said with a laugh. "I have to stay at the party for a while longer. But I'll be there in the morning. I promise."

"Kat," Milo said in a loud voice.

"Let go, kiddo," Bowie said, which only made his brother tug harder.

"Kat!" he said, louder still.

Panic welled up in Bowie as he recognized all the signs that Milo was rapidly heading for a tantrum. The boy wanted Katrina with them and couldn't understand why they had to leave her behind.

"Katrina is staying here with her family." He tried to guide his brother toward the break in the fence that led to the front yard, but Milo was really good at planting his feet, making himself immovable.

"Why don't I walk you to your car?" Katrina suggested, and Bo was a little embarrassed at the depth of his gratitude.

"I don't want to drag you away from the reception, but that would be helpful," he admitted. At the very least, it would take Milo away from the crowd in the event his brother launched into one of his full-scale nuclear meltdowns.

"No problem."

She walked with them through the lovely back-yard and down Riverbend Road to where he had parked. At the vehicle, she went so far as to get Milo strapped into his booster seat before she shut the door.

"Thank you. Again," Bowie said. "What did we ever do before you came? And how will we ever get along without you?"

Muted strains of music from the reception drifted to them here as she gazed up at him for a long moment, her lovely face in shadows, illuminated only by the moonlight and the glow of a streetlight down the street.

"You have to figure that out," she finally said briskly. "Sooner rather than later. I have a little more than a week here in Haven Point, and then I need to go back to Colombia."

"Don't remind me."

She gave him a sharp look. "That's not fair."

"What's not?"

"I'm having a hard enough time with my mother pouring on the guilt about my choices every time I talk to her. I don't need to hear it from you, too."

"That wasn't my intention," he said, though he wasn't entirely sure his words were completely truthful.

"You knew this was temporary from the beginning."

"Yes. I only meant he cares a great deal for you and you've been wonderful for him. He's made amazing progress the last few weeks. Can you blame me for wanting to see that continue?"

"I have obligations, Bowie. Places I have to be. I thought you understood that. My daughter is waiting for me. I care about Milo and wish I could stay longer, but it's simply not possible."

"I know that," he said.

"Do you?"

"You bring up Gabriela about every time you talk to me. I'm beginning to wonder if you're trying to remind me or yourself."

He could see at once that was the wrong thing to say. She drew back as if he had slapped her.

"Kat. I'm sorry."

"I need to return to the reception." Now she was the one who spoke in a stiff voice, so tight it was a wonder she could get the words out. "Thank you again for coming and sharing in this joyful day."

She turned around and hurried away in a flurry of flip-flops and plum silk, leaving him to wonder why he acted like an ass every single time he talked to her.

"Dahhhs," Milo said, tugging at her arm Thursday afternoon, nearly a week after Wynona and Cade were married.

The day was cloudy, with a low pressure system hanging over the area and wind tossing the lake into a froth of whitecaps. Katrina had a headache brewing, too, gathering just as surely as those clouds.

She really hoped the rain predicted for the area would hit and then move out before the weekend, when crowds would gather to celebrate Lake Haven Days in town.

"Give me five minutes, okay? I have to finish this email first before we go to McKenzie's house for you to see her dogs, Hondo and Rika. They'll still be there in a few minutes. Can you play with your cars until I'm done?"

He gave his put-upon look of disgust but plopped down on the floor of the family room next to the kitchen and started running his favorite purple car around the edge of the rug.

Katrina returned to her email, fairly sure she wore the same look of disgust as she gazed at the message on her laptop screen. Her headache gathered steam as she read the contents one more time.

According to Angel Herrera, they had to file yet another form with the Colombian national adoption agency, which would result in, naturally, more fees and yet more foot-dragging.

Katrina wanted to cry—to weep and scream and break something. Or lots of somethings.

Her daughter was slipping away from her and she didn't know how to fix it, and she was so tired of fighting this fight.

You bring up Gabriela about every time you talk to me. I'm beginning to wonder if you're trying to remind me or yourself.

Bowie's words had haunted her all week. Maybe she was as flighty as everyone thought. She told herself she wanted nothing as much as to have her daughter with her, but she couldn't seem to figure out a way to break through all the roadblocks in her way.

She returned to her reply email, which seemed wholly inadequate to convey the depth of her fear.

I have met every requirement asked of me, including providing all additional funds as requested. If you are unable to bring this matter to a satisfactory conclusion for all parties, perhaps I need to begin looking for another agency that can better meet my needs.

It was an empty threat, and Angel Herrera had to know it. She couldn't afford the time or resources to start all over. But she also couldn't let him continue extorting money from her and dragging out the proceedings. A child's future was at stake.

She reread the letter, tweaked a few words, took a deep breath and hit Send. The moment she did, her stomach felt hollow and her shoulders seemed to cramp with tension.

She really hoped she was doing the right thing. She had already been approved for the adoption. All these requirements for additional paperwork made no sense.

Katrina pressed a hand to her stomach, unable to avoid the grim premonition that the adoption was doomed.

She had just spoken with Gabi the night before via Skype and the girl had tried to reach out and touch the computer screen. "Come home," Gabi had ordered in Spanish in her bossiest voice.

"Next week," she had promised her daughter. She had hoped to have news for the nuns at the orphanage, but now she didn't know what to tell anyone.

Needing a little comfort, she pulled up the photo album on her tablet to the familiar pictures that helped keep her focused. She saw a picture of Gabi splashing in the little wading pool at the orphanage in the purple flowered swimsuit Katrina had bought her. Another with her features fierce with concentration as she threw a ball toward a few other children on the bleak concrete play yard. A third with her hair flying back in the air and her feet straight out as she tried to figure out how to pump her legs on the swings.

Would the girl ever be her daughter legally? And if she wouldn't, how could Katrina leave everything she loved, her family and her town and her career, to live in another country so she could be with her?

She didn't realize she was crying until she felt a small hand on her leg. "Stop," Milo ordered, in the same bossy tone Gabi had used the night before.

"Stop?" she asked with a sniffle.

"Stop. Sad."

The two words were perfectly clear, the most articulate she had ever heard him. He even did the hard consonants at the end of the words. He wanted her to stop being sad. His meaning was unmistakable.

Katrina was stunned on several levels. She couldn't forget that Milo had autism, which meant he wasn't always in tune with his own emotions or with other people's. The fact that he identified her sadness and expressed his displeasure in it was rather remarkable.

She managed a watery smile through her tears. "This is my daughter. Gabi."

"Ga," he tried.

"That's good. Gabi. I miss her and I'm…afraid I won't be able to bring her back here to live with me."

He patted Katrina's knee. "Stop. Sad."

Oh. He was trying to comfort her. Yet another breakthrough. She hugged him, something he usually didn't like. This time he let her hug him for about two seconds longer than usual before wriggling away and picking up his car again.

Her heart ached to know she would be leaving him in only a few days. What a cruel choice, that she had to leave one child she cared about in order to help another.

"Okay, that's enough of that." Katrina wiped her tears, slapped her hands on her thighs and stood up a moment later. "Let's go find us some dogs."

She decided on impulse to walk the short distance along the lake trail to Redemption Bay and McKenzie's house, where the Helping Hands were meeting that day. As long as the rain held off, a little exercise might benefit both of them.

He needed to work out a little energy, and she needed to clear her head. Fresh air was exactly what she needed, especially when it was Haven Point air—clean and cool and sweet with the scent of summer blooms and pine pitch and the lake.

"THAT KID SURE loves the water, doesn't he?"

A half hour later, Katrina sat on McKenzie's large terrace overlooking the lake, watching diligently as Milo stood at the water's edge. He had one hand on Hondo, McKenzie and Ben's brawny German shepherd, while he threw rocks into the water with the other.

"He really does," she answered McKenzie. "He would be happy all day if I let him stand there and throw rocks in."

"Ben used to love skipping rocks," Ben's mother, Lydia, said with a nostalgic smile.

"*Used to?* He still does," McKenzie said. "His record is eight skips."

"All my kids loved to throw rocks," Charlene remembered. "It's a wonder I ever had any left in my landscaping. If you're done with the black paint, would you hand it down?"

The Haven Point Helping Hands had gathered

to finish a couple of last-minute craft projects for a booth they were sponsoring the next day at Lake Haven Days, the town's annual summer festival.

Katrina handed the small bottle of paint in question to her mother, then continued sticking labels on the small bars of scented soap some of the Helping Hands had made for the booth.

She wasn't the best crafter, but she enjoyed hanging out with all the funny, smart, compassionate women who made up the Helping Hands. She would savor every moment, she told herself. This afternoon held an added poignancy, given her limited time left in Haven Point. This might be her last chance with them before she left the following week to return to Colombia and Gabriela.

While she listened to their chatter, she kept a careful eye on Milo. McKenzie had enlisted one of the high school girls who worked for her to keep an eye on the children who came with their mothers, but Milo could sometimes need a little extra attention.

He was her first priority here, and any craft projects had to come in a distant second.

"This was a good idea, to have our meeting here for a change instead of your claustrophobic work space where we usually meet," Linda Fremont said.

McKenzie only smiled at the barbed compliment. "Our summers are so fleeting, I want to spend every moment I can outdoors, don't you?"

Katrina didn't hear how Sam's mother answered.

She probably didn't need to. Linda rarely had a nice word to say about anything.

The conversation drifted, and she was content to sit and listen while she kept an eye on Milo. A few moments later, he appeared to tire of the rocks at long last and headed toward her, this time with Hondo following close behind.

"Bo," he said when he reached her side.

Her heartbeat kicked up a beat, and she couldn't resist scanning the lake for a certain gorgeous computer geek, though her rational side knew he wasn't anywhere around.

"Bo's not here, honey. He's working, remember?"

"Bo!" he insisted. "Bo. Bo-o."

He pointed at the gleaming restored Kilpatrick moored to the dock at the edge of the property, bobbing gently on the water.

"Oh. You're saying *boat*."

He nodded vigorously, and she smiled. "It's beautiful, isn't it?"

He reached for her hand and tugged it. "Bo!"

She had told him they would go on a boat and hadn't followed through, she suddenly remembered. "We can't go out on the boat right now. I'm sorry."

"Bo! Bo. Bo." He chanted the words, more insistent with every syllable. She could see he was heading for a meltdown, like those rising storm clouds of earlier, the ones that seemed to have churned a little over the lake, then blown away.

What he needed right now was food, she realized.

They had opted to craft first, eat later—which was fine for the women but not for a young boy whose mood was much more stable when he ate at regular intervals.

She reached for her backpack and the supplies she had packed along for exactly this eventuality.

"I've got a granola bar and some apple slices and peanut butter here. Let's walk over there and take a look at Ben's boat while we have a snack. What do you say?"

She took his hand and the paper bag with the snacks and walked across the lawn with him, then out along the dock. He was intrigued enough to be out over the water that he let himself be distracted from going on the boat. Holding his hand, she walked down with him almost to the end, and they sat on the dock eating the snacks and watching a kingfisher swooping into the water for its own snack.

By the time he polished off nearly everything she'd brought, he forgot all about going out on the boat and she led him back to the group, where a few other children had arrived.

"You're so good with him," Charlene said, with a definite note of astonishment in her voice. Katrina might have reminded her mother she *was* an experienced educator with excellent job reviews but decided to simply enjoy the rare compliment.

"He's a good boy," she said instead.

"Does he still have tantrums?" Charlene asked. "I know you said he did when Bowie hired you, but I haven't seen anything like that when I've been with the two of you."

"Once in a while," she answered. "I've sort of figured out some of the cues and a few strategies to head them off. Distraction is the best thing I've found."

"Bowie is going to have a tough time of things when you're gone," Charlene said.

As if she needed more guilt. "He'll be fine," she said, trying to convince herself as much as anyone. "He's hired a very well-known autism specialist to be Milo's nanny. I've spoken with her on the phone a few times this week, and she sounds more than competent. She's coming in Tuesday. That's supposed to be my last day."

"You're still leaving Wednesday?" Samantha asked, her expression plainly upset about the prospect.

"That's still my plan."

"We've hardly spent a minute together."

Yeah. Guilt. Her new best friend. "We're together now," she pointed out. "And we'll have plenty of time to hang out during the Lake Haven Days activities.

Sam didn't seem very appeased, and Katrina didn't know what to say to her. She could feel the friendship slipping away, and she hated it.

Fortunately, Lydia distracted Sam by asking her about a particular dress style she had seen at a boutique in San Francisco when she was there on a visit a few months earlier with her husband, and the conversation drifted.

After a few moments, she decided she better check on Milo, who had gone inside with Lizzie and a few of the children to explore Ben and Kenzie's well-outfitted game room. He seemed to be doing fine, watching with wide eyes while Jazmyn Barrett and Katrina's niece-to-be, Chloe, played Ping-Pong.

When she headed back to the kitchen, she found McKenzie replenishing a tray of snacks to take back out to the other Helping Hands. The chance to speak with her alone seemed too good an opportunity to pass up.

"I need to ask a favor," she said after a few moments of helping her fill the tray. "Technically, I need to ask Ben a favor, I guess."

McKenzie's eyes showed her curiosity. "Of course. Whatever we can do."

Warmth seeped into her. She loved knowing she could ask any of the women here for help and she would find it. "It's not for me, actually," she answered. "It's Milo. He's a little bit obsessed with boats, as you may have noticed."

McKenzie smiled. "I do believe I picked that up a little while ago."

"I promised him I would try to arrange a ride for him on a boat before I leave town."

"Oh! Ben mentioned that Bowie had talked to him a week or so ago about taking the boy out on his Killy when he had the chance. We've been so slammed with the wedding that I think we both completely forgot. I'm sorry."

"Please. Don't apologize. You have absolutely nothing to be sorry for. You threw together that wedding and reception basically single-handedly and did an amazing job."

"But we still need to get that boy out on the boat. Ben thought it was a great idea when Bowie talked to him. He was really looking forward to it. What about tonight?"

"Tonight!" She laughed at the typical McKenzie charge-forward response. "It's only the night before the biggest day of the year around here. Don't you have somewhere else to be?"

McKenzie took her mayoral responsibilities very seriously, which Katrina respected.

"Oh, tomorrow will be completely insane, but believe it or not, we're totally free tonight. We were just going to hang out together at home and maybe grill."

"Sounds like a lovely evening," she said, trying to ignore the envy roiling through her.

"It would be even better if you and Bowie and Milo joined us. Ben would love any excuse to take out the Killy, and it would be lovely to come back here with you and grill on the terrace."

"I don't know if Bowie has plans," she said quickly, before McKenzie took the idea and started running with it. "I should have talked to him first. He may need to work late."

"Ben can make sure he doesn't," McKenzie said.

"I'll text Ben now so that he and Bowie can work out all the details."

McKenzie's fingers flew over her phone before Katrina could protest.

"There," Kenz said a moment later. "Done."

Katrina wasn't at all sure how Bowie would feel about the whole thing. He had gone out of his way to avoid spending much time with her the last week—and she had done the same.

She had done her best to avoid Bowie since the wedding. He stayed late at Caine Tech most nights, and on the nights he came home at a reasonable hour, she made excuses to go hang out with Sam or visit other friends in Haven Point.

Trying to keep from spending much time with the man in person didn't keep her thoughts from straying to him way too many times a day than she knew was strictly in her best interest.

After Wynnie's wedding, she had faced the grim truth that she was falling for Bowie. She recognized all the signs in herself.

So much for her good intentions, her plans to remain cool and friendly but casual.

Every morning, she woke up with a little kick in her chest at the idea that she would probably see him for a few moments in the kitchen when he would hurry in—freshly showered, clean-shaven, smelling so delicious she wanted to nuzzle against him. He would grab a coffee, talk to Milo for a few moments, give her a polite greeting and then hurry to the office. It usually lasted all of ten minutes, but her pulse would race for much longer.

It was thoroughly ridiculous, and she knew it.

Now they wouldn't be able to avoid being together for at least a few hours.

"Oh, this is going to be so much fun!" McKenzie exclaimed. "The perfect evening. I can't wait!"

Though she knew it was foolish and would probably only add to her heartbreak when she left, Katrina had to admit she felt the same.

CHAPTER FOURTEEN

As the afternoon wore on and she and Milo returned home, Katrina tried not to check her inbox on her smartphone, which was now dry and working, but it was becoming increasingly clear that she would not receive an email response from Angel Herrera that day.

Considering it was late Friday afternoon and he had already demonstrated over the last several months that he never checked email on weekends, odds were good she wouldn't hear from him that day.

If he didn't respond by Monday, she told herself, she would start calling him nonstop until he spoke with her and told her the truth about what was happening with the adoption proceedings.

Aware she could do nothing about that particular problem from thousands of miles away, she tried to focus on Milo and his excitement about the coming boat ride. It didn't help her mental state that the very thing that had him vibrating off the walls was yet another source of anxiety for her.

"Bo?" Milo said.

Was he saying *boat* this time or *Bo*? She couldn't quite tell.

She looked up from the fruit she was chopping to the clock on the microwave of the kitchen. "He should be here soon," she said.

He had texted her an hour ago that he would be home before six so they could meet Kenzie and Ben. She couldn't tell by the terse text if he was annoyed at having plans made for him by two interfering women.

"Okay, I'm done with the strawberries. Do you want to add them to our salad?"

Milo nodded and climbed back on the chair next to the work island. With his tongue held between his teeth, he scooped the strawberries gingerly into the bowl that already held pineapple, kiwi and sliced bananas.

Just as he spooned the last of the fruit into the bowl, she heard the unmistakable sound of the garage door opening.

"Bo!" Milo said.

"Yes. That's Bo."

With that same ridiculous anticipation zinging through her, she hurried to finish the salad, adding the final ingredients just as he walked in.

"Hi," he said.

Her heartbeat seemed to accelerate to what were probably unhealthy levels. "Hello," she greeted him.

"Bo," Milo said.

"Hey, kiddo." He walked in and rubbed Milo's

head, a gesture the boy tolerated more easily than hugs and warm embraces.

He gazed into the bowl. "That looks good."

"I hope so. It sounded refreshing for a summer night."

"I guess we're going on a boat ride."

Why did he have to be so darn gorgeous and smell so good? She would have a much easier time being casual and friendly and distant if he didn't punch every single one of her yum buttons.

"I'm sorry," she said, then cleared her throat so her voice didn't squeak like a thirteen-year-old boy's. "I never meant to push you into it. I only mentioned to McKenzie that Milo would love a ride sometime and, well, you know how she is. Hurricane McKenzie. She kind of took the idea and ran with it."

"It's fine. I did mention it to Ben after we talked about it a while ago, but both of us have been slammed."

"Milo's looking forward to it, aren't you?"

"Boat," the boy pronounced, enunciating the *T* in an exaggerated way as they had practiced all afternoon.

Bowie's eyebrows rose. "That sounded great. Can you say it again?"

Milo complied, looking pleased with himself.

"Good work."

"He's been trying hard," she said. "Milo is a little excited for the boat ride, if you can't tell."

"That's the important thing." Bowie smiled and

held his hand up in a fist. After a moment, Milo tucked in his fingers and bumped his brother's much larger hand, and Katrina felt like they'd both fist-bumped her heart.

Oh, she was in trouble.

How was she going to make it through the next few days without completely falling hard for both of the Callahan brothers? She had no idea. She only knew she had to try.

"I CAN'T BELIEVE you've been here for two months and I still haven't taken you out on the Delphine," Ben said, shaking his head. "She's a beauty, isn't she?"

"Stunning," Bowie agreed. "I'll admit, I didn't quite catch the vision a few years ago when you started looking for a Killy, but I'm starting to understand now. This is a piece of art."

"My family knew how to build boats, that's for sure."

Ben rubbed a hand over the glossy wooden surface in front of him, and Bowie couldn't help thinking how different his friend looked out here. He was relaxed and lighthearted and *happy*, worlds away from the focused, serious, borderline obsessive-compulsive guy he was until a few years ago.

Back then, Bowie never would have guessed Ben might seem completely comfortable behind the controls of a sleek, elegant wooden boat on a lovely Idaho summer evening.

As the boat glided smoothly over the wake from

another boat, Bowie shifted his gaze to the back of the boat, where Katrina and McKenzie sat on either side of Milo like lovely bookends, one blonde and one dark-haired.

Bowie had no doubt who deserved credit for the changes in Ben over the last few years. McKenzie seemed to have helped Ben learn to slow down and enjoy his life more.

"It's a great legacy," Bowie said now. "You must be proud."

Ben looked amused. "I don't know about a legacy, great or otherwise. The Kilpatricks knew how to build boats. Let's leave it at that."

From hints Ben had dropped over the years—not to mention the fact that he'd once sold Aidan all his family holdings in Haven Point for a song—Bowie knew his friend's memories of this place hadn't always been pleasant. It was rather remarkable that he could seem to be so at peace here now.

"I appreciate you finding the time for this. I know you're as busy as I am when you're in town."

Ben still supervised the varied Caine Tech operations across the Pacific Northwest and California and traveled a great deal. Like Aidan, he now used Haven Point as home base and flew in and out with regularity.

"If you want the truth, I'm grateful to Milo for giving me an excuse to get her out. It's been too long."

They both glanced again toward the back of the

boat, where Milo had his face lifted to the wind and his eyes closed, as if memorizing every sensation. Funny, but he seemed as at peace as Ben did out here.

"He loves it," Ben commented.

Bowie felt a funny ache in his chest as he looked at this little boy he still felt like he barely knew finding such joy in a simple moment.

"Yeah. He does," Bowie said.

"If you decide you want one, let me know. I've got connections now in the wooden boat restoration world."

"I'll think about it," he answered.

That seemed like a huge commitment, way more than he was prepared to take on right now. He was still trying to figure out what to do with Milo. On the other hand, this could be a good way for the two of them to connect, especially after Katrina left.

"Seems like a no-brainer to me, especially since you've got a private dock there in Serenity Harbor that most boat owners would kill to own."

What would he do with a boat if he ended up not living here in Haven Point for much longer? Or if the autism specialist arrived and decided Milo might benefit more from a boarding school somewhere?

He hadn't completely discounted that possibility for his brother, as much as he disliked thinking about it. If Debra Peters thought Milo would thrive in a residential treatment school, maybe he owed it to his brother to try it out.

"I'll think about it," he repeated.

Ben appeared to accept that as they headed for the north end of the lake. A few moments later, he gestured to Bowie. "Here. Take over."

"What? Now?" He tried not to let shock show on his features.

"Yeah. Just while I grab a beer. Try not to hit anybody else. There are a bunch of idiots on the water this time of year who don't know what they're doing."

Um. He happened to be one of those idiots right now. He had rarely even been on a boat, forget about driving one. But how would he ever decide if he wanted one of his own if he never gave it a shot?

Ben didn't give him an option, anyway, he just got up and moved to the back of the boat toward the others and the cooler they had stowed aboard.

Somehow Bowie managed to negotiate around a few fishing boats and a hot rodder on a personal watercraft until Ben returned and handed him a beer.

"Sweet, isn't she?" Ben asked.

"She is, indeed."

For the rest of the ride, he tried to emulate his brother and simply enjoy the ride until they returned back to Ben and McKenzie's house on Redemption Bay as the setting sun was sending orange and pink rays across the water.

Milo complained a little about having to get off the boat, but McKenzie seemed to know just the trick to persuade him.

"We have steaks and hot dogs to grill," she said. "Is there anyone here who might like some?"

Milo raised his hand instantly, making the rest of them smile. Yes, he might have autism, but he was a six-year-old boy first.

He was even more excited when McKenzie went to the back door of the house and opened it for the two dogs, who were clamoring to come out and join them on the terrace.

Both dogs headed straight for Milo, who actually giggled as they licked at him, a sound Bowie had rarely heard from him.

"Better add a dog to that wish list," Ben said.

Katrina had been telling him the same thing, that his brother adored dogs and would probably thrive with a pet of his own. That was another thought that completely overwhelmed him right now.

"A boat and a dog? You don't think I have enough to worry about, with a new brother, a new job and a new house?"

"You'd be surprised at how quickly a guy can adapt to a different way of looking at the world."

Not that surprised, he thought a short time later as Ben grilled steaks and Katrina and McKenzie bustled around setting dishes out on the tablecloth Ben's wife threw over their patio table. He was already seeing the world differently than he had before that phone call informing him about Milo. He stood at the water's edge, keeping a careful eye on his brother, who was beginning to tire after his long day. Bowie could only hope they would make it through dinner.

He turned back to look at the scene and saw Katrina laugh at something McKenzie said. Her hair seemed to gleam like silky gold in the sunset, and Bowie was aware of an odd feeling curling through him.

Contentment, he realized. It all felt so…normal. Two couples, a pair of dogs and a kid, enjoying a beautiful summer evening beside a mountain lake.

Except one of those couples *wasn't* a couple at all. Katrina wasn't his. She had made it clear she didn't want to be.

Just like that, the feeling of peace shredded like a piece of paper caught in the propeller of Ben's boat. She was leaving in a handful of days. Every time he thought about it, he wanted to pound his fist into a tree.

"That's quite a ferocious look." McKenzie came up beside him and held out a plate full of appetizers that looked like mini tacos. "Is everything okay?"

Nothing was okay. His life had been spinning out of his control since the day he stepped foot in Haven Point. He picked up one of the appetizers to give himself a moment to answer.

"Sure," he lied. "Everything's great. Why wouldn't it be?"

"You've had a lot of life changes in a short time. It can't be easy for you."

Obviously she didn't have the same suck-it-up-

and-deal philosophy as her husband when it came to adjusting to major life changes.

"We're figuring things out, a little at a time." What else could he do?

"Are you enjoying Haven Point?"

"Is that an official inquiry, Mayor Kilpatrick?"

"No. I'm asking as a friend who genuinely cares about you and wants you to be happy. I know some of the Caine Tech transplants from the city have a hard time adjusting to the quieter pace here in Haven Point."

"I like the quiet," he said and was a little surprised to realize it was true.

"Katrina and Milo seem to get along," McKenzie observed. "She's great with him. I've enjoyed watching them together."

He didn't want to talk about Katrina—not when the thought of not having her in their lives left him feeling gutted.

"I don't know what we would have done without her the last few weeks," he said. His voice came out a little gruffer than he expected, which earned him an odd, intense look from McKenzie. He had to hope his tangled emotions about her weren't evident on his features.

Milo chose that moment to run over to Katrina to show her something he must have found by the lake. Bowie couldn't hear what they said, but he saw Katrina's smile and the complete trust his brother had in her.

McKenzie must have seen it, too. "What will happen when she goes back to Colombia next week? Are you worried about how your brother will handle it?"

With every single breath. "Yeah," he said, unable to clear that gruffness away. "That will be one more change we'll have to deal with, right?"

"With any luck, it won't take long to wrap up the adoption and she'll be back in Haven Point before we know it."

"Right." He wished he could find the same peace in the thought as McKenzie did.

"I hope the adoption doesn't take much longer. It's been such a long, frustrating process. Kat has thrown everything into providing a home for this little girl—all her emotional strength and financial resources. That girl never does things in half measure. I really hope she doesn't end up getting her heart broken by the whole thing."

"How would she?"

"If she can't untangle all the red tape, you know? She loves Gabriela already. It's obvious in the way she talks about her and how pleased she is to show off Gabi's pictures. After all her effort, Kat would be devastated if the adoption fell through. She would probably see it as one more failure."

"A failure of the system, you mean. How could it be hers?"

"She'll see it that way. Trust me."

"You've been friends a long time."

McKenzie gazed over at Katrina and Milo, now

throwing a ball back and forth while the dogs raced between them in glee.

"I was friends with Wyn first. She has been one of my best friends since I came to Haven Point in grade school. Kat is a few years younger than we are, but she was always skipping after us, wanting to play. She was so cute—small, freckled, with a big gap-toothed smile and blond braids. We were all a little protective of her."

"Why? Because of her seizures?"

Surprise flashed across her features. "She told you about those? That's usually a forbidden subject."

"Yes. She mentioned them."

"I think she would much rather forget that time in her life ever existed," McKenzie said, her eyes still wide with surprise. "Having epilepsy always set her a little apart—and being different can be tough when you're a kid."

Like Bowie, McKenzie sounded like she had learned that lesson through bitter experience. Bowie could relate.

"Her seizures could be terrifying. They would come out of nowhere and could be violent and intense. She missed a lot of school, so she was always behind, and other kids made fun of her for that. I don't think some of her teachers were very patient with her either. Kat pretended it didn't bother her, but of course it must have."

His heart ached as he imagined her, adorable and sweet and desperate to belong. He could absolutely relate. As they moved from place to place, school to school, he had tried so hard to fit in.

"That's one of the reasons Wyn always let her hang out with us. Though I've never asked her and thus have no proof, I also think it goes a long way toward explaining why Katrina became a teacher. She is passionate about all her students, but especially those with learning challenges. She won't tolerate a hint of bullying in her classroom, and she always stayed late to tutor anybody who might have trouble with the course work."

Bo wanted to tell McKenzie to stop talking. He didn't need more excuses to fall hard for the dedicated, wonderful woman who had seen the possibilities within his brother when everyone else saw only challenges.

"I also think that's one reason she's dated so many losers," McKenzie confided, glancing around to make sure Katrina hadn't wandered within earshot.

He *really* didn't need to hear this, Bowie thought, but he couldn't seem to prevent himself from asking the follow-up question.

"Why is that?"

"She needs a decent man to show her she doesn't have to keep proving herself—that she's enough, just the way she is."

Longing rose in him, wild and fierce. He wanted to be the one to take her by the hand and show her all the wonderful things he saw in her. Her courage, her strength, her kindness.

He was still reeling from that realization when
Milo raced over with the dogs close behind.

"Eat," the boy said.

McKenzie smiled. "I bet it's ready by now. If it's
not, we might have to start eating mosquitoes."

She opened her mouth and pretended to chomp
the air, making Milo almost smile.

How would he help his brother hold on to that
almost-smile when Katrina walked out of their lives?
He had no idea. Milo's impending heartbreak almost
made him wish he'd never offered her a job that day
in the supermarket.

Almost. But not quite.

CHAPTER FIFTEEN

"WHAT A LOVELY EVENING," Katrina said as Bowie drove the short distance between Redemption Bay and Serenity Harbor. "I'd forgotten how much I enjoy spending summer evenings on the lake."

"It was beautiful."

In the blue glow from the dashboard lights, his features appeared harsh, with more contrast and deeper shadows. She studied him freely here in the dark, trying to memorize the angle of his nose, the curve of his strong cheekbones.

She would miss him.

She curled her hands into fists on her lap, trying her best to ignore the ache of emotion in her throat. The evening had been beautiful not only because of their surroundings but because it gave her the chance to be with Bowie and Milo. She would have dozens of memories to store up and relive after she left them.

"So has Ben talked you into a boat yet?" she asked.

"He's working on it. I'm not convinced yet. Boat ownership is so much work. You know what they say about it, right? The happiest two days in a boat owner's life are the day he buys a boat and the day he sells it."

She smiled. "There you go. When you think about buying a boat, you can look forward to at least two happy days in your future."

"At least," he said, his teeth flashing white in the dim interior.

"Yes, they're a lot of work, from what I understand, but a lot of fun, too. Like most things worth having in life, right?" Relationships. Families. Careers. All took effort before one could savor the joy.

"I suppose that's true. Some people want to skip the work part and focus only on the fun."

That had been her, Katrina realized. She had loved the fun of dating but had never been willing to invest the time and effort to find something meaningful.

When they reached his house and he pulled into the garage, she climbed out and opened the door for Milo. The boy blinked at her, eyes bleary. They had put in a long day, and she couldn't blame him for being exhausted.

"Come on, sleepyhead. Let's get you to bed."

"I can do that," Bowie said. "You've been on duty all day."

"I don't mind," she assured him. "I won't have many more chances to help him into bed."

His features tightened briefly, but he said nothing as she ushered Milo into the house and down the hall to his bedroom. The little boy was too tired for a bath, so she decided to let him skip it, even though usually it was one of his favorite parts of his routine. She helped him wash his face and hands—all those dog germs!—and brush his teeth, then he slipped into his pajamas and climbed into his bed.

"No story tonight, okay?" she said when Milo had the covers tucked up to his chin. "It's been a long day and we read a bunch of stories earlier. Straight to sleep, bud, so we can have fun tomorrow at the parade."

She kissed his forehead, aware of that heavy ache in her chest again. Oh, she would miss this little boy. When she rose, he pantomimed holding a cup and taking an imaginary sip from it.

"You need a drink of water? Just a moment. I'll get you one."

"No need."

At the voice, she turned and found Bowie with his shoulder propped against the door frame, holding a glass of water. How long had he been there? Though she'd left his presence only fifteen minutes earlier, her heart still skipped as if she hadn't seen him in weeks.

He was the sort of man who could cause a woman to make a terrible mistake. Something irrevocably stupid, like lose her heart to him.

Not her, of course. She couldn't let that happen.

"Look at that." She forced a smile. "Your brother beat me to it."

He unfolded from the door and moved toward

the bed, holding out the water glass for his brother. After Milo took it and sipped what appeared to be about a tablespoon of water, he handed it back, then pointed to his forehead.

Bowie frowned in confusion. "I don't understand," he confessed. "You want me to put water on your forehead?"

Katrina hid her smile. "I think he wants you to give him a good-night kiss, like I did."

Understanding dawned on his handsome features. "Oh. Got it."

He set the glass on the bedside table and leaned in to kiss the boy's forehead in exactly the spot where her mouth had been.

"Good night, kiddo," he said, running a hand over Milo's hair. The boy didn't go so far as to smile—that was reserved for magical moments that involved dogs of some sort, apparently, or maybe boats—but he did wear a completely contented expression.

Milo had come so far in the few weeks she had been here. She wasn't vain enough to think she had much to do with it. She had only provided the structure and a few tools to help him feel comfortable enough in his new environment to begin to thrive.

With all her heart, she hoped he could continue the same progress after she was gone.

She turned on the sound machine he liked, and immediately the music of rippling water over river rock sounded in the room.

"Good night, kiddo," she murmured.

"Night," Bowie added.

He flipped the light switch off and closed the door behind Katrina.

Though neither suggested it, they moved together to the kitchen/family room that had become the hub of his home.

"He seemed to enjoy himself tonight," Bowie said.

"He went on a boat ride and got to play with two of his favorite dogs. In Milo World, that's pretty much the definition of the best day ever."

"It was a pretty good day in Bowie World, too," he said.

"You sound surprised."

He shrugged. "Between Milo and working to get my team operational at the new facility, I've been too busy for much socializing since I came here."

"Everybody needs a little downtime, even if they have to schedule it in. If you don't take it voluntarily, eventually your body will wear out and force you to find it."

"Apparently that's a lesson I have to learn again and again."

"We all need the reminder ocassionally."

"On that note, I think I'll go outside and enjoy the beautiful evening for a few more moments. Care to join me?"

The invitation shocked her, especially as they had so carefully avoided being alone together since the wedding. For a long moment, she didn't know what to say.

She knew what she *should* say, what any rational, self-protective woman with common sense would: *Thank you, but no. I'm going to go hide away in my room, where I'm completely safe from any temptation offered by a gorgeous man in the moonlight.*

What she *should* say and what she *wanted* to say were two completely different things. When she compared his invitation with the alternative—lurking in her room, pretending to watch TV and doing her best to forget that said gorgeous man was outside in the moonlight on his own—she knew there was really no comparison.

She could go talk to him for a few moments. It was too early for bed, anyway.

"Sure," she finally said. The moment the word was out, she wanted to call it back but couldn't figure out how to do it without sounding even more stupid.

"Would you like something to drink?"

"No, thanks."

The glass of wine she'd had at dinner was more than enough. She didn't tend to make the best decisions when she drank—as evidenced by half the men she had ever dated. Since it was hard enough to resist Bowie Callahan when she was stone-cold sober, she should probably avoid anything else that might cloud her mind.

"Water?" he asked.

"Yes. Thanks. I can grab it."

She pulled out a glass from the cupboard and filled it with ice and filtered water from the refrigerator, took a long, healthy, rather desperate drink, then filled it again.

He pulled out a beer and led the way to the terrace, flipping the switch on the globe lights as he did. The night was unusually warm for this high elevation, which usually cooled down dramatically once the sun set.

Her natural instinct was to chatter about nothing in order to fill all the empty space between them, but somehow, for once in her life, she was able to hold her tongue.

He didn't seem in a talkative mood either as he sank beside her into the other lounger that faced the water. He leaned back in the chair, closing his eyes with a heavy sigh.

He looked tired, poor man, working hard to make things happen at Caine Tech while dealing with new challenges in his personal life. She wanted to bring him a pillow and a blanket, to tuck it around him and hold him while he slept.

Oh, mercy. What was *wrong* with her?

"You and McKenzie seemed to have a lot to talk about tonight."

As soon as she said the words, she wanted to kick herself. It was none of her business whom he talked to and what they talked about.

He gave her a sideways look, somehow timing it just right so the moonlight slipped out from behind a cloud in time to bathe him in pale light. It still wasn't enough light for her to read his expression. "We were talking about you, actually."

"Me? And here I thought you were talking about something interesting—Haven Point politics or one of the charities McKenzie works for or something."

Why would *she* be a topic of conversation between them? McKenzie knew her better than just about anybody, except Sam and Wynona. She carried plenty of embarrassing secrets about Kat. Which of those had she opted to share with Bowie?

"She's a good friend who cares about you," he said, which put her mind at ease at least a little.

"I care about her, too. We've been friends forever. As long as I can remember. Grade school, anyway."

"That's what she told me." He paused. "She's worried about what you'll do if the adoption of Gabriela doesn't go through."

She had a wholly immature desire to clamp her hands over her ears to block out what he was saying, as if just entertaining the possibility could risk making her worst fears come true.

If that was the case, the opposite had to work, too. "It's going through," she insisted firmly. "I won't consider any other outcome."

"You can't always control the world. What will you do if the court doesn't approve the paperwork or this country doesn't allow her an entry visa?"

"I'll move to Colombia and become an expat," she said promptly. "If I can, I'll continue teaching

English down there. If not, I'll scrub floors or work in the orphanage kitchen or sell flowers on a street corner. It doesn't matter. I'll do whatever it takes to be with her."

He shifted his gaze to meet hers. "You would do that? Walk away from your family and your home everything familiar in your world—simply to be with a girl you didn't even know existed a year ago?"

She wished she had better words to explain what to most people probably made no sense whatsoever. "She's my daughter, Bowie. I love her. Mothers will make whatever sacrifice is necessary for the good of their children."

"Not all mothers," he said, his expression suddenly tight.

What had his childhood been like? He had given her hints here and there, and her imagination had filled in some of the gaps. She wanted to know more, though.

"Was yours really so bad?" she finally asked.

He said nothing for a long moment, so long she thought perhaps he would ignore her, then he turned and looked out at the lake. "Plenty of people had it worse than I did."

But plenty had it better. He didn't say the words, but she guessed them, anyway. He confirmed her suspicions a moment later.

"My mother was a sixteen-year-old runaway when she had me. I have no idea who my father is. I doubt even Stella knows."

"That explains how a man in his thirties could have a six-year-old brother."

"Right. She was sixteen when she had me, in her early forties when she had Milo. As far as I know, she didn't have any other children in between."

She couldn't imagine it. Sixteen, the same age as sweet Lizzie Lawson, barely a child. "How did she take care of you?"

"She had an insurance settlement from her parents, who were killed in a car accident before I was born. Before she ran away from foster care herself. It paid out a small amount monthly—though she usually blew it all by the second day of the month on booze or drugs."

"What about the rest of the month?"

"Stella was a survivor. I'll give her that. She was very much into doing her own thing, living without rules and not being responsible to anyone. Somehow she had a knack for finding others who shared her counterculture ideas. She would glom on to anybody who could take care of her. Us, I guess. One guy after another—or woman, depending on her mood. Sometimes we lived in a commune-type situation. It wasn't what you might call a traditional childhood."

She couldn't imagine it, especially coming from her sheltered, traditional small-town background with a mother and father who had adored each of their five children.

"With that much insecurity, I'm surprised you

weren't taken away and shuttled through the foster care system."

"I was, a few times, but she always managed to play the game enough to convince the family court she was competent to care for me. Those times were rare. More than likely, if child welfare services came sniffing around because a teacher or a neighbor reported something, we would just pick up and leave."

Oh. Poor boy. That must have been so hard on a kid, never settling in one place long enough to grow roots. No wonder he loved this beautiful house on the lake so much.

Katrina gazed at him, feeling that tug and pull of her heart again. Some part of her wanted to tell him to stop talking right now, aware that with each word she was coming to care for him more. At the same time, she wanted to know everything about him, all the pieces of the puzzle.

"You said you hadn't had contact with your mother for years. How old were you when you… parted ways?"

"I started making plans to leave when I was about thirteen. It took me about two years to put my strategy into action. I taught myself to use computers, earned my GED and got into MIT."

She stared, astonished at the sheer depth of accomplishment behind those simple words. "How can you say all that in the same casual tone I use to tell Sam I picked up new mascara at the grocery store today? You should be yelling it from every rooftop!"

His jaw tightened. "No. I shouldn't. I don't pat myself on the back at all. I did things I'm still not proud of. I was a hacker, Kat. I lied, I stole, I cheated my way into MIT. I learned Stella's lessons well and went after my goals without regard to the consequences."

"Nobody can cheat their way into MIT."

"They can when they have my particular skills," he said, with no trace of ego in his voice.

"Were you caught?"

"I would have been, probably. Instead, the guilt became too overwhelming and I came clean to the dean of my college a month into my first classes. I was lucky. The school could have pressed charges and made it so I couldn't be admitted into another computer science program in the country. Instead, they took pity on me and gave me a chance to prove myself."

She could picture him clearly—young, driven, brilliant. How could MIT not have recognized his genius? He had proved himself and more.

"Anyway, after I left for MIT, I didn't hear from Stella again. I looked for her a few years ago, but apparently she changed her name and moved to another state. The trust fund had run out years before, and I couldn't even trace her that way. She might have changed her name, but I don't think she changed her lifestyle at all."

"That's why you don't know anything about

Milo's background. Because he basically grew up off the grid like you."

"Yeah," he said gruffly. "I hate that I couldn't help him to have a better start in life."

A better start than *Bowie* had.

Unable to help herself, she reached between them and rested her hand on the back of his in a gesture intended only for comfort. After a surprised moment, he turned his hand over and intertwined his fingers with hers.

They stayed that way for a long time while a breeze teased the ends of her hair and an owl hooted in a tree somewhere nearby and something splashed gently out on the water.

She could feel the heat of him, sense each steady breath, and she didn't want to move a muscle for fear of disturbing the peace that swirled around them like the soft summer night.

She was falling in love with him.

The truth, cold and overwhelming, washed over her as if someone had just picked her up and tossed her into a storm-tossed Lake Haven.

No! She *couldn't* be falling for him. She refused to allow it.

Every Spanish curse word she had learned from the older boys at the orphanage raced through her head as the magnitude of her foolishness sank in.

How could she be so stupid? From the beginning, she had worried about this very thing and thought she had put protective measures in place.

Their conversation only confirmed it. What did the two of them possibly have in common? He was a genius who had graduated from one of the toughest universities in the world when he was still a teenager, while she had struggled to keep her grades up enough in high school to even get admitted into community college.

StupidKat.

The echoes of those childhood taunts seemed to ring off the surrounding mountains. He might be attracted to her, but it wouldn't last. It never did.

Bowie had the power to devastate her because she had stupidly handed it over to him.

How would she survive the next few days without making a complete fool of herself? For one crazy moment, she was tempted to march into his house and pack up her things. She could stay at her mother's house until her flight the following week—or maybe she could arrange an earlier flight.

No. She had told him she would stay until the new autism specialist arrived early in the week. That was only a few days away. Surely she could be tough until then.

She would start right now, by not throwing herself headlong into situations fraught with trouble. Like this one.

With considerable reluctance, she pulled her hand away and rose. "I should go to bed. Tomorrow will be a long day."

"Ah. Lake Haven Days."

"Yes. It's only the biggest day of the year around here. Our schedule is completely packed."

"Is it?"

"I promised Milo I would take him to the parade, which starts at ten. That means we'll have to hit the pancake breakfast at the fire station around eight so we can finish eating and make it to the parade route in time for the first floats. Then it's on to the boat races and the fair. If he's still up for it, we'll head to my mom's place for dinner before the fireworks."

"Wow. You weren't joking about a packed schedule."

She forced a smile, hoping he couldn't guess at the tumult of emotions churning through her. "The town celebration only comes around once a year. Might as well go big or go home, right?"

"You don't think that all might be a little much for Milo? What if he gets overstimulated from so much activity?"

"I'll be careful. I have a pretty good handle on his moods by now. If it looks like he needs a break, we'll return here for a rest."

He appeared to mull this over as they moved into the house but didn't speak until they had reached the kitchen.

"I'd better come with you," he announced.

She stared at him, completely caught off guard. She never would have pegged him for someone who would want to go to a small-town celebration. "What? Why?"

"You said it. Lake Haven Days comes around only once a year. This is my town now. I want to make a home here for me and for Milo. The people who work for me have done the same. Caine Tech is linked to Haven Point now, just as the town is connected to Caine Tech. It would be irresponsible for me to miss something this important to the sense of community."

She couldn't spend an entire day with him. She didn't have the strength for it.

"In that case, you can take Milo. I'll go with my family."

"That's not what I meant. Milo wouldn't enjoy the day nearly as much without you there to show him—us—around. You know this town and the celebration much better than I do. I don't even know where the fire station is."

"It's at the intersection of Lakeside Drive and Bristlecone Road. There. Now you know."

"He'll still want to have you with us. As do I."

Oh, not fair. How could she resist him when he looked at her out of those stunning blue eyes that made her want to divulge all her secrets?

She would have to resist him. She would simply have to suck it up and keep her focus on her future.

"All right. Bright and early, then. I don't like to be late for breakfast. The Haven Point firefighters make the *best* pancakes. Light, fluffy, melt-in-your-mouth deliciousness."

"Sounds perfect."

"Good night, then."

"Right." He paused. "I did enjoy myself tonight. The boat ride and dinner, yes, but especially out on the terrace with you. I don't talk about my past often. I prefer to focus on today and tomorrow instead of what I can't change about yesterday. Somehow I'm glad you know the truth about me, ugliness and all."

Oh. How was she supposed to resist him when he made it so very impossible? "I heard no ugliness, Bowie. Only a story of strength and character and survival, about a remarkable man."

She probably shouldn't have said that last bit. That suspicion was confirmed when heat flared in his gaze.

"Kat," he murmured, and she couldn't help her shiver. His gaze sharpened on the instinctive movement, and he stepped forward, eyes intent.

He was going to kiss her, and suddenly she wanted to taste him again more than she wanted to breathe.

"Stop me," he ordered.

She swallowed and shook her head slightly. How could she do anything else? The heat in his gaze flared to an inferno, and a heartbeat later his mouth devoured hers.

The kiss was raw and intense, fierce and wild and delicious. He *was* remarkable, and she found it incredibly addicting that in this moment he wanted *her* with a passion that stole her breath.

She wanted him, too, as she had never hungered

for a man's touch. She wanted to tug him into her bedroom and explore every hard inch of him.

And then what?

The question slithered into her subconscious somehow, and once it was there, it refused to budge.

In less than a handful of days, she was leaving. She had no idea how long she would be gone; she only knew that when—if—she returned, she would have Gabi with her and all her choices in life would change.

She couldn't have an affair with Bowie. She wanted meaning and permanence and stability, and he offered none of that.

Too many times before, she had traded her dignity and self-respect for a few moments of feeling cherished, valued, meaningful, only to discover the feeling was as fleeting and insubstantial as dandelion puffs.

When she found herself stranded in Colombia, she had made a vow to herself. Never again. She would have to know a man truly cared for her and wanted a future with her before she took the easy way to artificial intimacy.

But, oh, Bowie was tempting.

"You're making me crazy," he murmured in her ear, then trailed seductive little kisses from there along her jawline and back to her mouth.

It would be so, so easy to give in to these feelings. They were alone in his quiet house. What would be the harm in making love? At least she would have the memories. That was all she would have, though, and it would be cold comfort. She had enough regrets in her life. She suddenly couldn't bear the idea that caring for this man so much might one day be one of them.

She allowed herself a few more moments to savor the wild heat rushing through her, then forced herself to draw upon all her hard-won self-control. "Bowie. We have to stop."

His eyes looked dazed with arousal. "Do we?"

She pressed her lips together, tasting him there on her mouth. "I don't want to," she admitted. "If I could, I would stay here and do this all night— but we both know eventually kissing wouldn't be enough."

"Eventually?" he murmured.

The husky rasp of his voice sent tremors rippling down her spine. She wanted so much to sink into the kiss, into him, and let him sink into her in return.

What would she gain? Only more heartbreak.

"I'm sorry. I can't. Not with you."

She escaped the room before she said something else that would reveal the depth of her feelings to him.

CHAPTER SIXTEEN

WHEN THE ALARM on his phone trilled the next morning, Bowie was tempted to hit the snooze button, pull the sheet over his head and try to block out the whole freaking world.

His head ached like a mother, and his mouth held the sour taste of frustration and regret.

With no small amount of trepidation, he sat up in bed, and the movement sent pain clanging through him like he'd stuck his head in a tin bucket and Milo was gleefully pounding on it with a wooden spoon.

He had a hangover for the first time since his sophomore year in college, when some of the older students thought it was a funny joke to get the underage brainiac plastered.

He *never* drank too much. It was kind of a thing with him. When a kid grew up cleaning up after his mother's messes from drugs and alcohol, he either followed the example set forth in his childhood or found other ways to deal with stress, to relax and unwind.

Bo had always been firmly in the latter camp. He would take his bike for a long ride or go for a hard run. He didn't like being out of his head, not able to make his own decisions. But he had been so damn stirred up the night before when Katrina walked away—frustrated and aroused and angry, all the while aware of the ache in his chest that wouldn't go away.

I can't. Not with you.

What had she meant by that? He had stayed up half the damn night trying to figure it out.

On the surface, he might have thought she didn't want anything to do with him after he had stupidly told her the truth about Stella and their life, about MIT, about the choices he had made. But then he remembered the other words she had said.

I heard no ugliness, Bowie. Only a story of strength and character and survival, about a remarkable man.

He wanted to be that man. He wanted her to look at him with respect and admiration. He wanted her sweet smile and her kisses and her soft kindness that seemed to reach out and heal places inside he thought had long since scarred over.

He didn't know what to do with this jumbled ball of emotion in his gut. He had never felt like this for a woman before—never *wanted* to. Now he understood why. It hurt like hell, especially when she made it clear she didn't want him in return.

That wasn't completely true. She wanted him physically. Her response couldn't have been feigned—yet she had still pushed him away.

What had he been thinking when he volunteered to spend an entire day with her and Milo today at the Lake Haven Days celebration? He had a dozen urgent things on his docket and was certain his time would be better spent trying to tick off items on his to-do list than hanging out watching a parade full of tractors and marching bands. He could sneak into the office while everyone on his team had the day off and probably accomplish three times as much as a normal day when he had to field questions and deal with emails all day.

Good plan.

He sat for a moment on the edge of his bed, holding his throbbing head and trying to summon the strength to tell Katrina and Milo he had changed his mind and wouldn't be going with them, after all.

Shower first, he decided. He made his way to the bathroom and popped a couple of aspirin. By the time he showered and dressed, he felt halfway human.

He headed into the kitchen, following the siren call of coffee. Katrina was loading water bottles into a backpack, while Milo was playing with his cars on the floor, lining them up on the floor as he did, like his own version of the Lake Haven Days parade.

"Good morning," she said. Her voice sounded cheerful enough, but he saw a hint of wariness in her eyes as she studied him. Could she tell by looking at him that his brain threatened to explode out of his skull?

"Morning," he managed to answer. "Thanks for the coffee."

"Completely selfish on my part. There's bound to be coffee at the pancake breakfast, but it won't be nearly as good as the high-dollar stuff you have here."

He paid an exorbitant amount for a special blend from a tiny mail-order company in Costa Rica. He didn't spend much on clothes or women or fast cars, but he did like good coffee.

As he sipped, he felt the throb in his temples recede a little more.

"Do you want to take two cars to the celebration today?" she asked. "That way you don't have to feel obligated to stay all day. You can go to the breakfast and parade and then leave from there to do your thing."

He opened his mouth to tell her he had changed his mind and was going to skip all the celebrations. The words somehow clogged in his throat. He couldn't do it. All the reasons he had given her the night before—about community and finding his place in it—still rang true. Now he had the added impetus, the somber reminder that this would likely be his last chance to spend any significant time with Katrina.

Everything was about to change. Debra Peters would arrive early in the week, and Katrina would return to Colombia and the child she loved.

"I would think parking is an issue at an event

like this, where everybody in town wants to be in the same place at the same time."

"It can be," she acknowledged.

"Let's not add to the congestion, then. We'll take one car. If I need to leave, I can always walk back here. It's not that far, and it should be a nice day."

So much for his good intentions to stay out of her way until she left. When it came to Katrina Bailey, every plan he made seemed to disintegrate.

"There. That's the last of the supplies," she said as she zipped up her backpack. "We're ready whenever you are."

"Go," Milo said as he jumped up from the floor.

"We're going. Don't worry."

Bowie didn't miss that Katrina's smile to his brother didn't seem to extend to him.

As THE LAST floats in the parade went by, Bowie looked around, more interested in the parade watchers than he was in the actual event itself.

So this was what being part of a community meant. He saw fathers with children on their shoulders, older men helping their equally aged wives fold up blankets and lawn chairs, giggling teenage girls whispering behind their hands while a couple of guys who looked to be about sixteen casually posed with their chests out and their scrawny biceps flexed while pretending not to pay any attention to the girls.

"What do you think, Milo? How was your first parade?"

His brother lifted his gaze to Bowie at the question. He didn't smile with his mouth, but Bowie could see happiness beaming out of his sparkling eyes. Only the most hardened of hearts could have resisted smiling back.

"That good, was it?" he asked.

Five minutes into the event, it was obvious Milo had never seen a parade before, just as Bowie had suspected. He had been hypnotized from the moment the flag had marched past, carried by a local wounded veterans group followed by the scraggly high school marching band playing "The Star-Spangled Banner," to the last patrol car driving behind a float filled with what looked like youngsters from the local 4-H group showing off their baby goats.

For the first ten minutes or so, Milo hadn't even budged, had sat on the curb staring with wide eyes, enraptured by the entire spectacle of a small-town parade.

Bowie's brother hadn't even moved when those riding the float that advertised the local grocery store started throwing out handfuls of taffy for the kids. One piece of candy even hit him in the arm, but he still didn't pick it up until Katrina explained that the taffy was for anybody who wanted it, as long as they could move fast enough to grab the flying pieces.

He couldn't blame Milo for not knowing what to do. What kid wakes up expecting candy to be pelted at him out of nowhere? Still, Milo didn't race out until a sweet little girl in the group next to them brought a piece of candy over for him. Then it was a mad scramble as he filled a plastic shopping bag Katrina had thoughtfully provided.

"What about you? What did you think?" Katrina asked him. "I know as far as parades go, it's not much, but we like it."

"I'm glad I came," he answered truthfully. "I would have hated to miss the riding lawn mower brigade and their fancy tricks, riding in formation. I do believe my life is complete now."

She made a face. "Be careful. They're always looking for new recruits."

Before he could answer, Katrina looked over his shoulder and shrieked. He jerked around instinctively and came face-to-face with her sister, heading toward them.

Katrina rushed to Wynona and threw her arms around her as if she hadn't seen her in months. "You're back! I thought you weren't coming home from Banff until next week."

Wynona gave a rueful-sounding laugh. "You know Cade. He couldn't bear the thought that the Haven Point Police Department might have to run crowd control without him during the busiest weekend of the year."

"That was a short honeymoon," Katrina said.

"I know. But he's promised to make it up to me with a longer trip when things slow down after the first of the year."

A honeymoon lasting less than a week wouldn't have been nearly long enough for Bowie. He would want to keep Katrina to himself for weeks—and he had a feeling that still wouldn't be long enough.

Maybe he would take her to some gorgeous secluded beach in Tahiti, all sun-kissed skin and lazy afternoons, or a ski lodge in the mountains, where they could hole up together while a blizzard raged outside...

Where the hell did *that* come from?

Aghast, Bowie jolted his thoughts away from that dangerous direction. He wasn't having a honeymoon—with Katrina or anyone else. Long ago, he had figured traditional happy-ever-afters weren't meant for guys like him.

"Since you're home early, I hope that means you're going to dinner at Mom's place later," Katrina said.

"Yes. Cade has to work, but I'll be there. I wouldn't miss it, since this might be my last chance to see you before you leave."

Bowie didn't need another reminder that his own time with Katrina was limited. Every time the thought popped into his head, it brought along a sense of dread and impending loss.

"By the way," Wynona went on, "don't expect the usual quiet family get-together tonight. Charlene apparently decided it wasn't enough excitement to throw a wedding party for the whole town last week.

She's invited everyone in the Helping Hands over to watch the fireworks at her place."

Katrina rolled her eyes. "Thanks for the warning."

Wynona looked around surreptitiously and lowered her voice, though Bowie was close enough he could still hear. "And speaking of warnings, here's another one. I understand she's invited several eligible and unattached gentlemen."

He didn't miss the way Katrina's color rose. "Why would she do that?"

"You know why. This is her last chance. Mom's Hail Mary pass. She's desperately hoping you'll fall for somebody and change your mind about the whole adoption thing."

Katrina's blush intensified, and he wondered if she was avoiding looking at him out of embarrassment... or something else.

"Are you kidding?" she exclaimed. "I can't believe that woman. She really thinks I'm flighty enough that I'll suddenly meet a guy in one night and abandon months of effort and thousands of dollars...not to mention a child who is counting on me? So nice to know my mother has such a high opinion of me."

Though she spoke in a caustic tone, he saw the shadow of old hurt in her eyes that made him want to pull her close and kiss it away.

"Mom loves you and worries for you. You know she does. I'm settled, Marshall's settled—or as good as—Elliot is too far away for her to smother. This is just her twisted way of trying to make sure you're happy."

"It's her way of meddling in my life, like she's been doing all our life. She doesn't trust me and doesn't believe I'm capable of making my own decisions. I'm not StupidKat anymore. I haven't been for a long, long time. Why can't she see that?"

Again, he wanted to pull her into his arms, but Wyn beat him to it. "She's our mom. She wants to fix things. It's what she does."

"I'm not broken anymore," Katrina said. "But Charlene still sees me as her poor, pitiful daughter whose brain doesn't work the way it should."

"Everyone else knows better," Wyn said. "So what if she invites the entire Snake River rugby team? She can dangle all the carrots she wants, but that doesn't mean you have to take a bite out of one. You can be polite and friendly and totally uninterested."

"Or I can stay home," she muttered.

"Your choice, honey." A bell chimed on her watch, and Wyn looked down with a frown. "I have to run. My department has a booth at the fair, and I'm supposed to be there in ten minutes so I can take my turn handing out flyers and answering questions. I hope I see you tonight."

She hugged Katrina one more time, smiled at Bowie and Milo, then turned and disappeared through the crowd.

"You know," he said after she walked away, "we could probably see the fireworks just fine from Serenity Harbor. Just the three of us. I promise not to invite any rugby players."

He knew a few, but he wasn't at all inclined to introduce them to his...to Katrina.

She sighed, her color still rosy. In the late-morning sunshine, she looked soft and sweet and so lovely he had a tough time looking away.

She scooped up the blanket Milo had been sitting on. "No. I can't let her scare me away. I have people I care about whom I still want to see. Wyn and Uncle Mike. Marshall and Andie and her kids. I'll go." She paused. "You and Milo certainly aren't obligated, though."

"Fireworks and rugby players. We wouldn't want to miss that. Would we, Milo?"

His brother shook his head vigorously. Katrina made a face.

"Fine," she said. "Just be prepared. You heard Wyn. My mom is getting desperate—and she probably thinks you have home-field advantage, since I'm, you know, living in your house."

If only that were true, he thought with regret. She didn't seem to have any trouble rejecting him—as his aching head could still testify.

"What's next for our day?"

Katrina shrugged. "The possibilities are endless. We could go watch the softball game, or we could go to the tractor pull. Given what a boat fanatic he is, my guess is that Milo would most enjoy the toy boat races."

"Boat?" Milo said.

Bowie smiled at his brother. "Sounds like we have a winner. Let's go."

THIS WAS THE kind of evening that helped Haven Point live up to its name. The vast blue lake rippled softly in a light summer breeze, and her mother's backyard looked charming, with hanging lanterns in all the trees and red, white and blue bunting on the railing of the deck.

Katrina stood on the steps of the deck, savoring the *rightness* of the scene.

Neighbors talked with neighbors, Uncle Mike and a group of his friends played horseshoes in a corner of the lawn and a group of children chased each other around, their laughter ringing above the lapping of water and the rustle of the leaves in the stately maples ringing her mother's yard.

Only one thing ruined the perfection, she saw. Milo stood to one side, wearing that look of curious concentration as the other children ran past, as if he were a pint-size anthropologist watching a newly discovered civilization.

He didn't seem to mind his "otherness." She, however, minded very much.

She was about to step forward and enlist his help carrying dishes out to the long, cloth-covered tables when young Will Montgomery—soon to become her nephew through marriage and about a year or so younger than Milo—stopped next to him.

She couldn't hear what he said to her temporary charge, but a moment later, both boys were heading to the sturdy redwood swingset and play structure Uncle Mike had just finished constructing.

Gabi would love playing on that swingset with Will and Chloe.

The ache in her chest deepened. Her daughter should be here. With her open friendliness and her sheer delight in every small moment of life, she would absolutely love a party like this. The children would adore her, too. Katrina didn't doubt it for a moment.

What if she couldn't work through all the legalities and ended up having to relocate to Barranquilla with Gabi?

She didn't even want to think about that as she stood here beside the lake on a lovely summer evening. The fear lurked on the edge of her psyche anyway. Haven Point was her home, and she loved it here. Her family was here, a job she hoped to return to, even a couple of houses she had her eye on that would be perfect for a single woman with a child.

She wanted that dream. But if she had to, she would try to build a new life in Colombia with Gabi. What other choice did she have?

"That's the expression of a woman with serious things on her mind."

At the voice, she looked over to find the gorgeous Jamie Caine joining her on the step, wearing his charmer of a smile.

Everything was so easy with Jamie. With him, she could flirt and tease and slip right back into the role everybody expected of her.

"Yes. Deadly serious. I was wondering when you would finally make all my dreams come true and break away from Eppie and Hazel so you could come talk to me. And look at that. Here you are."

His laugh was low and sexy and made several women in the vicinity turn and stare—but did absolutely nothing for her. She didn't need to know why. The reason was over in the corner talking to Jamie's brother, Aidan, and a couple of guys she didn't know.

"Eppie and Hazel are two tough crackers. I don't like messing with them."

"You're a jet jockey who flies giant airplanes worth millions of dollars. You've been in combat, for crying out loud. Are you really afraid of two little old women?"

"Hell to the yes," he said, with so much genuine emotion in his voice she had to laugh.

Out of the corner of her gaze, she saw Bowie turn at the sound—not that she was staring at him or anything. His gaze shifted to her and then to Jamie, and she saw something hot there that made nerves jitter in her stomach.

At almost the same instant, Samantha Fremont approached Bowie with two drinks in her hands and gave one to him, earning a smile.

Katrina quickly looked back at Jamie, trying to squash her completely unreasonable jealousy. "Hazel and Eppie scare me, too," she admitted. "They're something, aren't they?"

He nodded. "And while we're speaking of dreams coming true," he said, with that same charmer of a smile, "when are you going to take pity on me and finally go grab a drink with me sometime?"

Jamie always flirted outrageously with her. Usually she enjoyed it and flirted right back. She never took him seriously, and that was just the way he liked it.

"We both have drinks, don't we?" She held up her own glass containing her mom's famous raspberry lemonade. "Why don't we count this?"

"I meant just the two of us."

"The closest person is ten feet away. If you close your eyes and try really hard, you could pretend you and I are alone on a moonlit lakeshore."

He laughed, which this time drew her mother's attention. Even from several yards away, she could see the hopeful expression on Charlene's face and had to fight her sigh.

She shifted her gaze away, then instantly regretted it when it landed again on Bowie, deep in conversation with Sam. Her friend's features were animated and happy, and as Katrina watched, Sam placed a carefully manicured hand on Bowie's chest. She was overwhelmed with the sudden ridiculous urge to race over and smack it away.

What was wrong with her? She had no claim over Bowie. She worked for him, that was it—and she wouldn't be doing that much longer. She certainly had no business wanting to dictate his social interactions. He could talk with anyone he chose.

Besides, hadn't she once thought someone like Sam would be good for him? Bowie needed someone sweet and kind and, especially, *available*.

A cloud of depression settled over her like a gnat swarm. She tried to swat it away by flirting with Jamie for a minute or two, but it was obvious to both of them her heart wasn't in it. She was almost relieved when Milo started heading for the water's edge and she had to extricate herself from Jamie to avert trouble.

Milo appeared unconcerned when she joined him.

"No water, remember? We talked about it."

He held up a rock and pantomimed throwing it in, and she decided that would be fine. Right now, she had to wonder if chucking a big boulder into the water might actually be cathartic.

"Go ahead," Katrina said. "I'll watch you from here."

She set her drink down so she could pull over a couple of her mother's molded plastic lawn chairs and angled them so she had a good view of both Milo and the party.

As soon as she picked up her lemonade and sank into one of the chairs, Wyn wandered over and sat down in the other.

"I suppose this is the closest we'll get to a going-away party for you," her sister said.

"I don't need a party. I'll be back home with my daughter before you know it."

"I'm going to pray that's exactly what happens," Wynona said.

"Don't jinx it. I can't consider the alternative."

Some of her own fear must have filtered through her voice, because Wynnie reached over and squeezed her arm. "I know. Same here. I don't want you to move permanently to another country. What would I do without my baby sis?"

"I don't want to talk about it. Let's change the subject."

"Okay," Wyn said, a wicked look in her eye. "I guess it's obvious Sam has a new crush."

Yeah, that wasn't a subject she wanted to discuss either. Still, she couldn't resist following the direction of her sister's gaze to where Samantha and Bowie still stood close together, engaged in conversation.

Sam was really putting out the vibe. Katrina knew her well enough to see all the signs. She wouldn't be going to so much trouble if Bowie wasn't somehow encouraging her.

"Looks like." She tried to give a casual smile, but she had a feeling Wyn wasn't fooled.

"They look cute together, don't you think?" Wyn said.

"Adorable," Kat said. The word came out more

abruptly than she intended and earned a searching look from Wynona.

Shoot. Her sister had been a trained police officer until a year ago, quick to read between the lines. She didn't need Wyn suspecting she might be jealous.

She didn't *want* to be jealous. It made her feel petty and small and stupid. She had been the one to encourage Bowie to ask Sam out. How could she be jealous that he decided to take her up on it?

If Wyn could read her emotions on her features, she decided not to say anything about it, much to Katrina's relief.

"Speaking of crushes," she said after a moment, "did I see you deep in conversation with Jamie Caine a few minutes ago? Anything interesting going on there?"

She couldn't help thinking how much easier her life would feel right now if that were the case. "You're as bad as Mom. That's why I don't dare talk to any man in Haven Point for long. If our conversation dragged on a minute or two longer, she would be ordering wedding cakes."

Wyn gave her a sympathetic smile. "For the record, Jamie is a great guy. You could do much worse. There's more to him than a charming smile and a flirty disposition.'

She knew that. She'd seen those same glimpses in Jamie's eyes. There were reservoirs of something deeper, something he worked hard to keep concealed, for reasons she didn't quite understand.

"I appreciate the advice, but I'm not looking for any guy, charming smile or not."

"Don't say that too loudly. Your priorities might shift a year from now, after things are settled with Gabi. You might change your mind about what you want."

"Maybe," she said in what she hoped was a noncommittal voice.

At that moment, Sam's tinkling laugh rippled out over the grass, and she couldn't prevent her gaze from finding her friend once again—and the man Sam apparently found so amusing.

When she shifted back to Wynona, she found her sister studying her with an intent, probing look that made her feel exposed and vulnerable, like a suspect in an interrogation room.

"Or maybe you've already figured out what you want," Wyn said.

She didn't dare look at her sister. Wyn knew her better than anyone. She must have seen the truth Katrina didn't even want to admit to herself.

She was in love with Bowie.

Despite her best efforts to keep him at arm's length, somehow he had pushed his way into her heart.

She was saved from having to respond by Milo, who wandered over to her and made the ASL sign for thirsty.

"You want a drink? Mine is almost empty. Let's go get something for both of us, buddy."

She took his hand and walked with him to the re-
freshment table, away from her sister's sudden scru-
tiny and the difficult truth she didn't want to face.

CHAPTER SEVENTEEN

"YOU MUST BE super good with computers," Samantha Fremont said, toying with the straw in her drink.

"Fairly good," Bowie said modestly.

"I sure wish I could figure out the accounting
software we're using at the store. Maybe you could
come in sometime and show me what I'm doing
wrong."

He gave a noncommittal answer—what did he
know about small business accounting software?—
and turned the subject by asking her about some of
the other businesses in town.

Bowie liked Samantha. She was sweet and funny
and so earnest as she asked him about his job, how
long he'd worked for Caine Tech, what he did there,
how he liked it.

During the ten minutes of their conversation, he
had managed to shove his tongue firmly in his cheek
and answered that he liked it fine and had been there
a long time.

He didn't quite have the heart to tell her he was
one of the cofounders of the company and had been
with Aidan and Ben from the beginning—and was

responsible for bringing to market some of the company's most innovative products.

A mere few weeks ago, he might have been interested enough in her to ask her out—eventually, maybe, once his life settled down a bit and he could breathe again.

That was before he'd been kicked in the chest by a certain teacher with blue eyes and wheat-colored hair and a mouth that tasted like strawberries and cream and heaven.

He searched for Katrina, almost without realizing it, and found her at the swingset, alternating between pushing Milo and doing the same for Andie Montgomery's kid Will.

As he watched Will pump his legs in and out and Milo try to figure out the movement, among much laughter and explaining from Katrina and Will, Bo felt that same jolt in his chest again, a breathless, restless, staggering ache he had never felt before.

He was in love with her.

The truth just about knocked him over, as if Milo had just kicked *him*.

He didn't know how he knew, since it was an emotion he was completely unfamiliar with, but somehow the truth of it settled over him like the twilight stretching across the lake.

He loved Katrina Bailey. Her strength, her dedication, her compassion. The sweet way she cared for his brother. Her determination to rescue a girl she had come to care about.

Now what the hell was he supposed to do?

"Are you okay?" Samantha asked. "You're looking a little pale and you were suddenly miles away."

He didn't know how to answer her. "Yeah," he finally lied. "Will you excuse me? I need to grab some water."

"Oh. Sure. I should grab the blanket out of my car for the fireworks, anyway." She paused. "It's a big blanket. There's room for two, if you want."

Shoot. How was he supposed to turn her down, wiping that sweet, hopeful smile away? "I've, um, got my little brother. We're kind of a package deal."

He wasn't all that sure how Milo would do with the fireworks, anyway, especially after the long day of stimulation they'd already enjoyed.

"Oh. That's okay. We can squeeze one more. Or maybe he'll want to sit with Kat. She seems pretty good with him."

Katrina was wonderful with him. Bowie would have loved her for that alone, even if not for the hundred other reasons.

"I'll have to see," he said.

She smiled broadly. "Sounds good. I'll meet you back here after dark."

Samantha took off into the house, and he grabbed a cup and filled it from the glass water jug that had floating blueberries and sliced strawberries in it. It made him think of Katrina again, the taste of her mouth and the heat of her skin.

Unable to resist, he scanned the party for her. At

first he couldn't see her, until he saw a slim figure
in a flowered pink sundress work through the crowd
and head through the trees toward the trail that ran
along the lakeshore.

His first thought was to worry that Milo had
gone wandering, but he found his brother still on
the swings, this time being pushed by Andie Montgomery. Satisfied that his brother would be okay
under her watchful eye, he headed after Katrina.

The sun had set, casting his surroundings in
shadow, though full dark would be another hour
away. For now, everything was muted and pale in
the lavender twilight except the lake, which seemed
to glow amber and peach. Birds twittered in the tall
trees as they prepared to call it a day.

He walked about a hundred yards from the house
until he finally found her. She sat on the lakeshore
on a bench placed along the trail that offered a beautiful view of the mountains rising up on the other
side of the water.

The sunset tinted her features the same amber of
the lake, and she looked lovely and a little sad. As
he watched her, Bowie had to fight the urge to rub
his fist against his chest as that ache intensified.

He loved her and didn't know what to do about it.

He should probably start by leaving her alone.
This was a grievous intrusion of her privacy. She
had obviously left the party so she could be alone,
and it was rude of him to stand here among the trees
and spy on her.

He turned, intending to slip back through the trees to her mother's house, when his foot nudged a rock that clattered against another one.

She turned her head, and in the fading light, he saw her features twist into surprise and then a sort of resignation. Since she had already seen him, he knew he couldn't just turn around and go back to the party now without seeming like some kind of creepy stalker.

Instead, he stepped forward and walked to the side of the bench. "Everything okay?"

"Sure. Just fine," she said after a beat. "Why do you ask?"

The words were obviously untrue. He wasn't foolish enough to claim he was an expert on Katrina Bailey by any means, but she *had* lived in his home the last few weeks. He could see the restlessness in her and, beneath it, something else. Something almost…sad.

He inclined his head the way they had come. "All your family and friends are up there with the food and the booze and the music, while you're down here by yourself."

"Maybe I just needed a moment to catch my breath. Sometimes a girl just likes to be alone once in a while."

The words stung. She obviously didn't want or need his concern. That probably went double—or triple—when it came to these new and frightening emotions twisting through him.

"Right. Sorry I bothered you," he said stiffly. "I was worried about you, but I can see that was unnecessary."

She sighed. "I'm the one who's sorry for snapping at you. Thanks for worrying about me, but I'm fine, really. Sit down, if you want."

He hesitated for only a moment before stepping forward and easing onto the bench beside her. The scent of her drifted to him, of strawberries and wildflowers and Katrina. He was aware of a little pang as he wondered how many more of these moments with her he would be able to steal before she left in only a few days.

"Is Milo okay?" she asked. "Andie offered to keep an eye on him. She's great with kids, but I still probably shouldn't have left him."

"He seems to be having a great time, as far as I can tell. Who knows? I doubt he has a lot of experience with social occasions like this or Wynona's wedding last week. It's probably a little different for him, attending a party where everybody's not stoned."

"You can never be too sure about Eppie and Hazel."

He had to laugh at the vision of the two spunky senior citizens toking away amid a cloud of smoke.

"Seems like a fun party," he said. "It was very kind of your mom to welcome Milo and me, when she barely knows us."

He saw a little color creep over her cheekbones.

"I don't think kindness had much to do with it. You heard what Wyn said earlier after the parade. She's desperate. I think she's still hoping you could convince me to stay in Haven Point and give up any silly idea of adopting a child."

Why would Charlene Bailey think *he* could have any influence on Katrina? Did she know something he didn't?

"To be clear, I couldn't, right? Convince you to stay, I mean." He had to ask.

She sent him a sidelong glance. "We've covered this ground already. I need to be with Gabriela."

He did his best to hide his disappointment. "I totally get that. She's a lucky girl."

She was quiet for a long time. "If those circumstances were different, would you…try? To convince me to stay, I mean?"

"In a heartbeat," he said, without a second's hesitation.

Her eyes were wide, and she gave him a half smile that made his heart flop in his chest like one of those lake trout coming out of the water.

"Why do you have to be so hard to resist?" she murmured.

"Why do you have to try so hard?" he countered.

She laughed a little, rolling her eyes. When the laughter faded, she gazed at him, eyes soft in the moonlight, and it seemed as inevitable as the sunset when she reached up and kissed him. It was poignant and tender and moved him beyond words.

He held his breath as emotions seeped through him. Though he wrapped his arms around her, he forced himself to let her take the lead in the kiss, to savor each slow, seductive moment of it, knowing that it might well be their last.

TENDERNESS SEEMED TO swirl around them like the whirlpools rumored in spots out on the lake, an inexorable force that she was helpless to resist.

She had no one to blame but herself. She had kissed him this time, had been completely unable to help it. She had slipped away from the party for a little breather, a chance to regain some perspective, and then suddenly there was Bowie and she had felt...safe.

Here in his arms, she didn't have to carry the weight of her worry about Gabi, about the adoption process, about her insecurities and uncertainties. She could simply savor this last chance to be with him, to let that whirlpool pull her down a little farther. Wouldn't it be lovely if she could stay here? If she didn't have to worry about anything else?

She sighed, hands in his hair, and gave herself up to the moment and the tantalizing heat of him. He seemed content to wait for direction from her, and she gave it, deepening the kiss and pouring all her newfound tenderness into it.

They kissed for long, delicious moments while the shadows lengthened and the sounds of her mother's party murmured through the trees, and her heart broke a little more.

She didn't want it to ever end, for reality to intrude once more—her obligations, her inadequacies, the sheer impossibility of them ever being together. Right now, this moment, would have to be enough.

They were wrapped together tightly, her hands exploring the strong muscles of his back, when she suddenly heard a gasp. Too late, she realized this might not have been the most discreet place for one last kiss, when her mother was throwing a party a hundred yards away. She turned and was horrified to find Samantha standing at the edge of the clearing with a look of utter betrayal on her face that cut into Katrina like a rusty saw blade.

"Sorry to interrupt," Sam said. Her eyes were two big green pools of pain and disillusionment. "I… The fireworks should be starting in a few moments and I…didn't want you to miss them. I told you I would save you a spot."

Her best friend in all the world—the one who had been kind to her when no one else was, who had shown her how to put on lipstick and listened to her gush on about a dozen different guys—didn't even look at her after that first blast of shock and disappointment.

"But I guess it looks like you were busy setting off a few fireworks of your own," Sam went on, her voice tight and hurt. "Sorry again that I interrupted. I'll leave you to it."

She turned and headed back along the lakeside loop trail toward the party, leaving a tense and awkward silence behind.

As much as she longed to be back in his arms, Katrina knew she should be grateful for the interruption. She was so weak when it came to him. One look and she lost any hint of common sense and turned back into a person she didn't like: the kind of stupid girl who would walk away from a great job to follow a guy she didn't even care for that much to another country.

The kind who would forget to consider her best friend's feelings.

A woman who for a few moments had actually been tempted to consider giving up the fight to help a child she loved and who needed her desperately.

For a man.

Once more, she was letting her emotions rule her head, letting her desire to be cherished and important make her forget everything important to her.

She stood up and moved toward the trail. "We should get back. I have no idea how Milo will do with the fireworks, and he might freak out if we're both missing."

He stood as well, looking as if he wanted to pull her back into his arms. Oh, she hoped he didn't.

"Kat," he began. "We need to talk about this... thing between us."

No. She couldn't bear it. "There is nothing between us," she said harshly. "Nothing real, anyway."

"Funny. It feels pretty real every time you're in my arms."

She felt tears burn behind her eyes but couldn't give in to them. Not here. Not yet. "Yes, I'm attracted to you. Big deal. I've been attracted to lots of guys before. Just ask Sam. She'll tell you."

Hating herself, she forced herself to go on. "That's all it is. Believe me, it will pass. And here's the thing. I'm not a shallow, silly girl anymore, willing to give up something important to me simply because some great-looking guy makes my toes curl. I can't be that girl. Leave me alone, Bowie. Don't kiss me again. I mean it."

For an instant, she thought she saw something deeper than male disappointment in his eyes, something dark and filled with pain, but she told herself she was imagining it.

Drawing on every last ounce of strength, she forced herself to pull away from him, to turn away and hurry back up the trail.

CHAPTER EIGHTEEN

BOWIE SEEMED TO take her words to heart. He worked all day Sunday, claiming another urgent problem at Caine Tech. In the morning, she and Milo went on one of her favorite hikes with Wynona and Andie Montgomery—plus Andie's children, the Montgomeries' adorable little dog, Sadie, and Wyn's beloved dog, Young Pete.

The hike gave her a good chance to talk a little more with her future sister-in-law and offered Milo a chance to interact with children. She was thrilled at the sweetness of Andie's son, Will, who quickly picked up a few ASL signs to communicate with Milo and seemed to take the other boy's sometimes odd behavior in stride.

Whenever she had cell service along the trail, Katrina tried to reach Sam, but the silence on the other end was deafening. Apparently Sam was screening her calls and ignoring her texts.

When they returned to watch the fireworks the night before, Sam had been nowhere in sight. Linda said she thought her daughter might have eaten some bad potato salad earlier in the day and she wasn't feeling well.

Katrina doubted the veracity of this claim but couldn't very well tell Linda she thought her daughter was lying to her.

When they returned from the hike and Sam still hadn't responded to any of her attempts to reach her, Katrina decided the situation called for desperate measures. The store was closed on Sundays, so she and Milo took a bike ride, with him on the tandem trainer attached to her mountain bike. He pedaled only half the time, but she'd been able to find one that had a seat back with a seat belt so it was more like a bike trailer for big kids that also had pedals and handlebars.

On their ride, they not so casually swung past the Fremont house, where Linda informed her Sam had gone to Boise for the day to have lunch with a friend from college.

"I told her I didn't think she was up to it after her food poisoning yesterday, but you know how stubborn she can be," Linda said.

Katrina knew that, all too well.

"It surprised me, when she told me her plans this morning, since she hadn't said a word all week about it. I would have thought she'd want to spend her day off with you. Maybe she thought you'd be too busy with him." Linda inclined her head toward Milo.

Or maybe she was angry and hurt and wouldn't ever speak to Kat again.

Now *she* felt like the one who had eaten bad potato salad. Depressed and not knowing what else to do, she said goodbye and took off with Milo again back toward Serenity Harbor.

Sam was her best friend and had been since the StupidKat days. She was loyal and funny and generally kind. Katrina hated knowing she had hurt her, that Sam felt she had betrayed her.

She *had* betrayed Samantha. She should have been more honest with her friend from the beginning.

What would she have told her, though? That Bowie had kissed her a few times? That she was afraid she was losing her heart to him, just like the dozens of other guys she had once been infatuated with?

No. This was different. She *had* lost her heart to Bowie. All those other guys meant nothing, not compared with this vast, aching reservoir of emotion. She should have told Sam something was happening to her, that her feelings for him were growing and changing, becoming more real than anything she had ever known.

Katrina hadn't said anything because she had been afraid to admit it, even to herself. As a result, she had hidden something important from her dear friend and had caused pain for both of them.

She had screwed up, and she had to make it right. She would be leaving Haven Point in three days.

Saying goodbye to Bowie and Milo would be tough. The thought of it left her feeling like her heart were being shredded apart, bit by bit. She didn't know how she could bear to leave Samantha behind, with her friend hating her.

SHE DIDN'T SEE Bowie at all through Sunday or Monday morning. She had been awake when he finally came home late Sunday night but didn't think it would be wise to tempt fate by going out to talk to him while she was in her pajamas and the house was dark and still.

When she headed into the kitchen to make breakfast for Milo, she found a note from Bowie, explaining that he had to run into work early and wasn't sure what time he would be home.

The note only confirmed her suspicion that he was avoiding her. How could she blame him?

Leave me alone, Bowie. Don't kiss me again. I mean it.

"Bo?" Milo asked.

She forced a smile, determined not to give in to her brewing headache or the depression that seemed to have settled into her bones. She had made a mess of everything since she'd been home.

"He's gone to work today," she told Milo. "It's just you and me. We're going to have so much fun together." It was her last full day with him before Debra Peters arrived the next day, and she didn't want to waste a moment of it.

"How about Mickey pancakes this morning?" she asked Milo. He nodded and gave her his half smile, then returned to his ever-present little cars.

Oh, she would miss him. Why did life have to be full of so many difficult decisions?

As the oil heated on the griddle, she mixed the batter, and when she judged the oil hot enough, she poured one circle, then two smaller ones for ears. She had a sudden random memory of making this at Sam's house, in the days when Sam's dad was in the hospital, dying of cancer. Sam had been thirteen, she remembered, and Katrina had done her best to be silly and make jokes and otherwise try to keep her friend's spirits up during those long, rough days.

Tears burned behind her eyes. She wasn't that silly girl anymore. She still loved her friend and wanted to fix this.

If Sam wouldn't answer her calls, she would track her down, she decided. On a Monday morning at 9:30 a.m. she had to be at the store, ready to open.

"Finish your breakfast, kiddo," she said to Milo. "We need to go for a walk into town."

An hour later, her stomach was still in knots when they approached the redbrick two-story building that housed Fremont Fashions. The door was locked and the sign hadn't yet been switched from CLOSED to OPEN, but she could see movement inside.

She rapped on the door and waited. Inside, she could see Linda make her slow way to the door. When she opened it, Mrs. Fremont wore her usual dour expression, as if she had just taken a bite out of something nasty.

"You're out and about early today," she said, by way of greeting.

"I really need to talk to Sam. Is she here?"

Curiosity flickered in Linda's gaze. "She's in the back, looking over an order of new purses that just came in from Genevieve Designs, the company run by Aidan Caine's sister-in-law in Hope's Crossing. They might be beautiful, but they're ridiculously expensive. Between you and me, I don't know how we'll ever sell a single one, but as usual, Samantha doesn't listen to me. You can go back."

Katrina glanced down at Milo, standing solemnly at her side. If this turned into a full-on fight and Samantha yelled at her and called her the ugly names she deserved, she didn't want Milo there to hear. He disliked conflict and would probably freak. "Do you mind keeping an eye on Milo?" she asked Linda. "He's usually happy playing with his cars."

She thought Linda might refuse, but the woman surprised her. She leaned down, her mouth lifting in the closest she came to a smile. "Milo, I know you enjoyed playing in the clothes the last time you were here. There's a clearance rack over there. You can't hurt anything there, and you can play with your cars inside all you want."

He appeared to consider this, then nodded and followed Linda to the round rack she indicated, slipping through the clothes to the middle, a secret little spot that probably seemed similar to the closet at home.

"I'll keep an eye on him," Linda said.

"Thank you."

With no more reason to dawdle, Katrina drew in a breath, steeled her nerve and headed to the back room of the shop. When she entered, Sam looked up from tagging some colorful hand-sewn purses. Her pretty features tightened, but after that first moment of hesitation, she went on with her work as if Kat hadn't even come in.

Katrina moved closer to the table. "Hey there. Did your mom tell you Milo and I stopped by your house yesterday?"

"Yes." The single word came out with the same sharp staccato as the label gun in her hand.

"She said you went to Boise to have lunch with a friend."

"That's right," Sam said. She didn't offer any further information and Katrina didn't ask, though she knew most of Sam's friends. They had roomed together in Boise and hung out with most of the same people.

She sat down on the chair across from Samantha, feeling miserable and awkward—emotions she wasn't used to experiencing around her BFF.

What if she couldn't fix this?

She let out a shaky breath. "Look, I need to talk to you about what happened with Bowie. What you saw."

The kiss that had destroyed her with that sweet, aching tenderness.

"What's to talk about?" Sam's movements were

jerky and abrupt as she pulled another purse out of the bag. "Obviously you saw a great-looking guy and you went for it. I would probably have done the same thing. Not if my best friend told me she was interested in him, of course. But that's just me."

Katrina winced as the barb struck home. She and Sam had always promised each other they would never let a man come between them—but here they were. "I'm so sorry, Sammy. None of this… I didn't want… Bowie and I are not in a relationship. I swear. Every time he kisses me, I tell myself it's the last time, and then…it happens again."

That was apparently the wrong thing to say. Samantha's mouth tightened. "So last night wasn't the first time."

Katrina couldn't lie. She shook her head, misery coursing through her like a black, endless river.

"Why didn't you tell me? Do you know how stupid I feel?"

She had bungled this whole thing from the beginning. She hadn't been honest with anyone, especially not herself. "You shouldn't. I'm the stupid one, Sam. You know I am. StupidKat, right? That's me. I should have told you after our first kiss but…I was in denial myself. I kept thinking each kiss was a one-off and wouldn't happen again."

"Are you sleeping with him?"

The question slapped into her like an unexpected tree branch on a hiking trail. "No! We've kissed a few times. That's all. It's…it's over. I told him the

other night after you found us not to kiss me again.
It's just… It's impossible and nothing can ever come
of it. I mean, look at me. I'm stupid TwitchyKat and
he's a genius who graduated from MIT when he was
still a teenager. Why would he even look twice at
me? It was only a few kisses. That's all. That's all
I can let it be."

She let out a breath, her throat so tight with emotion she could scarcely talk around it. "I'm so, so
sorry, Sammy. I never wanted to be *that girl*, the
kind who would be willing to ruin a friendship over
a man. Especially not *our* friendship. You're my best
friend and I love you."

Kat could feel tears welling up and did her best to
blink them away, but it was no good. A few dripped
out anyway.

Sam finally stopped tagging purses. She dropped
the gun and, eyes narrowed, gave her a long, hard
look across the table.

"Do you have feelings for him?"

A few more tears dripped out, and her nose
started to run. Katrina swallowed as all the truths
she had tried to deny rushed back. She remembered
the tenderness of his kiss, how cherished she felt in
his arms, the peace she found with him.

This was different from all those other infatua-
tions, as if every other guy she had thought she cared
about over the years had been practice, preparing
her to meet Bowie.

"I…I'm leaving in two days. My priority is Gabriela."

"That didn't answer my question."

She wanted to come up with a smooth lie, to make a joke, to be able to laugh off the question with her usual lighthearted humor. But she had lied to Sam enough and couldn't find the words to do it again.

Finally she nodded. "I don't want to have them," she whispered. "It's completely impossible, but…I can't seem to help it."

"You're in love with him." Samantha's voice rang with astonishment. The shock made her feel even worse, if possible. "After all this time, you're in love. With Bowie Callahan."

Why now? Why couldn't she have met him a year ago or a few years in the future, when both of their lives were more settled?

It didn't matter. The *when* didn't amount to anything. Their chances of a happy-ever-after were still impossible.

"It will pass. Like all the others."

"Are you sure?"

She wiped at her eyes to clear those pathetic tears that wouldn't seem to stop. "Look, Bowie is a great guy. He's brilliant and funny and kind. He's generous and remarkably compassionate, especially considering how he grew up, and he's trying his best to be a good brother to Milo even though it's frustrating and hard. He deserves someone wonderful in his life. Someone like you."

Sam surprised her by reaching for both of her hands. "Or you."

She shook her head and opened her mouth to argue, but Sam cut her off, giving their joined hands a little shake. "Seriously, Kat? I know better than anyone that you're not stupid. You never were. But I might have to change my mind about that if you're really going to sit there and tell me you're prepared to walk away from a guy who sounds like a freaking saint."

Relief flooded through her like the Hell's Fury River after heavy rain, and she sniffled. That sounded much more like the friend she adored. Did that mean Sam was ready to forgive her?

"He's *not* a saint. Far from it. He's impatient, he can be moody, he would be a workaholic without someone in his life to keep him balanced."

"And you can't be the one to do that because…?"

"I've made a commitment to Gabi, the first time I've been serious about anything in my life. I love her. She needs me and I…I need her."

"I don't understand why you have to choose between being with Bowie and being with Gabi. Work things out with her, bring her back here and then grab onto him and hold on tight."

"I don't know if that's possible," she admitted. "Things aren't going well with some of the adoption technicalities. There's a chance I might not be able to bring her home. I might have to stay there."

"Oh. Don't say that."

"It's possible." She still didn't have any answers from Angel Herrera. She'd tried to call him that morning, but the call went straight to voice mail. "If not, I may have to be the one to relocate to Colombia to be with her."

"I hope not." Sam mustered a smile. "I've missed you so much these last months. I don't know what I'll do if you move down there. I might have to pack up Fremont Fashions and move to Colombia with you."

Katrina wiped at her tears. "Let's pray it doesn't come to that. Although maybe your mom would meet a sexy Latin lover down there, grow her hair out of her poodle perm and learn how to dance the cumbia."

Sam laughed at that prospect. "I can't wait to meet Gabi. You love her, so I'm sure I'll love her, too. She's going to have to call me Auntie Sam."

"I'll make sure she does," she promised.

"I'm sorry I was such a bitch the other night and that I screened your calls and ignored your texts yesterday. My feelings were hurt—not because you were kissing Bowie but because you didn't tell me something was going on between the two of you."

Sam hugged her, and Katrina wrapped her arms around her friend, filled with the sweet relief of reconciliation. Things were still far from perfect in her world, but at least she hadn't forever lost a dear friendship.

"I should go find Milo. Your mom was letting him play in the clearance clothes rack."

Surprise registered on her face. "She was? Good. Maybe he'll ruin some of those hideous monstrosities so I can fill the space with some decent clothes for a change."

She laughed and Sam joined her. For a moment, it felt like old times, the two of them answering each other's sentences and reading each other's thoughts.

THE SENSE OF HELPLESSNESS—of circumstances swirling and writhing and swelling beyond his control like a tornado—was as familiar to Bowie as the rhythm of his heartbeat.

He hated it.

When he was a kid, he had never known what the day would bring—if they would have a roof overhead or get kicked out of whatever crappy apartment or camp trailer or friend's guest room they currently called home. Maybe he would wake up and find Stella passed out on the couch or a new guy living with them or no food in the cupboards because she had friends over who ate everything that didn't move.

There had been good moments, too. It always seemed harder to dredge them out of the old memory bank, but they were there.

Sitting by a campfire while she played guitar and sang in her husky contralto. Lying on a blanket in a sunlit meadow while they pointed out fanciful figures in the clouds to each other.

In the two months since learning of her death, he

had thought about Stella more than he had in all the years since he took off.

He had come to accept that she had been a fragile, damaged soul. Devastated by her parents' death when she was only a girl. Mentally ill, definitely—probably manic-depressive. She had certainly had substance abuse issues. She had needed help and had chosen instead to live an alternate lifestyle on the fringes of society, away from anyone who might have offered her that help. He would have felt nothing but pity for her, if not for Milo.

With a sigh, he looked out the window of the family room. Lake Haven seemed unnaturally flat, motionless, as if even the ripples and waves were holding their breath in anticipation of the coming storm.

"Here are the last of my things," Katrina said behind him, and he turned to find her setting down her battered suitcase on the floor. She looked beautiful, bright and sunny as a July morning. It made his chest ache.

"Mrs. Peters's room and the bathroom are clean and ready for her. Milo even helped me make the bed, didn't you, bud?"

Milo gave an impassive nod. His brother's reaction to Katrina leaving was part of the reason Bowie felt so uneasy. Milo adored her. Surely he should have *some* reaction to her departure instead of this unnerving calm.

He had explained to his little brother that Katrina was going away but that a new friend would be arriving that day. Bowie knew she had done the same, over and over. Was it possible Milo didn't understand? It was so hard to know how much filtered through.

"Are you sure you have everything?" he asked.

"Probably not." She gave a smile that was a little too wide and polished to be completely natural. "If you find anything else of mine, I would be grateful if you would drop it at my mother's place. She can either hold it for me or send it on."

That blade gouging into his heart gave another half turn. "Of course."

"What time is Debra due to arrive?"

"She spent the night in Nevada after leaving her previous job in San Jose. When she emailed last night from Winnemucca, she said she expected to arrive shortly after two."

That sense of helplessness swirled through him again, that useless wish that he could convince her not to leave.

He couldn't give in to it. "I'm expecting her any minute now. If you need to go now, I'm here. You don't have to stay until she arrives."

She raised an eyebrow with a look that plainly told him she wondered if he was trying to get rid of her. *Never*, he wanted to tell her. *Please don't leave.*

"I would like to stay until she arrives, if you don't mind. I'd like to go over my educational methods and where I've seen the most success with him."

"Thanks. I appreciate that."

She smiled a little, making that knife twist another half turn.

He had never been in love before. So far, it basically sucked.

"Would you be okay if I took Milo for one more walk while we're waiting?"

The prospect of *doing* something instead of sitting here waiting held vast appeal. He rose. "I'll come with you."

Surprise flickered in her eyes, and she opened her mouth as if to argue. After a moment, she closed it again and shrugged.

"Would you like to go feed the ducks?" she asked Milo.

Bo's brother pursed his lips as if his answer had the weight of a nuclear disarmament treaty. After a moment, he nodded with great gravitas.

When they walked outside, Bowie thought again that the air had a heavy, expectant quality and the sky was a strange color—not quite green, not quite purple but somewhere in between.

"We're supposed to have a big storm this evening with heavy wind," she said. "You may want to put away the patio umbrellas."

"I'll do that."

Under other circumstances, he might have credited the impending storm for this restlessness in him, but he knew better. It was all tangled up in the woman walking beside him and this painful tenderness scraping his insides raw.

"What have you heard from Colombia and the adoption? Anything new?"

She released a frustrated-sounding breath. "Crickets. It's making me crazy. I've sent a half-dozen emails marked Urgent to my attorney. I've texted him and tried calling, and he's not answering anything. The moment I get off the airplane, I'm heading straight for his office to make him tell me what's going on. I'm going there first, before I even go to the orphanage to see Gabi."

At the distress in her voice, he had to fight the urge to pull her into his arms and comfort her—or at least to reach for her hand and walk along beside her, with her fingers tucked inside his.

It would have made such an ordinary yet appealing picture: a man and a woman holding hands on a lake trail as a young boy walked ahead of them.

Instead, he mouthed the only platitude he could think of in the moment. "I'm sure everything will work out," he said. For her, anyway. At least she could have everything she wanted.

"Thanks," she answered.

The rest of the way to Redemption Bay, they talked about inconsequential things while Milo stopped every few hundred yards to throw a rock or a leaf or a pinecone into the flat water.

They were on their way back when his phone

beeped a text message. He pulled it out with a vague feeling of dread that was confirmed when he read it.

"That's the autism specialist," he said after he had answered Debra Peters. "She's on the outskirts of town and should be at the house momentarily."

If he hadn't been watching, he might have missed the brief twist of her features, a hint of shadow in her eyes. Was she regretting her decision to return to Colombia? Would she miss them?

When she spoke, her voice held no inflection other than superficial cheerfulness. "Great. We should probably head back so we can be there to meet her."

A million thoughts went through his head as they walked back, things he wanted to say to her before she left, but he didn't know where to start.

Finally when they reached his house, he knew he had to say something. He reached for her hand and gazed into her eyes.

"You've been amazing for Milo. I don't want to miss the chance to tell you that. You saw potential where no one else did and worked tirelessly to bring it out in him. I had been seriously considering sending him to a residential school, but you've given me reason to believe I might be able to provide him a stable home."

"You provide him love. That's the most important thing."

He looked at Milo, running his purple car around

the edge of the patio table, and drew in a deep breath. He did love him.

He hadn't known Milo existed for most of the boy's life. When he did find out about him, Bowie was ashamed to admit that at first he had resented the hell out of him, this strange, unique little stranger who required so much energy and patience.

Katrina had led the way, shown him how to open his heart to Milo and see the potential in him instead of only problems.

How would he ever thank her?

And how would he possibly carry on without her?

He had no freaking idea.

CHAPTER NINETEEN

S̲ome terribly petty part of her wanted to hate Debra Peters.

In her imagination, the woman looked like something out of Katrina's childhood nightmares, complete with hooked nose, wart on her chin and beady black eyes like the witch from *Hansel and Gretel*.

Instead, the woman was round and soft, with kind eyes, fashionably cut gray hair and a warm smile. She greeted Milo before she even bothered to greet Bowie and Katrina, which forever endeared her to Katrina. She seemed to have a deep understanding about the boy's unique needs and stepped in immediately, leaving Katrina feeling superfluous from the beginning.

Debra explained that until a few years ago she was a special education teacher whose emphasis was children with autism. After her husband died, she decided she wanted to see a little of the country and have the opportunity to focus on one child at a time.

The child she had cared for in her previous position was being mainstreamed into regular classes and no longer needed the kind of intensive help

Debra could offer—and didn't it work out perfectly, she said with a twinkling smile, that Bowie contacted her just at the moment she was thinking about looking for a new position, a new part of the country to experience?

She was perfect for the situation, exactly what Bowie and Milo needed, and immediately seemed to click with both of them.

Katrina was happy, she told herself. It would have been so much harder to leave the boy she cared about with someone unsuitable. It appeared that Debra would be more than adequate to take over.

She and Debra and Bowie spent a long time at the kitchen table going over Milo's routine and the therapies she had begun to follow with him. She was trying to figure out anything she might have forgotten to mention when her phone rang.

She glanced at it and her heart jolted. The caller ID had a Colombian prefix, but she didn't recognize it. Maybe Angel Herrera had a new number.

Finally!

The phone rang again, and she caught Bowie watching with a steady interest that somehow calmed her.

"I need to take this. Will you both excuse me?"

"Sure. Of course," Debra Peters said. Bowie nodded at the same time, and Katrina hurried out to the terrace, where she would have the best service, managing to connect the call an instant before it would have rung for the fourth time. "Hello. This is Katrina Bailey."

"Miss Bailey?" A heavily accented female voice said. "This is Consuela Moreno from the Colombian Family Welfare Institute. I'm sorry to tell you, we have a problem."

FIFTEEN MINUTES LATER, Katrina disconnected the call and sat unmoving, staring at the water whispering against the dock while the heavy, smothering air pressed in on her.

Serenity Harbor.

She made a rude noise in the back of her throat. What a stupid misnomer. She had found nothing like serenity here, only turmoil and pain.

Bile rose up, burning her stomach, her throat. She couldn't seem to suck in a deep breath, and it was taking all of her strength not to curl up on the chaise lounge and sob.

How was it possible to be numb, ice-cold and broiling hot, all at the same time? Somehow she managed it.

She couldn't give in. Not yet. She had to survive the next few moments while she said her final good-byes. Somehow she had to find the strength to go back inside Bowie's house and pretend everything was fine, that her world hadn't suddenly been devastated.

After that, she could climb into her car and completely fall apart.

She forced herself to breathe, deep and slow, for ten full counts. Though the nausea remained, the breathing helped push the worst of the turmoil back— enough that she felt strong enough to walk inside the house.

When she rejoined Bowie, Debra and Milo in the kitchen, Bowie's posture instantly went tense, and he aimed a swift look of concern in her direction. She had to ignore it. Not now. One word of compassion or solace and she would completely lose it.

"I'm sorry for the distraction," she said. She almost choked on the last word, which seemed wholly inadequate to describe what had just happened. "Is there anything else you need to know about Milo?"

The other woman shook her head. "I've been reading through your notes, and they're wonderful, filled with details and specific examples. I can't tell you how enormously helpful that will be. If I have questions that aren't covered, I'll reach out to you. You'll be available after you leave, won't you?"

Not easily. "Email will be the best way to reach me for now," she said.

"I saw your email address on the paperwork, so that will be great to have. Don't worry about a thing. We'll have so much fun together. Everything here will be fine after you go."

She could hang on to that, at least. "Good to hear. I guess this is it, then."

She might have thought her heart had been totally

shattered by now, but she still managed to feel a few new cracks as she forced herself to smile at Milo.

It was too much. The human heart wasn't designed to endure this kind of damage. A few more deep breaths gave her enough strength to walk over to where Milo played, to sit beside him on the floor.

He didn't lift his head for a long moment, until she was forced to plead. "Milo, buddy, can you look at me?"

He seemed reluctant to leave his cars but finally picked up his favorite purple sports car and turned to face her, though his gaze connected somewhere to the left of her.

That was the best she was going to get today, she decided.

"Thank you for letting me hang out with you these last few weeks. I've had so much fun. I wish I could stay longer, but...I have to go."

"Go?"

That word seemed to finally register, after all these days she had tried to tell him she would be leaving soon. His eyebrows lowered to a point above his nose, and his color rose. She really hoped he wasn't on the brink of a meltdown. That would make this difficult task so much worse.

"That's right. G-go." Her voice broke a little on the word, but she drew another deep breath. She felt Bowie approach them and couldn't let herself look at him. She would completely lose it if she did.

"You're going to have so much fun with Debra.

She knows just how to take care of you and do every-thing she can to help you get ready to go to a special class at school in the fall."

"School."

"That's right. School. Just like Ty and Will Mont-gomery and all the other children. Won't that be great?"

"Kat. School."

She had a fierce wish that she was returning to her beautiful classroom with the windows that over-looked the mountains, to the bulletin board she had prepared so carefully and the neat cubbies and the smell of chalk and erasers.

She had loved being a teacher but had walked away for the most ridiculous of reasons. Now she didn't know if she would ever be able to return.

"That's right. You'll go to Haven Point Elemen-tary School. That's where I was a teacher. You will love it. I promise. You'll have special teachers there who can help you learn and grow. You can even learn to read all the stories you love."

He looked back down at the car in his hand, and she could tell she was losing hold of his interest. "I have to go now, Milo. You be good for your brother and for Mrs. Peters, okay?"

She didn't know how much he understood, but he didn't protest when she hugged him for only an instant and kissed the top of his head. "Bye, bud."

He looked up, and this time she was almost sure he looked straight into her eyes. "Kat. Bye."

With that long statement, he turned around and returned to his cars on the floor. Well, she thought, at least one of them wouldn't be heartbroken when she left.

"I'll walk you out," Bowie said.

"I'd rather you didn't," she said.

"Too bad," he answered, his expression grim.

She didn't have the strength to argue, so she turned back to Debra Peters. "It was a pleasure meeting you. Best of luck to you. He's a…a good boy."

She smiled, then turned for the door quickly. Before she reached it, though, Milo intercepted her. He had his purple car in his hand, and he held it out to her.

"Kat."

Oh, she couldn't do this.

"I can't play right now, Milo. I'm sorry. I have to go."

She tried to hand it back, but he shook his head and pointed to her. "Kat."

She didn't know what he meant, and then suddenly those stupid tears welled up. "You want me to take your car?" she asked, hardly believing he would ever part with his beloved purple race car.

He nodded and waved, then returned to his toys under the watchful eye of Debra Peters.

It was all too much, more than her fragile heart could bear. A sob burst out, and she gripped the toy in her fist and pushed her way past Bowie and outside to his front porch, where heavy rain was falling, drumming on the roof.

How fitting. They had enjoyed near-perfect weather the four weeks she had been back in Haven Point with only a few little cloudbursts here and there, but now the clouds appeared to have unleashed.

"Katrina. Stop."

She tried to rush down the steps to her waiting car, but Bowie grabbed her arm. "What's wrong? Something happened in your phone call. What is it?"

She couldn't talk about this now. She *couldn't*. Not when Milo had just broken what was left of her heart. "It doesn't matter. I have to go. Goodbye, Bowie."

"Just like that? After everything we've shared, you're just going to walk away? What happened?"

"I…can't."

Another sob broke through her control, and it was like the time the Hell's Fury flooded a few summers earlier. A second sob burst through, then another until she could no longer hold them back. He grabbed her and pulled her into his arms, and she wept and wept, loud, horrible, noisy sounds she hated but couldn't stop.

"Don't cry, babe. Don't cry."

Just as she couldn't stop her tears, she also couldn't prevent herself from drawing comfort from his heat and his strength, as if those floodwaters were carrying her along and he was the only solid thing in the world she could hold on to right then.

THAT FEELING OF helplessness came back stronger
than ever. This was pain, raw and savage, and he
didn't know how to fix it for her, any more than he
knew how to convince her to stay.

"What's wrong? This isn't only about Milo.
Something else happened in that phone call. What
is it? Please don't shut me out, Kat."

She shuddered, her breathing coming in ragged
gasps as she tried to calm down. The sobs slowed
and then stopped completely.

"There. Now tell me what happened."

"I'm an idiot. That's what," she mumbled. "Stupid-
Kat. I'm no different from the girl who had to repeat
the second grade and went to remedial math class
until middle school."

"Knock it off," he said sternly. "Why do you say
that? You're a gifted teacher who has made an incredible difference in my brother's life and in the
lives of dozens of other children."

"Not my daughter's life. Not Gabi's." She said the
last word on a sob. Ah. He had suspected this had to
do with Gabriela. What else would have set her off?

"The phone call was about Gabi, wasn't it? Who
was it?"

She took a moment to answer as she stepped away
and pulled a corner of her sleeve up to wipe away
the crooked trail of tears on her cheeks.

"A representative from the ICBF. In English,
that's the Colombian Family Welfare Institute,
which is the authority that handles all international

adoptions in Colombia under the Hague Adoption Convention."

After the heartfelt sobs of the last few moments, he found the completely toneless words disconcerting.

"When I couldn't reach Angel Herrera, the attorney from the adoption agency I was using, I finally called ICBF to find out the status of my petition. That was a representative calling back to tell me that because I've missed the last three deadlines for filing information, my petition is being denied."

He frowned. She was hyperorganized when it came to paperwork. If he needed evidence, he only had to remember the detailed notebook she had left for Debra Peters about Milo. "That doesn't make any sense. You wouldn't have let those deadlines pass by on purpose. Did you explain that?"

"I tried. It doesn't matter. It's too late," she said, her voice lifeless.

"What happened?"

The raw devastation in her eyes, so at odds with her colorless tone, broke his heart all over again.

"Angel Herrera never filed the necessary forms. None of them. Something felt off there, from the very beginning. I should have trusted my instincts and gone elsewhere, but he was recommended by someone in the Barranquilla office of the ICBF and I didn't know where else to go."

He had done enough business around the world to know corruption could be rife in some places, especially in bureaucratic offices. Bribes and payoffs could be a way of life. Perhaps the original contact had been a cousin or an uncle of this Angel Herrera. They had seen a chance to rip off a gullible and rather desperate foreigner—a single woman—and they had taken it.

"I should have listened to my own gut, but…but I didn't. And now I'm going to lose her. I won't be able to bring her here and she won't be able to get the medical care she needs and she'll die."

"So we find a more reputable agency and reapply."

"How? It's all gone. All the money I spent, all the time and energy invested. Everything you've given me for helping you with Milo. I sent it all to Angel."

Fortunately, money wasn't a problem for him. He had never been more grateful for his success at Caine Tech. "We'll find a reputable agency and start over. It might take longer, but we'll figure it out."

She stared at him for a long moment while the rain pounded on the roof of his porch, and he saw a little glimmer of hope flash in her eyes, there and then gone in an instant. "There is no 'we,' Bowie. I can't drag you into this."

"I'm in it, like it or not. You helped me with Milo. Now it's my turn to help you with Gabriela."

"You already helped me. You paid me an outrageous amount and I basically threw it down the toilet. I trusted the wrong man—which, by the way, should be the title of my autobiography."

"You made a mistake."

"And an innocent child will pay for it!"

"Then let me help you fix it."

"You can't. She's my child. It's my mess, and I have to figure out how to clean it up."

"It doesn't have to be. We can fix it together. That's what I do, Kat. I find problems and I fix them."

"You have your own problems. This isn't one of them."

She was shutting him out, and he didn't know what to do about it. She had been doing the same since they met—drawing closer, then pulling away. He didn't know what to do, how to make her see what was in his heart.

He had to tell her.

Bowie gazed out at the whitecaps on the lake and the Redemption Mountains, solid and strong despite the rain. He had never felt so exposed, like a boat out on that water right now, being thrown in all directions by the storm with no protection.

Finally, he grabbed her hands. "It concerns you. That makes it mine. Would it make any difference in your willingness to accept my help if I tell you I'm in love with you?"

She stared at him, her eyes huge. He wished like hell he could tell what she was thinking. For a moment there, he thought he saw joy flash in those eyes. Now they just looked haunted, like the rest of her features.

"Don't say that," she finally whispered. "Please don't say that."

"Why not?"

"Because I know it's not true. It can't be true."

Those whitecaps around him seemed to rock harder, and he had to dig deep to steady himself. He had never told a woman he loved her before. He never would have guessed that when he finally did, she wouldn't believe him.

"I love you, Kat," he said, more firmly this time. "I want to help you. Please let me. We can fly down there and have this whole thing sorted out in a week. Two tops. We might even be back before the school year starts."

She slid her trembling hands away from his and scrubbed at her face. "I know what you're doing. It won't work."

"What am I doing?"

"I have a problem and you feel some…some sense of obligation to fix it because I helped you with Milo. You don't. You have enough on your plate. Milo, a new town, a new job. I can't ask you to take on this, too.

"You didn't ask. I'm offering."

"Because you say you love me."

"Because I *do* love you. I've never said that to a woman before and maybe I didn't say it in some romantic perfect moment, but it's the truth."

"You're attracted to me. It's not the same thing."

"You think I don't know the difference?"

"I think you're confusing attraction and maybe gratitude with something…something more."

Why was she so determined not to believe him? Did she have so little faith in him? Or in herself?

"Trust me. I know the difference," he said softly.

Her hands curled into fists at her sides. "I...I'm flattered," she finally said, her voice small and her features expressionless. "But I'm sorry, Bowie. I just... I don't feel the same way."

Of all the things he expected her to say, that would have been low on the list. "You don't?"

After the soft tenderness they shared, the quiet peace they found together? She had to be lying. Wasn't she?

Even the slim possibility that she meant her words made him feel like ice-cold lake water had just sloshed over his head.

"I'm sorry. I kissed you because you're great-looking and I'm attracted to you, but that's all. I should never have let things go so far."

Her words certainly had the ring of truth—but she was avoiding his gaze as she spoke, and he had to assume that was significant. Or maybe not.

"I could pretend I love you and let you help me adopt Gabi," she went on, "but that wouldn't be honorable. I won't use you that way. A different woman might be tempted, but that's not who I want to be anymore. I can't rely on the nearest available guy to fix my problems. I appreciate your offer. It was very kind and I'll never forget it, but...I have to do this myself. Now, if you'll excuse me. I really do have to go. Thank you for...everything. Goodbye, Bowie."

With that, she hurried down the steps and out into the storm, and he didn't know how the hell to stop her.

CHAPTER TWENTY

SHE DESERVED A freaking Academy Award, Katrina thought later that night as she sat in the window seat of her childhood home with her cat, Marshmallow, on her lap, gazing out at the storm that had continued unabated all afternoon and evening. The rain continued to click against the window, and she could hear the wind howling through the glass.

I'm sorry, Bowie. I don't feel the same way.

How had he taken one look at her and not seen her words for the blatant lies they were?

She had wanted so desperately to tell him she loved him, too. When she closed her eyes, she could still feel the echo of the joy that had surged through her at his words, at the hope that he could fix everything for her. It would be so easy to let him help her, and then she could have everything she wanted. Bowie. Milo. Gabriela. Together, all of them.

The picture shimmered in her head, shining and bright and beautiful. It was painfully within her grasp, and she only had to reach for it.

And then what?

Eventually Bo would figure out he didn't really

love her. She wasn't stupid enough to think they could have a happily-ever-after. What did she have to offer a man like him? He was a genius computer tech gazillionaire and she was a teacher who could barely manage to balance her checkbook each month.

She would only be prolonging the inevitable pain. That was fine for her, but she wouldn't put Gabriela or Milo through a painful breakup.

Telling Bowie she didn't love him had been her first award-worthy performance of the day. The other had been over the last few hours. Somehow she had made it through the evening, a family dinner with her mother and Uncle Mike, Wyn, Marsh and Andie, while holding on to the last vestiges of control.

She had told them all only that the adoption had hit a few snags and she didn't know when she would return but it shouldn't be long.

She was becoming pretty good at the whole lying-through-her-teeth thing.

She had no idea what she was going to do now, other than stick to her plan. Return to Colombia. Go in person to Angel Herrera and get her money back somehow, then take her petition to the Colombian Family Welfare Institute.

If she could, Katrina would have headed straight for the airport and camped out to get an earlier flight, but Samantha wanted to take her to breakfast and drive her to the Boise airport. Their relationship was still so fragile, she didn't want to disappoint her best friend.

Why did that matter, though, when she had disappointed everyone else?

The fight with Bowie burned through her mind, the hard, untrue things she had said to him.

I kissed you because you're great-looking and I'm attracted to you, but that's all. I should never have let things go so far.

I could pretend I love you and let you help me adopt Gabi, but that wouldn't be honorable.

Her heart ached at the memory, at the pain she had seen in his eyes, and she hated herself even more.

She was afraid.

That was the heart of it.

She was so afraid she didn't deserve a man like Bowie, that he could never truly love the real her.

Lightning arced across the lake, followed by the low rumble of thunder a few beats later. The space between the flash and the sound seemed to be growing longer as the storm moved away.

She should probably try to get some rest, though she didn't know how that would be possible when she was so wrung out and exhausted.

Maybe she would sleep here in the window seat. She only had to somehow summon the strength to grab a pillow and the colorful throw folded neatly at the foot of her bed. With a sigh, she managed to slide her feet to the floor, but before she could rise, her phone rang, the sound unnaturally loud in her bedroom, where the only other sounds were her breathing and the incessant rain against the window.

She pulled it out before it could wake her mother and Uncle Mike. One glance at the caller ID ramped her heartbeat into overdrive. Why would Bowie be calling her at ten thirty at night?

She didn't have the strength to talk to him. Not tonight, when she felt as emotionally wrung out as if she were out there in the lake being hit on all sides by wind and waves and lightning.

At the last second, she wavered and finally connected the call.

"Hello," she said softly.

"Katrina, this is Bowie. I know it's late. I'm sorry to disturb you, but it's urgent. Is Milo with you?"

She straightened at the undeniable thread of panic coiling through his voice. "No," she said, her heartbeat kicking up another notch. "Why would you ask? He's not in bed?"

It was a stupid question, and she knew it as soon as she asked. If Milo were in bed, why would Bowie call her?

He let out a long string of curses, made all the more startling because she had rarely heard him swear. "You were our last chance. I knew it was a long shot, but I'd hoped. I thought maybe he wandered over to find you somehow, though of course I'm sure you would have called as soon as he showed up. I'm sorry to bother you. I have to go. I need to call Chief Emmett and start a search."

"Wait. What can I do?"

Chilling silence met her question, and she realized he had already disconnected the call.

As soon as she lowered her phone, the panic exploded. It was raining, with lightning and thunder. Was Milo out in it somewhere?

Even though her hands shook and fear paralyzed her thoughts, she threw on her clothes in less than a minute and raced down the stairs and out the door.

She drove to Bowie's house in record time and parked in front just as her new brother-in-law showed up in his Haven Point patrol vehicle. Bowie hurried down the steps, the expression on his features a perfect match to the fear in her heart.

She fought the urge to go to him, to wrap her arms around him as he had comforted her earlier.

Later. For this moment, both of them had to focus only on doing everything possible to find Milo. She did hurry to his side, and he gave her a grateful look before he greeted Cade. "That was fast. Thanks for coming, Chief."

"Let's go inside, out of the rain, and you can tell me what's going on," Cade said.

They moved up the steps and into the great room of the house, where she found Debra Peters on the sofa, her eyes red and her features pinched.

"Oh, Katrina," she wailed. "I'm so sorry. Less than twelve hours into my tenure and we've lost him."

"I'm sure it's not your fault," she said, squeezing the woman's arm.

"Start at the beginning," Cade said.

"My younger brother, Milo, is missing. He's six years old, brown hair, freckles, about forty pounds and forty inches tall, last seen wearing blue pajamas with Superman on the front. He has limited verbal skills and autism, which will make it tough for him to answer back if searchers try to call out his name."

"I'm going to assume you've thoroughly combed through the house," Cade said.

"Every closet, every corner, under every bed. We've been searching for half an hour, since Mrs. Peters went in to check on him and found his bed empty."

"Is it usual for you to check on him in the night?" Cade asked Debra.

"I don't have a *usual* with him yet," she admitted, her voice wavering. "This is my first day. I only arrived this afternoon. I checked on him because I knew he was…upset when he went to bed. He had a meltdown earlier but seemed to have calmed down by the time his brother tucked him in."

"What upset him?" Cade asked.

Bowie's gaze flickered to Katrina, then back to her brother-in-law.

"As I said, he has autism," Bowie said. "It could be anything from a tag inside his shirt rubbing against his skin to a pillow out of place to having to use the wrong flavor of toothpaste."

Debra gestured to Katrina. "He missed Katrina.

He kept saying *Kat, Kat*, and grew increasingly upset when we tried to explain she wasn't coming back."

"That was the reason for the meltdown," Bowie agreed. "When we couldn't find him here, I thought maybe he went looking for her. That's why I called."

"Do you know anything about this?" Cade asked her.

"No," she whispered. "I haven't talked to him since I left this afternoon."

"You think he slipped outside?" Cade asked, nodding toward the security panel on the front door. "Looks like you've got a pretty intense security system here."

"I do, by necessity. But I disarmed it earlier when I went outside for a moment during a break in the rain to…clear my head."

He didn't look at her when he spoke, but somehow she had the distinct impression it may have been her fault he needed fresh air.

"I walked out on the dock for a moment, and it's possible he slipped out somehow when my back was turned and I didn't notice. I would like to think I would have heard or seen something, but I was… distracted."

He raked a hand through his hair, and he looked so upset and vulnerable that she again had to fight the urge to wrap her arms around his waist and promise everything would be okay.

It wouldn't. She knew that better than anyone. Sometimes happy-ever-after was just a fairy tale.

"We have to find him," Bowie said. "He's just a little kid who doesn't understand the world very well. I hate thinking of him being out there in this weather, cold and alone and afraid."

She couldn't seem to stop thinking about Milo's fascination with the water and that big lake out there, just begging for a little boy to wander into it.

"We'll do our best," Cade said. "I've already alerted everyone in my department and called in everyone on standby. They're all ready to assist in the search. Our first job is to set up a grid."

"While you're doing that," Katrina finally spoke up, "I'll check out a few of the places he and I liked to go together. The playground, the baseball field, the dog park."

"Better wait until we coordinate and can set up a search perimeter. We don't want to duplicate effort," Cade said.

She had loved Cade as a brother for most of her life. Only days ago he had become her brother in truth when he married Wynona. That didn't mean she would let him try to stop her when the stakes were this high.

She faced him, her mouth tight and her chin out. "No. I'm not waiting. Milo is out there somewhere in the rain, and I won't stand by and let something happen to him. Not if I can prevent it. You have my cell number. Call me with any updates if necessary, but I'm going to look for him."

"Fine," Cade said after a moment, his voice resigned. "But before you leave, you can start with giving us a list of his favorite places so I can send out people at the same time to cover more ground."

With every passing second spent inside and not out looking for Milo, her stress and fear ratcheted up a level, but she knew Cade was right. She went through the list of all the places she knew Milo enjoyed, and by the time she finished, she was nearly weeping, imagining the harm that could come to a little boy in all those places.

"We'll find him. Don't worry, Kit-Kat." Cade put a hand on her shoulder. "We're mobilizing everybody. The fire department, the county search and rescue. Marshall is sending as many deputies as he can spare."

"I'm going to head south on the trail between here and Redemption Bay. We walked that nearly every day, and he's very familiar with it. I'll stop first at the Lawsons' house."

"Good idea," Bowie said. "It's a short walk, and he loves their dog."

"Right. From there, I'll hit McKenzie and Ben's place and then report back in."

"I'll go on the same trail, in the opposite direction," Bowie said.

"Meanwhile I'll stay here to coordinate and send searchers to all the places you mentioned," Cade said.

"Got it."

She and Bowie headed out the back together, flashlights in hand.

"Kat. Thank you for coming so quickly," Bowie said, just before they would have parted ways.

"Of course." Time was of the essence, but she decided five seconds wouldn't hurt. She threw her arms around him for a tight, fast embrace, then stepped away. "We'll find him, Bo. Don't worry."

"I hope so," he said, his voice grim, before he hurried away.

Her heart pounded as she headed toward the Lawsons' house, shining her flashlight and calling Milo's name as she went. There were a thousand dangers for a little boy out here on his own.

How would they ever find him? He was wary around strangers and wouldn't be able to answer when searchers called his name, unless he knew them.

He must be so afraid.

"Milo," she called again, but the wind seemed to steal her voice and whirl it into the cloudy sky. "Milo!"

She was so afraid she had lost Gabi already. She couldn't bear to lose Milo, too. A sob escaped her. She loved Milo *and* Bowie. Why did she have to choose? Why couldn't she have Gabi and the two Callahan brothers in her life?

I do love you. I've never said that to a woman before and maybe I didn't say it in some romantic perfect moment, but it's the truth.

Another sob escaped, and she was aware of hot tears mixing with the rain on her cheeks. Bowie said he loved her, and she had pushed him away because of her fear.

Love was about trust. About taking risks and facing the rain together, even when you were afraid.

"Milo?" she called again.

Over the rain, she thought she heard something, a distant cry. She paused, heart racing as her gaze scanned the dark, spindly shadows of tree trunks in the direction of the sound. Had she really heard something or had it merely been wishful thinking?

There. The moonlight pierced the clouds momentarily, long enough for her to spy a pale blur about twenty yards away. Could that be a face? She squinted, but between the tears and the rain, her vision was blurred.

"Milo? Is that you? It's Kat."

"Kat." It was a barely there sort of sound, a whisper that could have been the wind, but she moved toward it anyway.

It wasn't the wind. She was sure of it. She recognized that sound. "Milo, honey, it's me," she called. "Come out."

"No, no, no."

She hadn't heard that chant from him in a long time, especially not on a distressed wail. "You have to," she said as she made her way through the thick undergrowth. "Everyone is so worried about you, especially Bo. He's very sad and scared for you. You can't hide away here, sweetie."

"No, Kat. No, no, no, *no*," he cried, louder still.

When she moved closer and aimed the flashlight at him, she suddenly realized the trouble. His pajama top had tangled in a low tree branch. He wasn't being obstructive. He was saying "no" because he couldn't move.

Another child might have made the connection to take off his shirt and leave it there, but Milo's panic had held him fast as much as the tree branch.

Relief rushed through her, and she hugged him. "We'll get you out of there. Hold on. Easy." She knelt beside him, heedless of the mud and pine needles, and lowered her head so she could wedge the flashlight between her chin and her chest while she worked to extricate his shirt. It was stuck fast, so she finally just yanked it out with a loud rip that made him jump.

"There we are. You're free. Come here, come here." This boy who didn't always like being hugged jumped into her arms and held on tight. She rocked back, falling to the mud. He wore only pajamas and was soaked through and barefoot. His little feet were freezing, and he shivered in her arms.

First order of business was warming him up. Though it was tricky with him holding on tight, she managed to pull off her own shoes and socks and the rain slicker and sweatshirt she had thrown on in a panic. That left her in a T-shirt and jeans—not enough for these conditions, but she knew it would be only a short time until she could get him home.

"Here you go. Let's get these piggies warmed up."

She pulled her socks, warm from her own feet, onto his feet and then slid him out of his ripped pajama shirt and put the sweatshirt in its place. It draped almost to his knees.

"Coat next," she said and pulled the rain slicker on over the sweatshirt. "There. Is that a little better?"

He nodded, and it seemed his shivering had subsided a little. They were relatively sheltered under the spreading leaves of a pine tree, and while all her instincts yelled at her to get the boy to safety, she knew it would take only a moment to put Bowie's fear to rest.

She supposed she technically should call Cade first to have him call off the search, but she would let Bowie do that. Her hands shook from relief as much as the cold, misty rain already seeping through her T-shirt as she found his number on her phone and dialed, slipping her shoes back on her bare feet as she waited for him to pick up.

"I've got him," she said before he could even say hello. "He's safe and he's fine, just wet and cold. We're on the lake trail just before the Lawsons' house. He was caught in a branch."

"Oh, thank God," he breathed, as much a prayer as an exclamation. "I'll come pick you up."

"No need. We'll meet you at your house. It would take us almost as long to walk up to meet you at the road as it would to just come home. Call Cade and let him know to call off the search, would you?"

"I'll do that." He paused. "Katrina. Thank you."

The emotion in his voice seemed to vibrate through her. "You're welcome. We'll see you in a few minutes."

"Bo?" Milo said when she disconnected the call.

"Yes. That's Bo. Let's get you home to him. Come on, kiddo. Piggyback time."

She crouched in the mud, and he climbed onto her back. For the first time since she met him, she was grateful he was small for his age.

"Can you hold the flashlight? That's it. Just shine it ahead of us."

With distant lightning flashes across the lake and the occasional rumble of thunder, she took off on the trail back to Serenity Harbor. The trail was slick with mud, so she didn't dare run, but she knew she needed to get him in out of the cold. The legs of his pajamas were still wet, and she could feel his occasional shivers against her back.

She had made it only about halfway back to Bowie's house when she saw the wavering light of a flashlight moving toward them at a fast clip through the trees. She caught glimpses of the dark figure carrying the light between the trees.

"Bo," Milo said, his voice gruff, probably from the cold and his earlier cries.

She wasn't sure how he knew, but it was definitely Bowie. The muddy trail didn't appear to worry him. He was running full out. He faltered a little when his beam caught them, then moved even faster, reaching them an instant later.

"There you are. You scared the hell out of me, kid."

He pulled Milo off her back and into his arms, and Milo hugged him back.

"He's cold," Katrina said. "We should get him back to the house, where he can warm up."

"One minute."

Though he still had Milo on one hip, Bowie wrapped the other arm around her and pulled her to him. He was as wet as she, but in that moment, she didn't care. She wrapped her arms around him tightly.

"Thank you," he said, then kissed her hard, adjusted Milo to a better position in his arms and raced back up the trail toward home.

AN HOUR LATER, she was warm and dry, wearing a pair of Bowie's sweats that fit her about as well as her own sweatshirt had fit Milo. The sleeves were rolled up and she had folded the legs of the bottoms up about four times. She didn't care. They were warm and dry, and that was all that mattered.

Bowie was ushering out the last of the searchers while she sat with Milo on the sofa in the family room off the kitchen, the two of them wrapped in a blanket.

She couldn't see the boy's face from the angle she was holding him but had a feeling he was asleep, judging by how still he had become over the last few moments.

Her suspicion was confirmed when Bowie returned, speaking on the phone, caught sight of Milo and immediately lowered his voice.

"Yes. Thanks. We're all good. Thanks, Aidan. Give Eliza a hug for me and tell her she can stop worrying now...Yes. I'll tell her."

He hung up and came over to stand near her. "I'm supposed to give you a message from Eliza Caine. She said to tell you that she's baking you three dozen of your favorite white chocolate macadamia nut cookies and also has a giant hug with your name on it when she sees you next."

She managed a smile. "Eliza makes fantastic cookies. And her hugs are even better."

He didn't smile in return, just continued watching her holding his brother.

"I'm almost afraid to let him out of my sight now," Bowie said, his voice gruff. "Maybe I should think about moving a cot into his bedroom."

She tried to ignore the shivers rippling down her spine at his low tone. "He was pretty scared out there. Maybe he learned his lesson about wandering outside."

"I hope so."

"How's Mrs. Peters?"

"Shaken up. She's never lost a client before. I told her to go to bed. For now, I managed to talk her out of resigning—especially after I assured her this was totally my fault. I can't believe I didn't notice when he slipped right past me."

"Don't beat yourself up, Bowie. You're not to blame."

His expression told her he disagreed, but he didn't argue. "I guess I need to take him back to bed. I'm sure you don't want to sit there all night holding him."

She wouldn't mind, actually, but Milo probably wouldn't be all that comfortable.

Bowie stepped closer, and those shivers came back as his hands brushed against her when he reached down to scoop Milo into his arms.

Unable to resist, she followed Bowie down the hall to Milo's room and watched as he set the boy carefully on the bed and tucked the covers back up around him. Milo didn't stir, probably too exhausted from his ordeal.

He brushed a hand over his brother's hair, then bent down and pressed his mouth to Milo's forehead, and her throat clogged with emotion at the sweetness of the gesture.

Oh, she loved him.

And she loved Milo, too.

She moved past Bowie and kissed Milo's forehead, too, heart aching. She tried to burn the scent of clean pajamas and his grape no-tears soap and shampoo into her memory.

"I'm so glad he's okay," she whispered.

"Thanks to you," Bowie said.

She knew that wasn't necessarily true. Someone

else would have found him, but she was grateful some instinct had guided her in that direction.

"I should go," she finally said, after they both left Milo's side and returned to the hallway. "I have a… long day of travel tomorrow."

"We need to talk about that," he said.

Yes. She needed to tell him she was sorry, that she had lied, but she didn't know where to start.

"I've been thinking about Gabi," he said, his voice firm. "I'm going to help you adopt her, and I don't want to hear any arguments."

"Bowie," she began, but he cut her off, his expression implacable.

"Stop being so damn stubborn and hear me out. I am going to help you adopt your daughter. No strings, no ulterior motives. I'm doing this because it's the right thing to do."

He looked so very determined, his mouth set and his jaw firm, and she fell in love all over again.

"Hear me out. Caine Tech has an entire division in Bogotá, including an excellent legal team. Their specialty is obviously not family law, but they do have contacts in the system and can find reputable, honest people in Barranquilla who will guide you through. I already talked to Ben and Aidan earlier this evening, before Milo disappeared, and we set the wheels in motion. Someone will be there to pick you up when your flight lands and will help fast-track all the paperwork necessary. We've also been in touch with the US Embassy, and they're prepared to fast-track her visa to the States and citizenship paperwork as soon as possible."

He had done all this earlier in the evening, before Milo disappeared. While she had been sitting around moping, feeling hopeless—weak and ineffectual—he had been taking action, making calls, planning a strategy. Even after she lied so cruelly and told him she didn't love him, he had been working to fix this for her, to help her achieve something dear to her heart.

How could she continue to doubt that he truly loved her?

"Bowie," she began, but her voice faltered, unable to break through the logjam of emotion in her throat.

"Save your breath. There's a little girl down there who needs a family—who needs *you*—and I don't care what it takes. We will make it happen."

She had been so stubborn, thinking she had to learn to count on her own strength. She did. But leaning on a man—when he was the *right* man, when he was good and kind and decent—didn't make her weak.

It made her smart.

He loved her. The joy of it finally washed over her, cleansing away all the stupid mistakes of her past.

Bowie Callahan loved her. She wasn't StupidKat anymore. But if she walked away from Bowie and the beautiful future they could build together with Milo and with Gabi, she would be living up to that childhood nickname and more.

"Okay," she finally whispered.

He stared at her. "Okay, what?"

"Okay. I want your help and…everything else."

He said nothing, just continued to study her, a wary intensity in his eyes.

He wouldn't make it easy for her, she suddenly realized—and he shouldn't. He had absorbed all the risk earlier by telling her of his feelings. In return, she had shut him down cruelly. It was up to her now to shove aside her fear and her pride and offer him the only thing she could.

"I will accept your help gratefully because it's the best thing for me and for Gabi. More important, because…I love you."

He continued gazing down at her, completely motionless as if he hadn't heard her, and for one fragile, tenuous moment, she wondered if she had just made a horrible mistake.

No. She wouldn't believe that. He loved her. He said he did. Despite the hard circumstances of his childhood—or maybe because of them—Bowie Callahan was a man of honor and integrity.

He wouldn't have said the words if he didn't mean them wholeheartedly.

She stepped forward and touched his face, the lean, beautiful sculpted features of the man she loved so deeply.

"I am sorry I lied to you earlier. So sorry. I was a coward. I've messed up so many times before and was terrified I would do it again—only this time, it would matter. This time it would devastate me. I love you, Bowie. I'm so sorry I lied and hurt you. If you give me another chance, I swear I'll find some way to make it up to you."

Silence. Those blasted crickets.

She wasn't sure how long she stood there, her heart flayed open to him and her fingertips absorbing the heat of his skin. A few seconds? A lifetime?

Just when she was beginning to think it was too late, that she had ruined any possible chance for her happy-ever-after, his mouth lifted into a sweet, beautiful smile overflowing with more tenderness and love than she could ever have imagined.

"That sounds promising," he murmured. He shifted his mouth and brushed his lips against her fingertips where she touched his face, then reached for her.

With a sob of relief, she threw her arms around his neck and kissed him fiercely.

"I meant it, you know," she said, a long time later. "I love you, Bowie. When I came back to Haven Point, I vowed I was done with men, that I was only going to focus on Gabi and the life I wanted for us together. But then you and Milo worked your way into my heart, and I realized there is more than enough room there for everyone."

"Good," he said, so much joy and tenderness in his eyes she nearly wept again. "Because we're not going anywhere. I love you and I know I'll love Gabi, too. I can't wait to meet her."

Of course she had to kiss him again after that. A long time later, she was in his arms on the sofa, both of them out of breath and disheveled.

"I love you," he murmured again, and she knew she would never tire of hearing it. "When I moved to Haven Point, I never expected to fall in love, but from the moment I met you in the produce aisle at the grocery store, somehow I knew my heart would never be the same. You know you're going to have to marry me, right?"

She stared at him, completely astonished. "M-marry?"

He shrugged against her. "Not tomorrow or next week but eventually. Gabi and Milo will have enough challenges to face in this world. They're going to need both of us to help them do that."

It wouldn't be easy, she knew, emotions overflowing into tears as she kissed this man she loved with everything inside her.

Life wasn't easy. But they could face those challenges together.

EPILOGUE

SERENITY HARBOR HAD been invaded.

Bowie stood in the doorway, taking in the chaos that had exploded in his backyard.

Children and dogs seemed to be everywhere, running, laughing, barking. Gabi and her cousins played a heated game of tag, joined by what seemed like every dog in town but was really only Rika, Hondo and Gabi's cousins' little pooch, Sadie.

At least thirty people sat in clusters talking or laughing, and more bustled in and out of the house carrying food to the long tables set up on the edge of his terrace while the delectable smell of perfectly charred meat wafted into the air from the vicinity of Bowie's barbecue grill, where Ben, Aidan and Marshall fought over the tongs and chief grill master rights.

Katrina brushed past him carrying her delicious fruit salad, and he stopped her long enough to sneak a quick kiss. His wife of six months stole his breath every single time he saw her, and he loved her more than he ever believed possible.

"Hey! You're going to make me drop this," she

exclaimed, though he saw her color climb and loved knowing he could still make her blush.

"I'll take it. Where do you want it?" he asked.

"Thank you. Anywhere you can find room on the table."

He headed toward the bulging table filled with potluck offerings and topped by a huge banner made by his sister-in-law Andie and her kids that read Congratulations, Callahan Family. Underneath it were all their names: Bowie, Katrina, Milo, Gabriela, all encompassed by a big red heart.

"Papa!" Gabi shrieked as she ran by, and he scooped her up and into his arms, this girl who had brought so much life and light and joy into his world.

She was the reason for this party, which was a celebration of their appearance that afternoon before a family judge where Bowie formally adopted her.

Katrina had gone through the lengthy, complicated process in Colombia the summer before on her own, though he and Milo—along with Debra Peters, who had become a cherished member of their family—had made frequent visits to see her, and they had all been together on the day Katrina finally brought Gabi back to Haven Point.

They'd considered rushing their wedding to expedite the adoption process. A married couple had an easier time of adopting than a single woman, and his position and financial resources wouldn't have hurt. Things might have been less complicated that way, but Bowie had sensed Katrina needed to stand on her own, at least at first. Gabi had been hers from the moment Katrina met the girl, and Bowie hadn't felt right about swooping in and solving everything for her, though his financial resources and Caine Tech influence had certainly smoothed the process the second time around.

"Are you having fun?" he asked Gabi now.

"Yes," she declared, throwing her arms around him and hugging him tight. The whole world would be a much better place if every person had someone like Gabi in his or her life to keep things in perspective.

"Love you," she said, kissing his cheek, and Bowie felt the sting of emotion that he didn't bother to blink away.

This sweet little four-year-old girl had turned what had already been a pretty damn good life into something unbelievably beautiful.

"I love you, too, pumpkin."

"Put me down now, *por favor*, Papa," she said, her bossy tone brooking no argument. He laughed and complied. She wriggled to the ground and took off, running after Will and Chloe and the other children.

He watched them for a moment until he caught sight of another person he loved, Milo, sitting by himself on the wooden glider bench he loved, petting his therapy dog, Cooper, a big, calm golden retriever.

Bowie headed over and stood beside Milo. "You're not playing tag with Gabi and your cousins."

Milo shook his head but said nothing. Milo's

speech had truly taken off over the last year, but he was still a man of few words. That was fine with Bowie, especially since Gabi chattered enough for the both of them.

He had worried a little about how Milo would deal with a little sister who also had special needs— especially having to share Katrina with her. He should have known better. From the moment they met at Gabi's orphanage, the two children adored each other. Milo, three years older, watched out for Gabi with a touching protectiveness and Gabi, in turn, dragged Milo into friendships and fun— sometimes whether he liked it or not.

"Everything okay?" Bowie asked the little brother he thought of as a son, this unique little creature who had completely changed his life.

The very best gift Stella had ever given him.

"Yeah," Milo said.

"Then what are you doing over here by yourself?"

The boy tilted his head in that serious way he had and studied the crowd, the other children, the various pets and babies and friends.

"Being happy," he said simply.

That emotion burned again, and Bowie wiped at his eyes, not the slightest bit ashamed of it.

"Mind if I join you?" he asked. Milo shook his head, and Bowie sat beside him, not saying anything, just savoring the moment.

Katrina came out again, this time with a tray of hamburger buns she carried over to the grill. When

she spotted them, she must have sensed the intensity
in his gaze—she was good at that, the most intuitive
person he'd ever known. When she walked toward
them, he caught the tantalizing scent of strawberries
and cream and the woman he adored.

"What's going on over here? You guys okay?"

Bowie pulled her down to his lap and kissed her
again while Milo rolled his eyes before hiding a
smile against his shoulder.

"We're better than okay," Bowie answered his
wife. "We're happy."

Her expression softened and she kissed him, then
rubbed Milo's arm. "Same here," she said.

Gabi ran past again at full speed, like she did
everything. Not one to let herself be excluded from
anything, the little girl stopped when she spotted
them all together and flung herself up onto the glider
to join them.

They all wriggled to make room, and the four
of them—his family—rocked together for a priceless moment while the sunlight gleamed on the lake
and water lapped against the dock and everybody
Bowie cared about talked and laughed and enjoyed
being together.

* * * * *

New York Times bestselling author

RaeAnne Thayne

welcomes you to Haven Point, a small town full
of big surprises, hope and second chances...

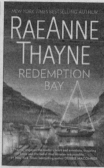

Order your copies today!

HQN™

www.HQNBooks.com

HARLEQUIN®

SPECIAL EDITION

Life, Love and Family

Save **$1.00**

on the purchase of ANY
Harlequin® Special Edition book.

Available wherever books are sold, including
most bookstores, supermarkets, drugstores
and discount stores.

Save $1.00

on the purchase of any Harlequin® Special Edition book.

Coupon valid until September 30, 2017.
Redeemable at participating outlets in the U.S. and Canada only.
Not redeemable at Barnes & Noble stores. Limit one coupon per customer.

52614949

5 65373 00076 2 (8100)0 12290

® and ™ are trademarks owned and used by the trademark owner and/or its licensee.

© 2017 Harlequin Enterprises Limited

HSECOUPMM0717

*Billionaire businessman Autry Jones swore off single
mothers—until he meets widowed mom of three
Marissa Jones just weeks before he's supposed to leave
for a job in Paris…*

*Read on for a sneak preview of
MOMMY AND THE MAVERICK
by* **Meg Maxwell***, the second book in the
MONTANA MAVERICKS: THE GREAT FAMILY
ROUNDUP continuity.*

"Right. We shook on being friends. But…" She paused and
dropped down onto the love seat across from the fireplace.

"But things feel more than friendly between us," he finished
for her. "There was that kiss, for one. And the fact that every
time I see you I want to kiss you again."

"Ditto. See the problem?"

He smiled and sat down beside her. "Marissa, why did you
come here? To tell me that doing the competition with Abby is
a bad idea? That she's going to get too attached to me?"

"Yup."

"Except you didn't say that."

"Because I don't want to take it from her. I want her to be
excited about the competition. To not lose out on something
when she's been dealt a hard blow in life so young. But yeah, I
am worried she's going to get too attached. All three girls. But
especially Abby."

"Abby knows I'm leaving for Paris at the end of August.
That's a given. Goodbye is already in the air, Marissa. We're
not fooling anyone."

"Why do I keep fighting it, then?" she asked. "Why do I have to keep reminding myself that feeling the way I do about you is only going to—"

"Make you feel like crap when I go? I know. I've had that same talk with myself fifty times. I wasn't expecting to meet you, Marissa. Or want you so damned bad every time I see you."

It wasn't just about sex, but he wasn't putting that out there. If she kept it to sexual attraction, surface stuff, maybe he'd believe it. Then he could enjoy his time with Marissa and go in a couple weeks without much strain in his chest.

"So what do we do?" she asked. "Give in to this or be smart and stay nice and platonic?"

He reached for her hand. "I don't know."

"Your hair's still damp," she said. "I can smell your shampoo. And your soap."

He leaned closer and kissed her, his hands slipping around her shoulders, down her back, drawing her to him. He felt her stiffen for a second and then relax. "I don't want to just be friends, Marissa. I want you."

She kissed him back, her hands in his hair, and he could feel her breasts against his chest. He sucked in a breath, overwhelmed by desire, by need. "You're sure?" he asked, pulling back a bit to look at her, directly into her beautiful dark brown eyes.

"No, I'm not sure," she whispered. "I just know that I want you, too."

Don't miss
MOMMY AND THE MAVERICK by Meg Maxwell,
available August 2017 wherever
Harlequin® Special Edition books and ebooks are sold.

www.Harlequin.com